I0667799

AND THEN

Blooms Love

And Then Blooms Love is a sweet faith-filled story of first love finding a second chance. Don't miss this tender and well-told debut!
—**Rachel Hauck**, *New York Times* and *USA Today* bestselling author

Reviewers are saying …

… this story is hard to stop reading because I wanted to find out what happened next. I consider that a hallmark of a good read.

…the author created characters with real problems I could relate to.

…I didn't want the story to end. In fact, I intentionally slowed down my reading towards the end, because I wasn't quite ready to say goodbye to everyone.

…the plot is very interesting, and the story moves at a nice pace.

…*And Then Blooms Love* is an intriguing story that kept me wondering about the characters.

…this book is a page turner.

AND THEN

Blooms Love

SALLY JO PITTS

Copyright Notice

And Then Blooms Love

First edition. Copyright © 2018 by Sally Jo Pitts. The information contained in this book is the intellectual property of Sally Jo Pitts and is governed by United States and International copyright laws. All rights reserved. No part of this publication, either text or image, may be used for any purpose other than personal use. Therefore, reproduction, modification, storage in a retrieval system, or retransmission, in any form or by any means, electronic, mechanical, or otherwise, for reasons other than personal use, except for brief quotations for reviews or articles and promotions, is strictly prohibited without prior written permission by the publisher.

This book is a work of fiction. Characters are the product of the author's imagination. Any resemblance to actual events or persons, living or dead, is entirely coincidental.

Cover and Interior Design: Derinda Babcock
Editor(s): René Holt, Deb Haggerty
Published in Association with the Seymour Agency

PUBLISHED BY: Elk Lake Publishing, Inc., 35 Dogwood Dr., Plymouth, MA 02360, 2018

Library Cataloging Data
Names: Pitts, Sally Jo (Sally Jo Pitts)
And Then Love Blooms / Sally Jo Pitts
214 p. 23cm × 15cm (9in × 6 in.)
Description: **She is determined to forget him …**

Hurt by her former fiancé Clifton Davenport, new flower shop owner Emme Matthews is working hard to establish a successful business and provide for the three-year-old child she is raising. Financial woes plague her, and she is forced to accept a floral job for a special dinner at the Davenport plantation. Not wishing to upset the event, Emme stays behind the scenes, only to learn the dinner is to announce Clifton's engagement.

Identifiers: ISBN-13: 978-1-946638-97-7 (trade) | 978-1-946638-98-4 (POD) | 978-1-946638-99-1 (e-book.)

Key Words: contemporary romance, inspirational, weddings, beach read, financial woes, unrequited love, South, women's fiction, leaving a legacy, small town romance

LCCN: 2018947124 Fiction

Acknowledgments

I want to express my gratitude to all who gave of their time and efforts toward this book making it into print.

Special thanks go to my wonderful, persistent, thorough, and encouraging critique partner, Marcia Lahti.

To Susie May Warren, Rachel Hauck, and Beth Vogt of My Book Therapy—I am grateful for your story crafting assistance.

Kudos to Deb Haggerty of Elk Lake Publishing Inc., editor René Holt, and Julie Gwinn, my agent with the Seymour Agency, for believing in this project.

To my beta readers—Erin Tom Landphair, Janet Russell, Kelly Christopher, and Jennifer Vaughan-Birch, I appreciate your comments and suggestions.

Very special thanks go to my husband, LaVelle, for his prayers, love, encouragement, and endurance during the long hours I spent absorbed in story.

And most of all, thanks to the Lord, my Savior, for his precious promises that demonstrate how he works in life's troubles and circumstances.

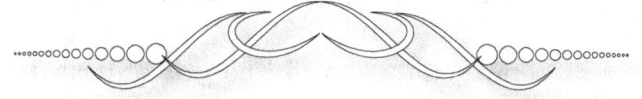

Trust in the Lord with all your heart,
And lean not on your own understanding.
In all your ways acknowledge Him,
And He shall direct your paths.
Proverbs 3:5-6 NKJV

Chapter 1

Could she steal ten minutes of quiet before life found her? With a devotional book squeezed under her arm and a steaming mocha latte in hand, Emme Matthews crept down the stairs of her living quarters to the flower shop below. First light was ushering a new spring morning into Hamilton Harbor, snuggled in the crook of the coastline on Florida's Panhandle. She didn't want to miss the show.

C-r-e-e-a-k

"Shh." She lifted her foot from the squeaky step and listened. No stirrings came from three-year-old Richie's room. The plink of water dripping in the work sink downstairs provided the customary white noise. Floral fragrances sparred with the musky scents of new carpet and freshly painted walls.

Only two more steps.

But when her bare foot touched the hardwood floor at the bottom of the stairs, a warning alarm shrieked from the refrigerated floral display case. Emme jumped. Hot coffee sloshed on her hand and the devotion book skittered across the floor. She plunked the cup on the work table, ran to the sink and shoved her hand under the faucet to let the water cool her skin. Sunlight pushed through the front display window, exposing a layer of condensation on the cooler's glass doors.

"My flower shipment." The words spilled from her mouth. She snatched the cooler door open. Inside, a blend of sweet odors filled her nostrils. The damp shelves and sides of the refrigerated case were barely cool to the touch. The daisies were holding up, but the daffodils had begun to nod.

"Please, please, please stand tall." No way she'd give voice to the florist's dreaded wilt word. Talking to plants had a therapeutic effect, and these flowers needed encouragement. "You can make it. I'll get help as soon as I can." She closed the door and ran shaky, damp fingers through her long hair, snagging on the tangles.

The sun spotlighted a plaque on the wall proclaiming her newly purchased Flower Cottage as one of Hamilton Harbor's cornerstone businesses. Emme swallowed hard. The lingering taste of her forgotten latte coated her dry throat. She had a reputation to uphold. More importantly, she couldn't squander the tiny foothold she'd carved as proof she could provide a stable home for Richie.

"Who are you talking to?"

Emme whirled about, clasping her hand to her throat. "Richie. Don't sneak up on me like that."

"I didn't sneak."

The three-year-old rubbed sleepy eyes. Entrusted with Richie's care by her dying cousin, he had been Emme's ward since she held the tiny miracle shortly after his birth.

"Sorry, buddy." Emme tousled Richie's messy curls. The pants of his blue-and-red Spiderman pajamas once touched his ankles, but now rested mid-calf. "You just startled me. The flower case isn't cooling right."

"You can fix it."

Sweet boy. He should talk to the daffodils. His eyes homed in on her, tugging at Emme's heart. He trusted her. So had the bank loan officer, or she wouldn't be a business owner. But was she worthy of their trust?

She straightened Richie's cockeyed shirt. "Thanks for the vote of confidence." She had repaired so much around the 1930s Craftsman home that she was on a first name basis at the do-it-yourself store. "This task, I'm afraid, is beyond my ability."

Emme took Richie's hand. "Let's get you some breakfast while I call a repairman." The stairs groaned beneath her feet. Plans for quiet time with the Lord and making her van payment on time unraveled with each step.

"Emme? Pam Boswick here."

The late morning call stirred Emme's adrenaline. "Pam, hello." She pressed her finger to her ear to shut out the clatter created by the refrigeration repairman.

"I heard you took over the Flower Cottage in Hamilton Harbor."

"You heard right."

Richie tugged at her shirt and pointed to his alphabet phone, needing a battery.

"That shop has a good reputation. You should do well there."

She glanced at her drooping flowers and the repairman prostrated in the bottom of the cooler. "I hope so."

"I have a job smack dab between you and Tallahassee. My usual florist in the area is booked, so I thought of you."

Emme's heart-rate did a two-step. In college, she'd worked with the popular event planner on occasion. A job with her might cover the cooler repair. Richie nudged his toy in front of her.

"The order is for a special dinner, March sixth, being hosted at the Davenport Colonnades."

Emme halted her search in the junk drawer for a AA battery. The cooler cackled. Enthusiasm drained and puddled at her feet. Colonnades was the one place she never intended to step foot again. Doing so would be too painful.

"I … uh … I'm afraid I have a conflict that evening."

"Oh? Too bad. I looked forward to working with you again. Let me know if anything changes."

"I will. Please keep me in mind for future jobs."

The call ended. Richie tugged her arm. She spotted a AA and with trembling fingers snapped the battery into the toy phone.

The repairman rested his rear on his heels and gave his verdict. "I got 'er runnin', but from the look of it, you're gonna need a new fan motor and gaskets. Probably run you three hundred, give 'r take, and I'll have to order the parts."

A weak whistle escaped Emme's lips. Her cooler was essential. "Please, order what you need."

With the repairman barely out of the parking lot, heavy footsteps reverberated on the wooden decking leading to the back door. The tall form of Izzie Ketterling, Emme's floral assistant, entered the room mouth first. "I hope that repairman came here for flowers."

"Afraid not." Emme let out a shaky breath. "The cooler needs three hundred dollars' worth of TLC."

Richie rushed to Izzie, who knelt to greet him. "Yikes. We could all use a little TLC. Give Auntie Izzie a hug."

"Cool boots," Richie said, wrapping his pudgy arms around her.

Izzie smoothed Richie's hair and tied a bandana at his neck. "Now you're ready to ride the range with your stuffed animals."

"Thanks, Auntie." Richie hurried back to the children's corner. Izzie wasn't the boy's real aunt, but Emme loved the sense of family she offered him.

"What's up with the boots and bandanas?"

Izzie wore a red kerchief tied at her neck, a peasant blouse, a mid-calf A-line skirt, and silver cowboy boot earrings.

"I was in a Western sort of mood today."

Emme gave her a bemused smile. Friends at church called them yin-yang opposites. Izzie's short, black, stand-at-attention hair, dark eyes, and white blue-toned complexion contrasted with Emme's long, honey-blonde hair, blue eyes, and fair pink-toned skin. Izzie added her inventive skills to what she wore, while Emme focused her creativity on floral design.

"Well, cowgirl, you need to mount up and make hospital and funeral home deliveries." Emme hesitated and added, "I had to turn down an order."

"Turn down?" Izzie straightened her posture. In boots, she topped Emme's five-foot-five by a good six inches. "Have you lost your senses? Who called?"

Emme stood, hoping the action would help give credence to her quick decision. "Pam Boswick."

"As in highly-sought-after-event-planner Pam Boswick?" Izzie's voice cranked up an octave.

Emme nodded and jabbed a plastic cardholder pick into the funeral spray. "The job was for the Davenport Plantation."

"That's it?" Izzie's words popped like heat hitting a kernel of corn. "So what if it's flowers for El Creepo and his mother. You should jump at the chance."

"Jump? Jump at the chance to be humiliated by the Davenports again? You've got to be kidding." Emme slumped onto her stool.

"No. *You* must be kidding." Her "you" came out like the poke of an index finger to the chest. "It's your chance to shine and show Clifton what he gave up." Izzie swept her arm in an overhead circle. "We can lasso and brand 'em with Flower Cottage finesse before they know what hit 'em."

Emme rolled her eyes. "Where do you come up with this stuff? This isn't a rodeo. The assignment is a dinner— a special dinner party at Colonnades. Mrs. Davenport would never stand for me having the job."

"You don't know that for sure."

"I do." Pressing the palms of her hands on the worktable, Emme pushed herself up. There was little chance Mrs. Davenport's "not good enough for my son" rating had changed. "I won't risk the shop's reputation by looking bad in front of Pam."

"What about the little matter of your expenses?"

"I've got some savings left."

"And next month, then what?"

The florist cooler fan belched a metallic clinking noise, bringing Emme and Izzie to silence. The rattle turned to a jingle, then to a rhythmic hum.

Emme started to breathe again. Izzie spoke the truth. She couldn't afford to turn down jobs, not if she expected to pay her bills and provide for Richie.

But getting involved with the Davenports had nearly destroyed her once—twice might finish her off.

Clifton Davenport brought the Kawasaki all-terrain vehicle to an abrupt stop, kicking up a white, puffy cloud from the graveled road outside greenhouse seven. Chalky dust coated his nose and throat as he hurried inside.

"Carlos, you okay?"

Carlos looked small in the midst of the fifty-foot glass enclosure with tables of bedding plants spanning its length. He held a blood-soaked handkerchief against his forearm. Water dripped from a jagged pipe above his head. The droplets plunked into puddles at his feet. Damp, musty potting soil, mixed with overturned sweet-smelling petunias, scented the air.

"The ol' water line broke, but I got the main to the greenhouse shut down. Now the water's not gushing. I'll work on the pipes."

Clifton lifted a brow and shook his head. Lifting the cloth covering Carlos's arm revealed a long, bloody gash. "I'm more concerned about patching you. Henry can fix the pipe."

Steering Carlos to the work sink and shelving, Clifton grabbed the first-aid kit. Putting kits in all the main work areas was at least one good decision he had made since taking over plantation management.

"I was just tryin' to adjust one of the spray nozzles overhead. These bedding plants need to be ready for shippin' next week."

"I appreciate your efforts but hate you got hurt in the process." Clifton held Carlos's arm under the water faucet. "Let's clean this wound first."

"Okay, Doc." Carlos, who had worked at the plantation as long as Clifton could remember, gave a wink of appreciation. "Doesn't seem so long ago you had to be doctored for a bad cut from that crazy chop to your leg during Christmas tree season."

"You're right, my motivation for EMT training. Thankfully this cut isn't too deep. No need for stitches. Looks like a good cleaning with antiseptic and a bandage will do the trick." Clifton took out cleansing wipes, Betadine, sterile gauze and tape.

"I miss those days when families came here on the Christmas train to pick out a tree," Carlos said.

Clifton lifted his eyes and tried to read the older man's expression. Where Carlos was going with this conversation he couldn't guess, but he did know when Carlos brought up a topic he had a definite purpose.

Carlos peered at Clifton, brows raised, and waited for a response.

"Me too," Clifton answered.

Beaming, Carlos pressed on. "I especially miss watching you as a kid, trying to impress the little blonde-haired girl who used to come with her parents."

"You mean Mary Elaine?"

He nodded, wiping at drops of water still clinging to his arms.

"Yup. Your first love."

Bingo. His objective revealed. Carlos's comment took him back to his plight as a nine-year-old boy, so smitten by blond, blue-eyed Mary Elaine Matthews, he'd almost chopped his leg off watching her stroll through the rows of Christmas cedars.

Clifton snapped a piece of adhesive tape from a roll and eyed Carlos. "Anyone ever tell you you're nosy?"

Carlos's grin filled his cheeks, turning his eyes into narrow slits. "Maria, every day. Wasn't that long ago that little girl became the big girl you brought home from college."

Which left him with two scars—one etched on his leg, the other on his heart. "Why the sudden interest in my love life?"

Holding the gauze on his arm while Clifton secured the bandage with tape, Carlos lifted his shoulders. "I guess because I heard there's supposed to be a special engagement announcement tonight."

His statement seemed to beg an answer. Instead, Clifton averted his gaze and concentrated on returning the first-aid supplies to the plastic box.

"I always thought you and your childhood sweetheart were well suited." Carlos wasn't giving up.

"Mark it down. Appearances may not always be what they seem." But if Clifton was honest, he'd have to admit Mary Elaine was his first love—possibly his only love. Dwelling on that revelation was not the direction his thoughts needed to go. Not with his betrothal to Renata Mendes on the verge of becoming official.

"Well, your new girl … she seems pretty nice. At least she gives that appearance."

"Indeed, she is." Clifton snapped the kit closed. "Keep the cut clean. No more strenuous work today."

"But if I wrap my arm with a plastic bag—"

"Go home, Carlos," Clifton called over his shoulder. "Take care of your arm."

Not looking back, Clifton hurried out the greenhouse door with dredged up memories nipping at his heels.

The crunch of the ATV tires on the road accentuated the gritty thoughts crisscrossing inside Clifton's brain—responsibilities, engagement, Christmas trees, Mary Elaine. Why did Carlos have to bring her up?

Clifton lifted his head and let the breeze flow over his face in hopes of clearing his mind. He moved past the greenhouses to the open stretch of potted lemon, orange, and tangerine trees. A field of freshly upturned soil lay ready for new planting. The fragrance of early citrus blooms combined with the rich scent of earth prodded his sense of pride in the Davenport estate. The land had been in his family since 1821 when Spain ceded the land to the territory of Florida. But his stomach contracted around a cannon ball of shame. He'd sold a portion of the family property to Renata's father for cash flow.

Arriving back at the office, Clifton climbed the stairs on the outside of the building. The office was housed in the loft of a converted barn. His footsteps echoed on the hard wood floor as he moved past watchful eyes gazing down from the portraits of his forefathers. All sported the straight-bridge Roman nose he'd inherited.

His father's portrait, at the end of the hall, captured his characteristic pleasant manner with the slight uplift to the corners of his mouth.

"Dad, I wish you were here to advise me on this engagement. I don't want to mess things up with Renata like I did with Mary Elaine."

Clifton had proposed to Renata before her father announced his intentions. As a wedding gift, he planned to deed back the plantation property he'd purchased. But as a result, their marriage now smacked of a business obligation.

Were he and Renata really right for each other? A common bond had brought them together. Or was it her ability to secure the Davenport heritage? Should he accept Mendes's generous wedding gift? What gnawed at him was his inability to grasp his true motivation for marrying Renata. Was it bond or rebound? Doubt pressed his chest, making breathing difficult.

Scrutiny from his father's eyes in the portrait penetrated something deep inside Clifton—still prompting him to follow his gut feelings and leave his old impulsive ways behind. His dad had often stated, "Son, you have remarkable God-given instincts. You just have to get your timing right."

Clifton inhaled the familiar aroma of lemon oil held in the century-old walls. The smell bathed him in memories punctuated with regrets—regrets for mistakes made on his quest to learn the right timing his dad had talked about.

A phone message on the oak desk, once his father's, caught his attention. Written in Ms. Peacock's hand, the note let him know the order for Carolyn's Flowers got reversed. *Needed 100 whites and 50 purple snapdragons.*

"What else can go wrong?" Clifton grabbed the yellow invoice orders from the wire basket on his desk and flipped through them. Nothing for Carolyn's Flowers. He pulled up the business program on his computer and checked recent orders for Carolyn's Flowers. The last one recorded was the month before.

Snatching up the phone, he punched "two" for the veteran receptionist and bookkeeper. Voice mail picked up, redirecting calls to his business cell phone. Clifton returned the desk phone to its cradle, letting out a deep exhale. "Ms. Peacock has a dentist appointment."

"Talkin' to yourself?"

His brother, Gavin, lumbered into the office with bright pink rose corsages in hand. Younger by a year, Gavin stood an inch taller, wore his dark hair a bit longer, and always managed to look neat—his Davenport Nurseries T-shirt tucked into his jeans.

"I think talking to myself is my new normal."

"I've heard the practice is fine until you start answering yourself." Gavin's smile faded. "Hate to tell you, but the fan motor in greenhouse three is smoking."

"Get it turned off." Clifton barked an abrupt response, his focus still on the phone message from Carolyn's Flowers.

"I did. Lighten up. I just wanted to let you know. I called Henry about repairs."

"Good. He'll be busy." His words clipped. "He has to fix a water pipe in number seven." Clifton grasped the message from Ms. Peacock. "Who took this order? I can't even find an order form for white and purple snapdragons."

Gavin set the corsages on the desk and reached for the note. "That must have been the day we went to pick up supplies in Tallahassee. I transferred the office calls to Eduardo. He was pruning fruit trees—"

"Doesn't matter now. We have to correct the mistake." Clifton raked his fingers through his short, bristle haircut. The office chair creaked as he leaned back. "I'm sorry I snapped at you. It's just—"

"Pre-engagement jitters?"

"Maybe." Clifton pointed to the corsages Gavin had laid on his desk. "What are those for?"

"The ladies attending the banquet tonight?" He posed his answer in a way that questioned Clifton's faculties.

"Oh."

An uncomfortable burning seized Clifton's throat. He worked with the business end of plants, trees and flowers, hardly ever thinking of the end use, much less etiquette.

"Renata showed me two dresses she might wear tonight and asked my opinion. I thought these flowers would look nice on the one she decided to wear. Mom's wearing off-white, so pink works for her too."

"You even know what Mom is wearing?" Before Gavin could answer, Clifton threw his hands up in surrender. "I concede. You got all the good manners, thoughtfulness, and creative genes."

Gavin smirked. "Not a big deal. I cut some roses at the house, wrapped the stems with a little floral tape, and stuck a pin in them." He picked up the corsages and went in the break room. Raising his voice, he said, "I'm putting these in the refrigerator. Don't forget them when you leave."

Clifton rummaged through his top desk drawer for a pack of Rolaids. He took two, crunched on the minty relief for his distressed stomach, and shoved the remainder of the roll in his pocket.

"Sometimes I feel like this whole engagement thing is just some weird play. Once the curtain comes down, the drama will be over and I can relax—just be me, whatever that is."

Gavin walked back in the room shaking his head, his demeanor now solemn. "You're dwelling on Mendes's offer to gift back the family property when you and Renata marry. Instead you should be excited about marrying someone special."

Gavin slumped in the chair in front of Clifton's desk. "It's my fault. I should have paid more attention to the risky investments Nix made when he took over after Dad died. Then selling the property wouldn't have been necessary."

Clifton stiffened. Leaning forward in his chair, he spoke in earnest. "Fault? It's my fault for running off to South America leaving Bolton Nix to push us to the brink of bankruptcy. It's Mom's fault for not learning the business. It's Dad's fault for dying on us. It's the economy. In the end, it doesn't matter who's at fault."

Clifton pushed back from his desk and stood. "We've been over this how many times?" He paced on the floor planks behind the desk on a path so familiar he knew the distance between every knot hole.

"The plan to let Mendes purchase part of our property with a buyback clause seemed the best way to keep the family property intact." Clifton stopped and pressed his hands to his lower back. "But Mendes muddled everything when he said he planned to give the property back as a wedding gift." Clifton raised his shoulders and the palms of his hands. "It's like we're obligated to marry now. And Renata can't understand my concern."

Using the tips of his fingers, Clifton massaged his forehead then grasped the back of the desk chair. "The stress of getting this new computer program working must have addled my brain. I know I should be running around telling everyone how lucky I am to have a beautiful, fun-loving, intelligent girl like Renata willing to marry me." He sank back into his chair and let out a heavy sigh. "Most guys would give anything to be in my shoes."

Gavin stared at his brother. "You're right. Most *would* want to be in your shoes."

Clifton glanced at his leather slip-ons, dusty and dirt-encrusted from the muddy greenhouse floor. Being in his shoes right now was a messy business.

Chapter 2

Emme struggled to maneuver the boxed flower arrangement lodged in the rose-covered arbor. She gave the box a shove, wincing as she scraped her knuckles on The Flower Cottage front gate. "Here's the last item." Emme released the container with a thud onto the tailgate of Izzie's Suburban.

Draped over the car's front seat, Izzie made room for floral supplies. "You could have waited for me to help with that load."

Emme took a deep breath, touched her red knuckles and tried to calm her rapid heartbeat. Could heart palpitations be a sign of insanity? "I managed. But I guess it would have been easier to move the van and load the car in the back."

She attempted to ignore Izzie's "I-told-you-so" head-wagging.

"I'm just preoccupied." Emme blew at a pesky wisp of hair hanging over her eye. "I have to keep reminding myself that I need this Davenport job and should be grateful Pam still hired us after I turned down the venue."

"You bet." Izzie backed out of the front seat and bumped the car door closed with her hip.

Warm March sunlight penetrated the shield of oak trees in Feldman Park surrounded by once-stately homes. A bead of perspiration trickled down Emme's cheek and landed directly in the center of a Gerber daisy. "I've discovered a new way to water plants—sweat on them." She wiped at the moisture with the back of her wrist.

Izzie joined her at the rear of the car. "Gives a whole new meaning to working by the sweat of your brow."

Emme pressed her damp, aching hands against her slacks. "My face and hands are wet, but my mouth goes dry when I think of stepping foot into Colonnades again."

"Shoot. I can't wait. They'll be ooing and ahing and wanting to know where Pam came up with the super-florist."

She might not be a super-florist, but she was a professional floral designer. If she didn't have to face Clifton or his mother, she could handle this job. Couldn't she? "I hope everyone likes our work."

"Of course they will. You are your own worst critic. The Brazilian flag of flowers is a knock out."

Emme clasped her stiff hands. Attaching mesh wire to a wooden frame for the flag had taken its toll on her fingers. "We'll see. I promised Richie I'd let him see the finished result. As soon as I get him settled after school, I'll join you at the plantation with our Brazilian masterpiece."

"Speaking of Brazil, you've got to see today's business news." Izzie pulled a newspaper page from the back of her SUV. Holding it up for Emme to take in the headline, Izzie read aloud.

"Brazil's Mendes Enterprises joins with America's Davenport Plantation." Izzie peered over the top of the paper. Even in the humidity, Izzie's spiked, ebony hairdo stood as stiff as the netting in their supply box. "Imagine, two worlds connect right here in the panhandle of Florida. Who'd have thunk it?"

"What I think is the Davenports get enough publicity." Emme kicked at the grass bordering the sidewalk, releasing its earthy smell.

"Listen to this." Izzie flicked the page with her thumb and middle finger and read as if exposing a juicy scandal. "Clifton Davenport announced a coalition with Brazilian oil magnate, Leonardo Mendes, that will broaden market exposure by offering rare orchid varieties. Mendes and his associates, in town this week, are being hosted at the plantation."

Izzie stopped reading. "Speaking of exposure, I bet this reporter would drool over the tidbit that flowers provided for the Brazilian dignitaries are designed by Clifton's former fiancée."

"Can't happen." Emme adjusted the packing around a flower arrangement. The heavy floral scents in the confined space wrapped a shroud around her soul. Might as well be a funeral wreath. When Clifton put their engagement "on hold," he drove a stake in her heart. But what did it matter? First love getting a second chance was a distant dream. Harsh words ended their relationship four years ago—a fact she knew pleased his mother.

"I still think you should let sorry Clifton and his mother know you're the one running a successful flower shop, good enough to be selected for their event." Izzie tossed the newspaper back into the SUV. "And raising a three-year-old son to boot."

"No." The word was sharp and distasteful in her mouth. "The term successful is a stretch. We've covered this ground. His mother would fall faint—or whatever Southern ladies do—thinking I couldn't handle their elite affair."

"All the more reason to show her you can."

Emme shook her head. "I'm telling you, she'd ask Pam to get another florist. She never thought I could do anything worthwhile, and she especially didn't think I was good enough for Clifton."

"Did she tell you that?"

Emme wasn't proud she'd pressed her ear to the wall to listen to Mrs. Davenport talking to her husband, but the eavesdropping helped her know where she stood. "Not directly."

"Well then—"

"Trust me. If our work is to be considered on its merit, you've got to help me stay out of sight. I'm counting on you."

With Izzie's penchant to dress on the wild side, going unnoticed shouldn't be difficult. Her helper's ensemble today included three-inch hot pink espadrille wedge pumps, accenting a bright pink ruffled top tucked into a zebra-striped skirt. Emme should be close to invisible in her white slacks and yellow T-shirt topped with a practical white work apron.

Izzie pushed her lips into a pout, "You can't hide the fact you're Mary Elaine Matthews, florist extraordinaire, forever."

Emme crossed her arms in front of her. "I'm keeping a low profile, not hiding. Besides, you're the one who labeled me with my initials."

"Well, M.E. rolls off the tongue easier than Mary Elaine."

"I suppose. And providentially, M.E. evolved to E-m-m-e and just happens to give me a fresh identity."

"Whatever. You should tell him you own this shop. He deserves to know."

"Deserves? The guy gives me a ring, then runs overseas at his mother's bidding, and you think he deserves anything from me?"

"Correction." Izzie held up her palms and pushed at the air. "He'd get what he deserves by seeing the talented, beautiful, creative girl he gave up." She pressed fists to her hips. "Besides I thought he received some kind of university fellowship."

"He did. But I guarantee you his mother pulled the strings for him to get the appointment."

"I'm just sayin'—he called and tried to talk to you. You're the one who told him you never wanted to see or hear from him again."

"Well, he could have tried harder if he really cared." Emme slammed the rear car door closed. "Whose side are you on anyhow?"

"Yours, but—"

"Can we just get back to work?"

Izzie relinquished a shoulder shrug, then, with gray eyes twinkling, she said, "I know we can't jeopardize this job, but couldn't we deliver just a few black flowers?"

Emme stared at her friend a moment, then threw up her hands in surrender and laughed. What would she do without Izzie's humor to keep her sanity? "I get your drift, but all I want to see in black around here are my business books."

"Okay. Okay. Have it your way." Izzie bobbed her head, sending her silver doorknocker-sized earrings swaying.

Emme pushed hard against the decorative tip of a post on the iron fencing surrounding the Flower Cottage. With her friend's help, the job would be successful. "Davenport Plantation is thirty miles from here. We'll give them our best, then there'll be no need to cross paths again." She massaged the indentation pressed into her hand. "In the meantime, I'll remain out of Clifton's and his mom's sight, while my trusty assistant handles things up front."

Izzie gave Emme a snappy salute. "Right-o. I doubt there's any need to worry about being seen. Pam will be the one checking the banquet decorations."

"You best be on your way before the flowers do turn black in this heat."

As Izzie pulled away from the curb, Emme blew tense air from her lips. Soft bayside breezes nudged creaky retorts from the sign reading "The Flower Cottage since 1972" that hung from the trellis. Reentering the gate, she took a moment to admire the house painting job, of daffodil yellow with green shutter accents, she'd tackled on her own. The quaint two-story Craftsman home fulfilled a part of her childhood fantasy. But the other part—the love-of-her-life part—was sadly missing.

She stooped to pick up a rosebud broken off while loading the boxes. Two bluebirds skittered along a low-hanging oak limb. One took flight leaving the other alone.

Emme sank to the bench seat encircling a huge magnolia. The tree's oval-shaped leaves had provided the inspiration for garlands to embellish the mantle and dining table at the plantation. Would her "past tense" fiancé touch the smooth leaves latched in clusters to thirty-five feet of twine? What would he say if he knew she had designed the floral displays? Would he care?

"Designed by who?" he'd ask.

"The Matthews girl," his mother would respond, tartness in her tone.

"Matthews …" he'd tap his finger to his lips. "That name is familiar."

"You know," his mother would scoff, "the little waif with the alcoholic stepfather you fell head over heels for in your younger, foolish days."

"Umm. I have a vague remembrance …"

Emme opened her palm and studied the flower she'd picked up. "Too bad you'll never reach full-bloom." She fingered the red blossom, releasing its sweet perfume. The bruised petals felt soft in her hand but sent a hard reminder of a history with Clifton she needed to forget.

Emme turned off the two-lane highway onto the winding paved road leading to Colonnades. Her stomach was a trap for frenzied butterflies. She made her way along the drive lined with varying shades of pink azaleas and enormous oak trees. Her heart pounded against her rib cage, ignoring mental pleas for calm. Traveling the drive brought the taste of bittersweet nostalgia.

On the final turn, the imposing manor came into view—a grand display against the afternoon sky's blue canvas. A single gray cloud hung over the house—a sign of impending doom? Or perhaps a label marking Davenport ancestral pride.

Her tires bumped over steel train rails no longer in use. A lone railroad passenger car stood on the right side-lawn, surrounded by rose bushes. The sight transported her to six-year-old Clifton in his red-and-green elf cap greeting her family on the Christmas tree train.

Ahead, the columned porch where she and Clifton, nearly twelve years later, were welcomed by Clifton's father on a weekend visit from college. He was a gracious Southern gentleman; his mother, cordial but cool.

Emme shook her head, trying to erase the memories. Focus. Pam had instructed her to park alongside Chef Ormond's catering van on the east side of the house. She sent a quick text to Izzie—*I'm here*. She barely had time to unhook her seat belt when Izzie rushed out the side door as fast as her high-stilted shoes and snug skirt allowed.

"Thank goodness you're here. Pam is anxious to get the flag set up. Mrs. Davenport wants to approve the display."

Buzzards displaced butterflies and soared across Emme's insides. Her hands, white-knuckled, clenched the steering wheel. "I can't go in there."

"Don't worry." Izzie gave Emme's shoulder a reassuring touch. "The lady of the house hasn't been in the dining room. I asked Pam to let us set up the display before notifying Mrs. Davenport. Come on."

Heart be still. Emme slid from the van seat. She could do this. Put one foot in front of the other. The van. Remember the van payment. She brushed her hand over the Flower Cottage logo painted on the side.

Izzie opened the rear van doors. "Wow. I bet Brazil's flag never looked so good. This display oughta knock Ms. D's socks off."

"I doubt Mrs. Davenport owns anything so mundane as socks."

They pulled the three-by-five-foot structure from the van, careful not to disturb the water tubes holding each flower stem and made their way through the kitchen service entry.

Inside the tall ceilinged kitchen, Chef Ormond, dressed in a white chef's jacket and traditional toque, worked within a white cloud of flour he shook from a sifter. The aroma of sautéed garlic and onion, tended by his assistant, rose in the steam from a skillet on the gas stove. The odor made Emme's stomach tighten.

"Afternoon, chef." Emme quelled her inner turmoil, opting to show an unruffled face. She and Izzie had worked with Chef Ormond on a couple of other catered events. "Everything going okay?"

Chef peered at Emme over dusty wire-rimmed spectacles. "Food, good—help, not so good. Can't depend on anyone these days." He whacked an egg against a mixing bowl, opened it one-handed and began punishing it with a wire whisk. "Whatever happened to your word being your bond?"

"Someone let you down?" Izzie asked.

"The couple I was counting on to serve tonight aren't coming. Seems they skipped town owing their landlady a week's rent." His feverish whisking produced a yellow mixture the color of sunflowers.

"What are you going to do?"

"I don't know. I left a message with my brother and sister-in-law, but I think they went out of town."

"What kind of help do you need?" Emme asked.

"One person to serve and another for clean-up. The job will pay seventy-five each for the evening. Know anyone who could work?"

Izzie's brows shot upward. "Seventy-five bucks? I waited tables to get through school and I'm free for the evening. Count me in."

Chef's eyes glistened. "You're hired. Emme, how are you with washing dishes?"

"I'd like to help, but I need to get back to my little boy after we finish the flowers. I'll try to think of someone."

Chef Ormond nodded his thanks, then took notice of their creation made with white, blue, yellow and green mums.

"Nice work, ladies. It's a flag of …?"

"Brazil." Izzie said. "What do you think?"

Chef clicked his heels and made a sharp salute leaving a diagonal line of flour on the side of his face. "I'd sing their national anthem if I knew it."

Emme relaxed a bit. She could handle this event.

Pam Boswick, in her signature black-rimmed glasses with large round lenses, met them as they made their way from the kitchen into the dining room. She helped them move the display around the alcove wall that shielded beverage service and the kitchen door from the banquet room.

"You girls have done a fantastic job. Love, love, love the arrangements for the banquet table and the flag is absolutely beautiful." Pam wore her black hair in a page boy that shimmered in the light of crystal chandeliers that bedecked the high ceiling. She spoke with expressive sweeping gestures to emphasize her words. "I just found out tonight's dinner is not only to honor dignitaries from Brazil, but an engagement announcement."

Emme's grip on the flag frame slipped. Izzie steadied the structure.

"Let me help. We need this in one piece." Pam held the frame in the middle and helped position the floral display across from the head table.

"We have a stand for the flag in the van," Izzie said.

"Good. Lean the frame against the wall for now."

"Whose engagement?" Izzie asked.

"One of the sons. There're two, I understand."

Emme's knees turned to rubber. Clifton had a younger brother, Gavin. Could he be getting engaged? Or was it … Emme couldn't control her heart rate, gone on a roller coaster ride.

Pam pulled her phone from her pocket. "Mrs. Davenport wanted me to call when the flag arrived."

"No need to call, I'm here."

The unmistakable voice of Rosemary Davenport preceded her. Emme flinched and bolted for the alcove leading to the kitchen, plastering her back to the wall. Each beat of her heart thundered in her ears. Squeezing her eyes closed, she concentrated on controlling her breathing. If only she could become one with the wall. She listened to the voices.

Mrs. Davenport said, "Gavin told me he saw the florist van arrive."

Pam replied, "I was just calling to let you know."

"Hmm … the garlands and flowers …" She was about to pass judgment. Emme held her breath. "… are exquisite." Emme's eyes popped open.

"Beautiful work, I agree. Meet Izzie Ketterling with the Flower Cottage."

"Nice to meet you."

"Very nice work."

"What happened to Emme?" Pam asked

Izzie replied, "Uh … she went to get the stand for the flag."

Mrs. Davenport hummed. "Ah, the flag."

Emme heard footsteps cross the room.

"Isn't that green a bit light?"

Izzie answered Mrs. Davenport's question. "Mums absorb dye to change their color which results in natural, muted tones."

"The effect is quite lovely, but I'd hate to disrespect their flag with the wrong shade of green."

Emme had heard Mrs. Davenport's "but" the night Clifton announced their engagement. "Lovely maybe," she'd overheard her tell Clifton's father, "*but* lovely doesn't make her good marriage material."

Izzie suggested, "We could darken the green with a touch of spray paint if you like."

"I see, but I don't want you going to extra trouble if it's not necessary." There was a pause. "I'll send Clifton to check the flag. He won't want to displease his future father-in-law."

Emme gripped a fistful of apron. The roller coaster inside dropped, taking her breath away. Clifton was the one getting engaged.

Chapter 3

The afternoon sun streaked beams of light through the blinds in the Davenport business office.

"Sorry about the order mix up, Carolyn. We'll have the extra whites you were shorted sent out immediately." Clifton ended the call and looked at Gavin.

"Can you have Eduardo cut the snapdragons?"

Gavin stood, grasping the back of the chair he'd been sitting in. "Sure. Don't forget the corsages. They should be presented by you tonight."

"Appreciate it. I couldn't function without you, brother."

"Not when it comes to business. I'm glad that's your department."

Clifton knew Gavin was sincere. He wished he was worthy of his brother's trust. His phone sounded. He rolled his eyes toward Gavin, "Mom."

Gavin beamed. "More engagement party details, no doubt. I'm leaving."

Clifton threw a hand up in a half-hearted wave, "Thanks." He grabbed a form to record the Carolyn's Flowers order before the matter left his head, then answered his phone.

"Hi, Mom."

"What took you so long to answer?"

"Business."

"Let Gavin take care of things at the nursery. Don't you realize the dinner tonight is very important?"

"They're businessmen, not royalty."

"One of those men is going to be your father-in-law, and he holds the fate of Davenport properties in his hand. By the way, where's the ring?"

"Ring?" He knew precisely what ring she meant but didn't want to remember. Grandma Davenport presented the heirloom to him ceremoniously on his sixteenth birthday. Given to her on her sixteenth birthday, she decided the special diamond and ruby studded ring should go to her first-born grandchild with instructions to save it for his future bride.

"Grandma's ring."

"Mary Elaine still has it."

"What?" He jerked the phone away from his ear, switched to speaker and lowered the volume. He'd told Mary Elaine to keep the ring, thinking they would get back together. Another example of his gut instincts misleading him. She had moved on, and he needed to do the same.

"Clifton, why on earth ... Renata should have that ring."

"Renata picked out what she wanted. She wouldn't be satisfied with that old-fashioned style ring anyhow."

"If Grandma knew—"

"Grandma is dead and gone, but I'm sure she would understand."

"Oh, Clifton, that ring should stay in the family. Knowing the stepfather of that girl, it's probably been pawned by now."

"The guy had a bum rap." Clifton drummed his fingers against the wood desktop. "If that's what you called about, don't worry. The ring for Renata is taken care of." His mother was perfectly happy to have him handle business matters, but when it came to his personal life, meddling was her skilled expertise.

"Fine." The word landed with a distinct "not fine" tone. At least she did change subjects. "I need you to check on the dinner decorations."

"Why? I thought you said the florist came highly recommended."

"I know. But I need you to look at the floral Brazil flag display. It's pretty, but not the right shade of green."

"If the display looks good I'm sure everyone will be pleased."

"But Mr. Mendes has a critical eye. I don't want him offended if the colors aren't right."

"What do you expect me to do?"

"I'd just feel better if you checked. The florist said they could spray the flowers a darker green, but I don't want them to go to all that trouble if you think it's okay. Besides, spraying the flowers might make them look worse. Just look at the flag ... please."

"I'll take care of it."

"Promise?"

Clifton formed the three-finger Boy Scout pledge. "I promise." The only two words that would get him off the phone. Then, of course, he had to do what he promised.

He ended the call, finished the order form and entered the information into the computer. Along with managing minor crises, dealing with worn equipment, and generating an income greater than expenses, Clifton's latest focus had been on computerizing the family's business. Clifton arched his back and rubbed the tense muscles in his neck. "Lord," he whispered, "I may need your help to get through this day." He scrubbed the palms of his hands against his face.

The phone rang again. His mother. He let it go to voicemail, then listened to the recording. "Check the flowers in the dining room too." Clifton pulled the roll of antacids from his pocket, tossed the last two remaining into his mouth, and stood, ready to make the half-mile journey to Colonnades.

Clifton strode past the caterer and florist vans and entered the kitchen, filled with aromas accented by garlic and lemon. Chef Ormond's skilled use with a French knife made rat-a-tat chopping noises.

"How are things going?"

Chef never looked up. "The food? Fine. The help? Another story."

"I can sympathize."

Chef remained busy, pushing chopped lemon slices into a blender. "If you're looking for Pam, she left in a rush, something about music."

"That's okay, I don't need her. I'm just here to see how the floral arrangements are coming along."

"I took a peek at the banquet hall. The decorations—superb." He touched his fingers to his lips in bon appetit fashion.

Clifton raised his eyebrows to try and muster enthusiasm. A simple vase with a few fresh flowers would suit him, but not his mother—or his soon to be father-in-law. Father-in-law? That reality hadn't taken hold yet. He was still trying to come to grips with the idea of a wife.

Sucking in a deep breath, he received a whiff of fresh bread as he walked past the ovens. Normally that smell sparked pleasant sensations, but today—not so much.

Just take a day at a time. Each day holds enough trouble in itself. *Is that you, Lord?* Clifton made his way through the kitchen door into the banquet room, sending up a prayer as he walked. *Lord, I pray I've had my trouble quota for the day.*

The table setting looked nice enough. A woman, with black hair in a permanent state of fright, was busy adding accent flowers to a garland on the fireplace mantle.

"Afternoon."

The girl jumped, dropping a bright orange zinnia on the floor. "Oh, hi. I didn't hear you come in."

"Sorry, I didn't mean to startle you. I'm Clifton Davenport." He retrieved the flower she'd dropped and handed it to her.

"Thank you. Nice to meet you. I'm Isabella Ketterling, but everybody calls me Izzie."

She stood tall in elevated shoes, only a couple of inches shorter than his six feet. Huge earrings that could have been salvaged from a plumber's tool box swung from her earlobes.

"Well, Izzie," Clifton cleared his throat, "I'm just checking to see how the decorations are coming along." He turned his attention to the table. "Outstanding job on these arrangements." Clifton checked his watch and turned to scan the room. "There's supposed to be a flag of Brazil?"

"Uh ... my ... uh friend ... well, she's not just my friend, she's my employer. I help out, you know. She ... I guess you'd call me her assistant ... anyhow, the florist shop owner, that's it, the shop owner, we took the display outside to spray a few of the flowers a deeper green, so you could judge which looks best."

"I just need to see the flag."

"Uh ... I'll go get it for you."

"No need. I'll go outside."

Why was she so nervous? Maybe his mother did have reason for concern. He'd hate to have a tacky display or worse, dishonor Brazil's flag.

Izzie scurried ahead, speaking over her shoulder. "We set up several feet from the kitchen entry to prevent any spray coming back on the house."

He followed the spiky-haired woman, wearing a hot pink top and striped skirt that a zebra might mistake for a loved one. What if they got that creative with Brazil's flag? Izzie disappeared behind the Flower Cottage van. He heard muffled speech and then the van door open and close on the opposite side.

What was the deal? Was the florist incompetent? Maybe the day's trouble wasn't over after all.

Emme's cell phone buzzed in her holed-up position inside the van. She wrestled the phone from her pocket, gave the screen a quick swipe to silence the ring and answered the call.

"Ms. Matthews, sorry to bother you, but this is Larry at Low Price Auto Sales."

Emme crawled to the back of the van, cracking her knee against a box. Stifling a yelp, she answered, "Yes?"

"Just a reminder. Your van payment is due today." His voice leaned more toward pleased than sorry.

"There's a grace period, right? Eddie told me a week's extension wouldn't be a problem. I should have the money for you by next week," Emme said in a hushed voice.

"Eddie no longer works here. The due date is the due date, and I'm having trouble hearing you."

"Sorry." Emme pushed a couple of boxes in front of her to create a noise barrier in the back of the van she was in danger of losing. "But I'm right in the middle of a big job that will make the payment."

"Ms. Matthews, business is business, but I'm willing to work with you. You can make the payment next week if I get the eighteen percent penalty fee tomorrow."

What a guy. The oil from the guy's words could grease a tractor. "Eighteen percent?"

"It's in the contract."

"Right." Emme had a vision of the $12.08 balance in her savings account, drained by the cooler repair. No way she could function without her van. Emme peeked out the rear window at the catering van. Chef's plea for help could be her salvation.

"I'll have the fee for you tomorrow."

"By nine o'clock."

"Count on it."

Emme ended the call. The van side door rumbled open and Emme shrunk behind the boxes. The cold hard metal of the rear van doors pressed into her back.

"Relax. It's me." Izzie's barbed hair appeared first as she poked her head into the van.

Emme let out a breath. "Thank heaven."

"Clifton's a looker." Izzie wiggled her eyebrows up and down like a flashing neon sign.

Crawling forward on hands and knees, Emme squinted in sinister fashion at her friend.

"Along with being a bum for what he did to you, of course."

She backed up for Emme to have space to exit the van. "I see who wears the pants in that family."

"And who would that be?"

"His mom."

Emme held a bull dog stance on the van floor and raised a brow. "Figures. What makes you say that?"

"He called his mother to report that the green would be acceptable once we sprayed them."

Emme raised up, bumping her head against the open-door frame. "Acceptable?" Ignoring the bump, she jumped from the van and brushed at the bits of leaves and dirt pressed in the knees of her slacks.

"Well ... better than not."

"I suppose. His attitude just burns me." She turned and gestured toward the display. "As hard as we worked on that flag, and it's just acceptable?" She turned back to Izzie. "And now I've got sleazy Larry hounding me for the van payment."

"I thought you had an extra week."

"Me too. But Larry informed me the guy who told me I could have extra time no longer works for him."

"Now what? I know you are counting on payment from this job to get us over the hump for the month."

"If I pay an eighteen percent late fee by nine tomorrow morning, he said he'd hold off a week."

"And that comes to ...?"

"Close to sixty dollars. Looks like Chef Ormond has his dishwasher for tonight—me."

Chapter 4

"Five forty-five." Emme read the time on the digital display in Izzie's Suburban. "We must have set a record getting dressed and back here in less than two hours."

"Yup. Changed from floral designers to chef's worker bees—Superman-like." Izzie wheeled into the mansion drive, parked beside Chef Ormond's van, and pushed the gear shift into park. "All I had to do was change. You had to get Richie settled with the sitter too."

"I'm blessed to have Mellie, ever-ready to watch Richie. But I could have used Superman's phone booth for changing." Emme unsnapped her seatbelt and stepped out of the car, adjusting her black slacks and tucking in her white shirt. "It's hard trying to dress with a seat belt on. I hope my van appreciates me moonlighting."

"You think your van cares?"

"Ought to. I'm saving it from the clutches of Low-life Larry. You should have stopped me from dealing with him."

"You gotta be joking." Izzie's eyes opened wider than the conservative quarter-sized earrings she wore for their evening job. "Me? Stop Ms. Independence? When you decide, you put your choice in a choke hold." Izzie demonstrated with clenched fingers held to her neck, then motioned for Emme to follow her.

"I might be a little headstrong at times," Emme muttered to Izzie's backside and continued straightening her outfit.

When Izzie opened the service entrance door leading to the kitchen, the savory aroma of roasting meat mixed with the distinct, yeasty scent of fresh bread rode the air currents.

"Whoa. The PB and J we inhaled doesn't compare to those smells," Izzie said, sniffing the air. "Maybe we can dine on leftovers."

"Normally I'd agree, but my tummy's having trouble enough handling the peanut butter and jelly." Her brain, nerves and stomach all questioned her wisdom in returning to the plantation.

Inside, Chef Ormond, busy lining asparagus bundles in baking dishes, issued orders to his assistant in Spanish.

"We're back." Izzie announced.

He glanced in their direction and motioned to a short hallway across from the kitchen. "Good. I put vests and ties for you in the cook's quarters." He turned his attention back to the stove.

"The cook has his own quarters," Izzie said in "la-di-da" fashion.

"Probably expected in mansion circles." Emme followed Izzie to a small neat room of simple design with a twin bed, dresser, and wooden rocker. Black vests and ties were laid out on a tan duvet bed cover.

"You know how to tie one of these things?" Emme asked holding up the black strip as if it were a lifeless worm.

"I do." Izzie grabbed the tie, hung it around her neck, and began manipulating. "I learned from a waiter when I worked at a summer resort."

Emme sank into the rocker and watched Izzie's tying expertise. "What am I doing here? If it weren't for that Larry guy dunning me for the van payment, I'd never have come back tonight."

"Relax. You'll be in the kitchen most of the time. I've got you covered." Izzie picked up the other tie. "Stand up."

Raising Emme's collar, Izzie worked the tie into a knot. The tightening at her neck added to the tension rising in her throat. Emme took a look in the mirror. The white shirt made her fair complexion paler. "This must be what servants feel like when they're preparing to wait on royalty."

"And for seventy-five bucks, I'll wash their royal feet if they want."

"What do I do if Clifton or his mother walk in the kitchen?"

"Are you kidding, royalty wouldn't step foot in a kitchen."

"Well ... he's not really royalty."

"Quit worrying. I'm sure he'll stay right beside his intended."

"His intended. You had to remind me."

"Sorry."

Emme pulled the holder from her hair, letting the tresses tumble down to her shoulders. She tugged at her hair to camouflage the left side of her face. "How's this?"

"My, my, where did Emme go? We could always put a bag over your head for a fail-proof disguise."

"Funny. But I'm serious."

"Okay. So cover your face with your hair." Izzie flung expressive hands outward. That will be the plan if anyone shows up that might recognize you. Now, let's get to work."

Emme pulled her hair back to form a loose knot at the nape of her neck and tugged at her tie.

"You'll be fine." Izzie gave Emme's shoulder an encouraging pat.

In the kitchen, Chef Ormond switched to boss mode. "Set out the tableware and condiments. Follow my sketch." He pointed to a paper sitting on the counter. "Dessert and salad will be served from the kitchen, so stack those plates by the trays."

Normally being told what to do chipped at Emme's self-sufficiency but not having to be responsible for the decision-making tonight filled her with an odd comfort.

Izzie grabbed a stainless-steel serving cart and pulled it next to the tableware. "You gather the plates, I'll collect the cups and glasses, and we'll go from there."

By 6:30, the table appointments, salt and peppers, butter dishes, dressings, and breadbaskets were in place, water glasses filled, and the buffet in the alcove was prepared for hot and cold beverage service. Emme sucked in a breath, pleased with what they had accomplished. The candles flickering in the floral arrangements presented a peaceful ambiance. Classical music played softly in the background.

Izzie stepped back to take in the total effect. "Romantic, huh?"

A hollowness settled into Emme's chest. "Yeah, romantic." Could the contrast in her engagement to Clifton and tonight's fanfare be more different?

"Engaged?" Mr. Davenport's broad smile had seemed genuine. He rose from his chair, hugged Emme's neck and shook Clifton's hand. Mrs. Davenport had remained seated—her posture stiff, hands tightly clasped—and allowed only a slight upturn of her lips. She motioned to her husband, "Richard, there is something I forgot I needed to talk to you about. Excuse us a moment?"

When they left the room, she'd told Clifton, "Now is the perfect time for me to run to the bathroom." But when she went down the hall, she wasn't prepared to hear the words voiced by Clifton's mother.

"She is NOT good enough for Clifton. She has that alcoholic stepfather. A disgrace."

"You can't blame her for his actions," Clifton's father responded.

"Regardless. Don't you see? She will be a black mark on our good name. Clifton needs someone who is not just lovely, but extraordinary."

"In Clifton's eyes, she is. You must accept that."

"Accept? I don't have to accept her."

"You'll only alienate Clifton and drive him away if you push your negative attitude. Now pull yourself together. Let's not ruin this time for them."

Emme never made it to the bathroom. When she returned to the living room, Clifton was preoccupied with a phone call from his brother. Chin trembling, a painful tightness in her throat, she had blinked back tears.

Her breathing had been shaky that night, not unlike tonight.

"I'd best get started washing dishes."

She retreated to her dishwashing station. Minutes later, Izzie pushed through the kitchen door.

"They're here."

The two words made Emme's quickly eaten sandwich do the swing in her stomach.

Izzie stepped over to Emme and lowered her voice. "Mr. Mendes was impressed with the flag. The girl with Clifton gave him a hug when she saw the display. He told her the flag was Gavin's idea."

"True. Pam said Gavin had the idea and made the request."

"Gavin got a big ole' front hug from Clifton's girlfriend too. Her name's Renata by the way, but she doesn't compare to you."

Emme stepped up her scrubbing speed. The night's employment was her ticket to saving her van. Nothing more. What Clifton did was none of her business.

Chef Ormond and Tony loaded the main course plates on a tray for Izzie and she was off again. She returned with the used salad plates and delivered them to Emme. "Chef, your chicken cordon bleu is getting rave remarks."

"Good to hear."

By now, fresh scents of orange, lemon, coconut, and chocolate sweetened the air. Chef motioned for Emme to join him while he took parfait glasses lined with strips of banana from the freezer and placed them on a tray.

"Dessert is a lemon sorbet creation with sauces offered separately. Emme, you hold the sauce tray while Izzie serves the topping of their choice."

"Uh ..." Emme looked to Izzie for help.

"Can't I put the sauces on the table for them to pass?" Izzie asked.

"No, no, no. My dessert is magnificent." He leaned forward, eyes wide. "But only when served properly. The typical guest thinks more is better when they pour on the sauce which is simply death by drowning and ruins the sorbet." Chef's eyes glistened with moisture.

Izzie's spiky hair didn't budge as she bobbed her head up and down. "We're here for you, Chef, whatever you need."

Chef returned to his task arranging the glasses taken from the freezer.

Emme's jaw went slack. Izzie patted her shoulder. "Our plan will work, Emme. The guests are so absorbed in conversation, they won't look at us. Do that thing with your hair. The lights are low. I'll be back after I clear the dinner plates."

Emme dried her trembling hands and went to the cook's quarters. She loosened her hair from the holder and mechanically draped her hair to cover one side of her face. Didn't someone say if you act like you belong, no one will notice?

When she returned, a tray had been readied with the chilled parfaits. Chef added scoops of sorbet and a sprinkling of toasted coconut to the glasses while his assistant placed the sauces in small pitchers on another tray.

Chef clicked his heels and instructed Izzie. "Announce the dessert is a special sorbet creation for the bride-to-be. Mrs. Davenport said she loves banana splits. Then explain the choice of sauces."

Emme swallowed down the sour taste in her mouth. Special creation for the bride-to-be? Mrs. Davenport evidently found someone good enough for Clifton.

Chef Ormond pointed to each sauce as he recited descriptions. "The brown sauce is a fresh raspberry with dark chocolate; the red, a strawberry almondine. The orange sauce is a tart favorite made with orange and kumquat juice, and the last is my signature lemon zest butter sauce—a refreshing creamy blend and an especially nice accent to the sorbet."

Izzie repeated the sauce descriptions and left the kitchen to deliver the sorbets.

Emme stood by the kitchen door, chanting, "I can do this, I can do this," to herself.

After a few moments, Izzie stuck her head in kitchen door, "Ready with the sauces?"

Emme had difficulty swallowing. "I hope so."

"You'll be fine. They're definitely not expecting the florists to be serving dinner. Now is your chance to witness their shindig first hand."

Emme took a deep breath and carried the tray through the kitchen door. How hard could acting like she belonged be? The room, that earlier had carried a warm cozy feel, struck her as chilling. The flickering candlelight cast variant shadows that distorted the features of the twenty or so dinner guests. Hopefully the dismal lighting obscured her face. She relaxed a bit and joined Izzie, at the head table.

The girl named Renata, seated beside Clifton, tapped the coconut with her long slender parfait spoon. "You were so thoughtful to remember my favorite dessert."

"I'd like to take credit, but …" Clifton leaned forward to see his brother seated on the other side of Renata. Clifton's brother shrugged, "I suggested the dessert, and Mom put in the order."

Renata turned to Gavin. Even in low lighting, the girl's good looks managed to shine through. "Gavin, the flag and now, a special dessert." She nudged Clifton. "You have the most thoughtful brother ever."

Clifton ran his finger around the rim of his water glass and looked as if he'd like to be somewhere else. Emme knew the feeling.

Izzie recited the sauce selections for all to hear, then asked Renata, "Your sauce, ma'am?"

"Chocolate-raspberry, please."

Clifton suddenly raised his head and eyed Izzie. "Aren't you the florist I talked to today?"

Emme flinched and the tray jerked upward. Izzie lost her hold on the chocolate sauce which collided with the lemon pitcher. Emme made a desperate attempt to balance the tray, but not before the entire pitcher of chocolate sauce tumbled off the tray, landing squarely in Renata's lap.

My new dress—ruined." Renata pushed back from the table. The empty pitcher rolled from her lap and clattered to the floor.

Clifton grabbed his napkin—his first opportunity to make a positive contribution during the evening. He dabbed at the oozing mess spilling over the gathers on the front of Renata's lavender evening dress.

Gavin adjusted the room's dimmer light switch. The texture of the room moved from shadowed and soft to harsh reality. The two waitresses had retreated to the kitchen.

Clifton's mother, in take-charge mode, stood. "Everyone just stay seated." She hurried over and hovered. "Clifton, hand me a spoon and empty cup. Sit still dear, while I scoop up the biggest part of the spill. Such a lovely dress. I do hope it isn't ruined."

The floral designer Clifton met earlier in the day returned with a bowl of water and a clean cloth. "Thank you. Is it Ms. Ketterling?"

"Yes. Call me Izzie, please."

Clifton accepted the bowl and cloth, then handed them to his mother,

To Renata, Izzie said, "We are so sorry for the mishap. If you will bring us the dress, we'll have it cleaned."

"I should think so," Mrs. Davenport said. "You should also deduct the cost of dessert that none of us have been able to enjoy."

Clifton could see his mother's demands put Izzie on the spot. "I'm sure we can work something out."

To her credit, Renata spoke up. "I hate all the fuss over an accident. Please, everyone, enjoy dessert minus the chocolate sauce." She held out her arms to reveal the obvious. "I'll change and be right back."

"Let me walk you upstairs," Clifton said. Suggesting seemed awkward. But why? In South America, he had been comfortable with Renata. They both shared the loss of a parent to cancer and had grown to care for one another in that common bond. But here, their relationship seemed different. When she arrived in the States with her father and his cohorts, Clifton felt he'd been placed under a microscope for scrutiny.

Their footsteps were muffled against the carpeted stairs and polished mahogany bannister leading from the foyer to the second-floor bedrooms.

"What should I put on?"

"Uh ... well, I like your red dress."

She looked at him puzzled. "Won't that clash with my corsage?"

"Does it matter?"

"Of course. Gavin's taking pictures after our announcement. I don't want the flowers you gave me to look bad."

"When it comes to colors and picking ensembles, I'm afraid I'm not your man."

She glanced at him, her lips upturned. Was that a forced smile? "With these flowers, my choices are a flowery sundress or a white pant suit. Is a pant suit suitable for this occasion?"

"I don't know. Why not?"

They stood at the landing at the top of the stairs.

"Would you mind checking with Gavin while I get out of my dress?"

Clifton shrugged. "No problem."

Clifton punched in Gavin's speed dial number. He answered in a hushed tone.

"Put on your fashion consultant hat. Renata wants to know if she should wear the flowery dress or white pant suit and are pants acceptable at our fancy dinner?"

Gavin actually had a response right away. How did he do that? "The corsage would be lost in the flower print. Tell her to wear her white lace top, and the pant suit will be fine."

"Where did you learn fashion stuff?"

"Nothin' to it. Some of us got it; some don't."

"You got that right. That's why I stick to white, black, or khaki."

Renata poked her head out of the guest room door. "What did he say?"

"The white pantsuit with the lace top."

Her dark eyes sparkled at the suggestion. "Good idea. I'll be right out."

Clifton stepped to the railing. The chandelier created a checkerboard of bright and shadowed light on the dark wood floor of the foyer below. Every time he looked at the front entrance, he was reminded of Mary Elaine's first impression of the entrance to Colonnades. "Awesome," she'd said. Her enthusiasm had made him look at what he'd always taken for granted in a new light. The chandelier and staircase were beautiful, and he'd never taken time to appreciate them. Could Renata teach him to appreciate the aesthetic side of life?

The doorknob rattled behind him, and he turned to see a stunning Renata. The white pant suit contrasted with her dark hair and bronze complexion. She had her chocolate-soiled dress in hand.

"What do you think?" She turned about to present a 360-degree view.

"Very nice."

She smiled at him. His remark seemed to please her. Dress for him didn't carry so much weight.

"Can you pin on my corsage?"

"I'll try." His mother had helped pin on the flowers earlier.

He took the flowers and long sharp pin from her extended hand. Attempting to attach the flowers to her lapel took him back to a fraternity dance and laughing with Mary Elaine when the corsage he pinned on her kept falling off. The flowers became ragged, and she finally put them behind her ear.

"My track record for pinning on corsages is not good."

"Oh? Have you tried often?"

"Nope. But often enough to know Mom is a better pinner. We'd better get back downstairs. Mom has had sufficient time to register her complaints about the dessert service I hope."

When they returned downstairs, conversation was buzzing as everyone finished dessert. Only Renata's uncle's seat was vacant. Izzie brought coffee cups and placed them at Clifton's and Renata's place settings.

Renata handed her dress to Izzie. "I appreciate your offer to get my dress cleaned."

"Absolutely. Again, I am so sorry."

"I want to apologize too," Clifton said. "I'm afraid I startled you, but I was surprised to see you were both florist and waitress."

"Just helping out Chef Ormond. I'll bring your sorbets. Sauces are on the table. Chef made up more chocolate sauce."

Clifton's mom shared something that made Mr. Mendes laugh. The atmosphere had brightened. Izzie returned with the sorbets and poured coffee for Renata and Clifton.

His mom leaned over to him. "Mr. Rodrigues stepped out to take a call. When he returns, I think you should announce the engagement."

Clifton rubbed the back of his neck and adjusted his collar. He grabbed his linen napkin and squeezed. Beautiful girl, beautiful occasion. How hard could it be to make a statement about their plans to get married?

When Rodrigues entered the room, Clifton knew he had to get the announcement over with. He stood, clinked a spoon against his water glass, and cleared his throat gone dry. "Everyone. Again, I welcome our esteemed guests to my family's home for this special occasion. It is my pleasure not only to welcome you as our companies merge interests, but to announce that Renata has agreed to marry me."

Everyone smiled. Some applauded while some leaned to their neighbors to get the Portuguese translation. Only Rodrigues wore a grave expression. He walked briskly to Mr. Mendes and stooped down to speak in his ear.

Renata stood. "And I am a lucky girl to have a special man who wants to marry me."

She leaned over and kissed Clifton on the cheek and sat back down. Heat rose on his neck.

Uncle Jorge straightened and stood stiff behind Mendes. Mendes's face had visibly reddened, his eyes bulging. Something had happened. News of a relative dying? An oil spill? Upset his daughter kissed Clifton on the cheek? The big man stood so suddenly his chair flipped backward and hit the carpeted floor with a thud.

"Special man?" Mendes bellowed. He slammed both fists on the table. Everyone stopped talking and turned to stare.

"What do you take me for?" He seemed to look directly at Clifton. Was there someone behind him? He checked. No one there.

"You didn't think we would find out?"

He definitely directed that question at him.

"You think that we come from some third world nation and are stupid?" He pushed the fallen chair out of the way.

"Are you talking to me, sir?"

"You bet I am."

Rosemary Davenport stood. "What in heaven's name are you shouting about?"

"Suppose you tell us, Mr. Clifton Richard Davenport."

"Tell you what?"

"That if you married my daughter you would be a bigamist."

Clifton's jaw went slack.

"Absurd!" Rosemary protested.

Renata stood. "Papa what are you talking about?"

"I'm talking about a report I just received. It seems the special man here is already married."

Chapter 5

Emme's hands still trembled in the hot soapy water. She concentrated on each dish with its gilded edge, horrified at the thought of breaking one. She didn't want to create any more problems for Chef than she had already.

From the dining room, she heard applause and raised voices. The happy announcement must have been made.

Izzie pushed through the swinging door, sending a wave of cooled air into the warm kitchen where the aroma of chicken cordon bleu still clung to the air.

"You are not going to believe what just happened."

Emme carefully placed the plate she'd washed onto the drain board. She turned to see Izzie holding Renata's soiled dress in her arms like a soldier carrying a dead comrade.

"Oh, I might. That must be a three-hundred-dollar item we're going to have to spring for."

"Forget the dress. There may be no engagement or wedding."

"No?" Chef Ormond's eyebrows touched the edge of his chef hat.

"What are you talking about?" Emme asked.

"Clifton's already married. When one of the men from Brazil delivered the news, Mendes blew his top."

"He's married?" Emme stared at Izzie.

"Mendes accused Clifton of being a bigamist if he married his daughter."

"Incredible." Emme clasped her wet hands together. "What did Clifton say?"

"Nothing. He just stood there with his mouth open."

Emme stepped back, shaking her head. "No denial? I can't believe he'd do something like that." Even with all the pain of Clifton's walking out on their engagement, she had always believed he was basically a good person. Was she that bad a judge of character? Did he marry someone during his overseas travel? "Why would he be willing to marry Renata if he was married to someone else?"

"The guy must have some kind of marriage fetish," Izzie said.

Chef crossed his arms and rubbed his fingers against his chin. "You girls want to fill me in on what you're talking about?"

"Clifton and I were engaged before we graduated from college, but he changed his mind and went to Europe instead," Emme said.

Chef shook his head. "And I made you go out there. You should have told me."

"You're right." Emme dropped her head and eyed the stained dress. "We should have told you and now ... we don't expect you to pay us with the mess we've caused."

"And we'll take care of cleaning the dress of course," Izzie said.

"No. You'll be paid once you finish clean-up. But the dress, I leave that to you."

The kitchen door swung open and Gavin Davenport walked in.

Instinctively, Emme ducked into the utility room and pressed herself against a wall of mops, brooms and cleaning supplies. Encircled by the strong odor of disinfectant, she listened to Gavin speak.

"I wanted to thank you for a wonderful dinner, Chef Ormond."

"I'm glad you enjoyed it," Chef answered. "Sorry for the chocolate sauce mishap."

"Those things happen. I ... uh ... just wanted to let you know you can start clean-up. The party is over."

Emme waved goodbye as Izzie pulled out of the parking area behind the florist shop. She stood in the warm evening air, holding the soiled lavender dress. The clear night sky presented a black backdrop to show off its bright stars.

She and Clifton had held hands and examined those stars on a similar night outside Westcott Hall on the Florida State campus.

"Did you know if you draw an imaginary line from the Big Dipper, it points to the North Star in the handle of the Little Dipper?"

Clifton turned her chin toward him, hugging her close, and resting his chin on her head. His breath on her hair had warmed her heart.

"No. But I do know I want you to marry me." His lips brushed hers sending a tingle through her body. Her answer came in a long deepening kiss that dizzied her head. When she opened her eyes, he pulled a ring from his pocket. A diamond-and-ruby-studded silver band shimmered in the moonlight.

"It was my grandmother's. She gave me the ring with instructions that I give it to the love of my life." She could still hear the deep resonance of his voice.

She'd nuzzled her head under his chin, feeling the steady rhythm of his heart next to hers as they gazed at the North Star.

She still had the ring he gave her. What ring did he give Renata? What about the mystery bride? Did he have a sack full of his grandma's rings?

The stars winked. Emme lowered her eyes and took in reality—her gravel parking lot and the florist van she was struggling to make payments on.

How foolish she'd been. And now what deception was Clifton involved in? She'd refused his overseas calls. She wanted him to complete the program abroad, get his wanderlust worked out and hopefully get beyond his mother's interference—to truly be ready to come home to her.

But he must have adhered to the philosophy of "love the one you're with." Did he marry in Europe, before he went to South America and Renata? Were the rumors true that the plantation was in financial trouble? Could he stoop so low as to marry someone for her money? Would Clifton try to step over a legal line that could jeopardize his and his family's future?

She kicked at the gravel beneath her feet, sending a puff of dust up to agitate her nose, making her sneeze. A reality jolt.

Clifton's sincerity was not her worry. She walked toward the back door of her shop and fingered the soft threads of the dress draped over her arm. She had her own concerns—checking on her son, relieving Mellie, and dealing with a chocolate-covered dress.

Clifton sat, shoulders hunched, on the loveseat in the Colonnades living room. His mother tramped a trail in the deep pile carpet. Tracing the floral pattern on the textured brocade had been a way to occupy his hand during tongue lashings he'd received in the past, like the time he yanked the axle from his dad's new Buick trying to pull a friend's car out of a ditch. The grandfather clock ticked off the seconds approaching 10:30 p.m.

Clifton studied the copy of the marriage certificate Jorge Rodrigues had handed him after the dinner guests, including Renata, filed in funeral procession from the dining room at Colonnades.

The document showed that he and Mary Elaine Matthews were married by Carlton H. Gadsden on December 12, four years earlier and was duly returned, filed, and recorded in Marriage Book 22, page 544 on December 15, signed by the clerk in Judge Carlton R. Gadsden's court. The paper failed to indicate the vows and signatures were made during a mock wedding presentation for a college sociology class.

"Clifton, why on earth did you use real paperwork? Making a ridiculous mistake was just the sort of thing I wanted to prevent. Thank goodness I was able to get you into that overseas graduate program."

Clifton's brows shot up. "You? I applied for that program months before I was accepted."

"Don't look so shocked. You know openings like that aren't determined by credentials only."

"You arranged for me to get that appointment?"

"Let's just say I dropped a strong suggestion and reminder of our alumni support." She stopped her pacing. "Don't be so upset. You might never have met Renata."

"That's right, and I'd still be with Mary Elaine." Heat flushed through him. Mary Elaine was right. His mother did engineer their break-up.

"You do know that girl probably lured you into that ridiculous engagement to get a father for her baby." Grabbing the back of an upholstered chair, she prodded. "You *are* certain that child of hers is not yours?"

"Yes. I am sure," he growled. "We've had this conversation. I know where babies come from."

He did know where babies came from. The child was not his. Learning Mary Elaine's child was born nine months after he left for his overseas program still stung. Had she been involved with someone and needed a father for her baby? If that was the case, wouldn't she have tried to seduce him? That was far from the truth. Or did she get involved on the rebound—thanks to his mother's meddling? Whatever the case she had moved on, and he had to accept the fact.

He stared at the photocopy and punched the redial button on his phone for the third time.

Finally, Carlton picked up. "Hello frat brother. What can I do for you at this late hour?"

"Give me an explanation." Clifton brought Carlton up to date on the dilemma.

Carlton's reaction matched Clifton's. "How did that happen?"

"That's the question I need you to answer."

Clifton's mother crowded him, trying to listen in on their conversation. He might as well let her hear rather than repeat everything. He put the phone on speaker.

"Who signed the certificate?" Carlton asked.

"A Joyce R. Dayton, Clerk, County Judge's Court."

After a few beats of silence, Carlton said, "I put those papers in the stack to be shredded in Dad's office. Someone must have picked them up and filed them."

"How can the marriage be made official if we were just pretending?"

Clifton's mother latched onto that idea. "If his dad's the judge, can't he fix the problem?"

"Can your dad correct the mistake?" Clifton asked.

"He's on a South American mission trip and won't return for another week. Problem is, as a notary, I had legal authorization to perform the marriage, and we used real paperwork. Remember, we wanted everything to look authentic. I never dreamed the paperwork got filed."

"We got an A on the assignment—A for authentic. So … I've been legally married four years?"

"If the papers were recorded, you have been."

His mother took in a sharp sniff and crossed her arms. She was not making the situation any easier.

"Now what do I do?"

"What about an annulment?" Carlton said.

"Annulment." Clifton repeated. His mother held her hands in a tight, prayerful squeeze. "Maybe that will work." After an exchange of regrets over their stupidity, Clifton ended the call.

"Annulment, that has to be the answer," his mother said, eyes wide with hope. "I'll get Horowitz on the phone."

She grabbed the phone and punched in some numbers to reach the family attorney. "Jerrilyn, this is Rosemary. I'm sorry to call so late. No, no. I'm not calling about the benefit. I need to speak to Holton. It's important."

Clifton's mother put her hand over the mouthpiece and whispered, "We're in luck. He's still up."

She explained the situation and handed Clifton the phone. "He wants to talk to you."

Clifton rubbed sweaty palms on his slacks and took the phone. "Hello?"

Attorney Horowitz wasted no time on salutations but got right to the point. "If you expect to clear up the matter, you'll have to find the girl. I can have papers drawn up for signatures in my office."

"I have no clue how to find her. She did live in Tallahassee."

"Get a private investigator."

"Who do you recommend?"

"Hold on."

Clifton heard the rustling of papers over the phone. He brushed his hand across the rough surface on the couch until Horowitz came back on. "Call Lake Spencer. He's a retired lawman we often use."

Horowitz read off the number while Clifton stepped to the writing desk to write it down.

"Call him and get back with me as soon as she's located."

"Thanks, I will."

His mother stopped her pacing along the carpet and turned to Clifton. "Will what?"

"Call a private investigator to find my wife."

"Wife." She bumped the heel of her hand against her forehead. "This is crazy." She sank into the chair by the fireplace. "How could you have done such an idiotic thing—pretending to get married to that girl?"

Clifton breathed in deeply. He raised his shoulders, tightened then released his neck muscles. "It wasn't idiotic. We had a sociology assignment. Role-playing a wedding was part of our presentation."

"Why did it have to be with that Mary Elaine girl?" His mother pounded her fist against the arm of the chair. "I still say she wasn't right for you. Her and her obnoxious stepfather. And now you're trapped in …" she wrestled with the word, "… marriage."

Rosemary wrung her hands and stood again. "For heaven's sake, get Grandma's ring back when you find her. But mark my words. She'll give you some excuse, and the ring is probably long gone."

Clifton stood, his head ready to explode. "Don't hold back, Mom. Say what you think."

"Make fun if you like, but for the sake of the family and your father's memory, don't mess up things with Mendes."

"You think I want to? But I have to tell you, since Renata's dad announced he would deed the property he purchased back to Davenport ownership as a wedding gift, I feel like some kind of gigolo—expected to provide male companionship in exchange for lavish gifts."

"Clifton, don't be foolish. You've dated Renata for two years. Marriage was in the air long before Mr. Mendes offered the gift."

"I'm just telling you how his offer makes me feel."

"Think of him deeding the property back to us as a dowry. Isn't it a custom in their country? Besides, she's a wonderful girl and adores our plantation. She'll step right into the charities I'm involved in, and you two will make beautiful children."

"Sounds like choosing a horse for good breeding purposes." He did his own pacing in front of the fireplace, then returned to the discomfort of the loveseat. "Where does love enter in?"

"Don't be silly. Many a marriage has started for economic purposes. Marriage is a partnership that love grows from as it's nurtured."

Clifton grasped his head with both hands. "Look, I have no intention of messing things up, but more to the point, will Renata still want to be engaged? I think her uncle was more than gratified to make the discovery of this surprise marriage. I'm under constant scrutiny when he's around."

"He's just extra protective about his niece. After all, Renata's mother was his sister. Both Renata and her uncle will be okay once the marriage mistake is taken care of."

Clifton's mother spoke with an assurance Clifton didn't share.

"Gavin's talking to Renata now to smooth things over."

Pressing his hands to his thighs, Clifton pushed himself up from the loveseat. The memory of former tense discussions in the room were returning. "I need some fresh air."

Rosemary folded her arms and nodded.

Clifton couldn't get to the veranda fast enough. Closing the French doors behind him, he leaned his head back to take in the night sky. Mentally tracing an imaginary line from the Big Dipper to the Little Dipper, he located the North Star as Mary Elaine had taught him. Where under that star was she tonight?

Crush, puppy love, infatuation—those tingling feelings that pricked every nerve in his body when he had been near Mary Elaine—wasn't that what love was all about? Was he trying to manufacture with Renata something that only happens once and is never meant to be experienced again in quite the same way?

He got along well with Renata. Mr. Mendes had been grateful for Renata's interest in Clifton and the Davenport plantation after her mother's death. Could his good standing with Mendes be repaired? And what about Renata?

"Clifton." His mother broke into his respite. Would the night ever end?

Stepping inside, Clifton faced Gavin, who gave him a look suitable for an alien emerging from a UFO. "I got things smoothed over with Renata as best I could. But, where were you? You should have been giving her some reassurance."

"Look, I told her I'd clear up the confusion. But with her father's attitude, I felt I'd better stay away."

"You've got a point there. Renata is shocked and hurt, but she is willing to wait and see what you find out."

"I appreciate your talking to her."

The phone on the living room desk rang. Clifton's mom stopped, retraced her steps on the carpet trail, and answered. "Rosemary Davenport." She rolled her eyes in Clifton's direction, and mouthed, *Mendes.* "Yes, he's here."

Clifton took the phone from his mother's outstretched hand. "This is Clifton."

"I want to make myself perfectly clear. No wedding. No deal."

He hung up.

He had made himself perfectly clear.

Chapter 6

Emme reached in the cooler where the repairman had worked his three-hundred-dollar fix. Selecting some bold Asiatic yellow lilies with burnt red centers along with red roses to go with purple gladiolas, she began to work on a funeral spray. The soiled dress had been delivered to the cleaners, and the interest paid to "low-life" Larry. With Richie at preschool and arrangements made for Mellie to pick him up, Emme settled into her creative self to turn out the morning orders.

The floral foam crunched as she secured each flower in place with precision. But with each new addition to the arrangement, her focus strayed.

Had Clifton tricked Renata? Emme had known Clifton since they were kids. She couldn't wrap her mind around him being capable of bigamy. She picked up a long-stemmed rose. The sight of the deep crimson petals served as a reminder of her shared history with Clifton.

When she allowed the memory to rise, her heart ached for the boy who grew to be a man and had once said he wanted her to be his wife. Could that spirit in Clifton have changed so much? No way would he marry Renata if he were already married. But Rodrigues produced proof, and Clifton had offered no denial. *Face it girl, Clifton is not the man you thought he was.*

"Ready to rock and roll?" Izzie entered the back door with sausage biscuits and lattes in hand. She was dressed in an orange ruffled top over psychedelic-print skinny jeans of pink and orange. Her golden chandelier earrings glittered under the fluorescent work light as she set down the cup tray and paper sack.

"Might as well be ready. Time rolls on anyhow." Emme peeked in the bag. "Eats from McDonald's sound good. I've only had some juice while Richie had an on-the-go juice box and granola bar breakfast in the van. Thanks for picking up breakfast."

"You are most welcome." Izzie pulled paper-wrapped biscuits from the bag and set them on the work table. "Better bless these and thank the Lord for his cycle of births and deaths that give people a reason to send flowers."

"Will you do the honors?" Emme loved to hear Izzie's up-close and personal prayers.

"Sure." Izzie locked hands with Emme. "Lord, we need you to help these biscuits go to work in us, so we can produce some knock-out arrangements for our clients. And while I've got your attention, would you please send some more paying customers our way? Amen."

Emme squeezed Izzie's hand. "Amen to that. Speaking of paying customers, Pam called. Gavin contacted her and indicated our wedding design services would be needed for the Davenports ..." Emme crooked her fingers into quotation marks. "... once some personal snags had been handled."

"Did she know about the fracas last night?" Izzie asked.

"I'm not sure what she knows."

"I'd say bigamy is an awfully big snag. Maybe he's one of those professional husbands."

"Who marry women for what they can get from them?"

"Yeah. I read about a guy who had twenty wives. He targeted widows with money, charmed his way into their lives, then took what he could and moved on."

"Clifton sure didn't ask me to marry him for money."

"Maybe that's why ..." Izzie stopped mid-sentence.

Emme jabbed a gladiola into the styrofoam base.

"Go ahead and say it. Maybe he broke our engagement because I had no money."

After a silent moment, Izzie said, "With this girl's taste in clothing, he'll need plenty of money to keep her outfitted as she is accustomed."

Emme crumpled the sausage biscuit wrapper into her fist, strangling on the last bite of biscuit in the process. Eyes watering, she sipped on her latte to wash down the crumbs lodged in her throat. "Great. If the cleaners can't get that stain out, we're going to need a money source of our own."

Izzie crossed her arms in front of her. "You know your mom and Frank have offered to help while you're getting the business started."

Aggravating tears attempted to rise in Emme's eyes. She blinked triple-time to push them back.

"I'm a big girl now, and I can stand on my own two feet. How about starting a twenty-five-dollar-size new baby girl flower arrangement?"

Izzie reached for a pink kitty-shaped container. "It wouldn't hurt to have a helping hand, so you can stay on your feet while you're on your road to self-reliance, you know." She trounced on Emme's self-imposed independence.

Emme said, "When Frank drank up my college fund, I knew then I would have to meet life challenges on my own."

"Have it your way, but you're web-weavin' again. Remember Pastor Creighton said depending on yourself is like leaning on a flimsy spider web."

"Yes, but we're expected to do our part."

"Sometimes recognizing your weaknesses and accepting help is doing your part."

"I just don't want to burden others with my financial woes."

"Well, like I said, Clifton's girl has high-priced taste he'll need to provide for. I looked up the cost of a dress similar to the one she wore last night—one hundred ninety-nine smackeroos."

"Serves him right," Emme said wiping at her eyes with the heels of her hands. The sausage biscuit formed a heavy lump in her stomach. She forced her back straight, selected another yellow lily for her arrangement, and stabbed the stem into the foam. "Clifton Davenport will have to work out his problems, and I'll do the same. For now, we've got to get these flowers ready for delivery."

"Yup. I think we should pray Clifton takes care of the mess he's in, so we can get his wedding job."

"Why not?" Emme forced a smile, grabbed a tissue from under the counter, and dabbed at the moisture blurring her vision.

The shop phone rang.

"There's our call now." Izzie held up a piece of greenery in victory stance.

Emme answered the phone. "Flower Cottage."

"Is this Mary Elaine Matthews?"

"Yes. Can I help you?"

"I have a client interested in speaking with you, would you be available around noon today?"

Emme looked at orders on the work table that needed to be delivered by noon. "Just a minute." Emme put the phone to her chest. "Someone wants a consult at noon. Can you handle the deliveries?"

"Of course." Izzie followed her answer with a whispered, "Whoopee!"

Emme hung up. A smile nudged her cheeks, "Potential business for the flower shop."

"And I have an interior design consult later this afternoon." Eyes gleaming, Izzie, raised her hands, filled with pink tissue paper for the welcome new baby order. "Thank you, Lord. you work fast."

Emme's expression transformed from a smile to a wrinkled forehead. "Strange though. He asked if my name was Mary Elaine Matthews. I didn't think anyone around here knew me by that name."

Clifton opened the trellis gate to The Flower Cottage. Growing plants, trees, and shrubs was his occupation, but seeing the plants in this setting, with the vine-covered trellis and mounds of impatiens lining the walkway, spoke more of a home than a business. Bees worked at drawing nectar from pots of purple petunias hung along the iron fencing. The wings of a hummingbird buzzed as he sucked juice from a feeder hanging from an oak limb before flitting away.

"I found her," the private investigator had reported just over an hour ago. "She owns and operates the Flower Cottage in Hamilton Harbor."

"Are you sure?"

"The business is registered to Mary Elaine Matthews with the State of Florida. I called and the female answering the phone identified herself as Mary Elaine Matthews."

He had checked his own account listing for The Flower Cottage after receiving the investigator's call. The client information sheet replaced the name Mellie Tidwell with Emme Matthews.

Could Emme Matthews be Mary Elaine? Did she handle the flowers for last night's dinner? As he stood at the threshold of the cottage, he recalled that Mary Elaine had once said her dream home was a cottage surrounded by flowers. The back of his throat constricted when he tried to swallow. She had moved on with her dream, better off without him.

Clifton grasped the doorknob, cold to his touch, and entered the shop. His foot activated a buzzer, sending shockwaves through his body. Sweet floral scents washed over him. He pulled at his collar as perspiration ran between his shoulder blades.

A woman's voice called from upstairs. "I'll be right down." Was the voice Mary Elaine's? He couldn't be sure. Mary Elaine's mother? Her name was Nan.

His "okay" came out high-pitched and broken. He cleared his throat and tried again. "Okay." Better. He sat on a wicker stool at the counter and surveyed the shop while waiting.

The display window boasted springtime, with pots of daisies and hand-crafted butterflies suspended above. A classic Lionel O-27-gauge freight train was poised ready to weave its way through tunnels and over bridges around the flowers. Clifton knew his Lionel trains. He'd studied many catalogs and planning layouts, sharing the hobby with his dad. His mother had packed away his old set and cleared the train room to use as a TV room when Clifton left for college.

A play area next to the window held toys and books. In the back was a large work table covered with stem clippings, plant materials, and bits of pink and blue tissue paper. On the customer counter in the middle of the shop were two albums labeled Flowers for All Occasions. A picture frame displayed a towhead boy in a striped shirt with pudgy cheeks and a big smile. Somewhere deep in his mind, he'd filed a hope that his mother's announcement that Mary Elaine had a baby could be mistaken. But he had seen her with the child at his dad's funeral and here was tangible evidence. The boy had her blue eyes and blonde hair.

Maybe he should have let the attorney confront Mary Elaine with annulment papers. The wicker stool creaked under his weight. Floral fragrances nudged at his senses. *No, fixing the situation was his responsibility.*

Footsteps sounded on the stairs. Clifton caught a glimpse of the woman's profile before she turned to face him. A shot of adrenaline tingled through his body. The question of whether the owner of the Flower Cottage was the same girl he had hoped to marry was now answered.

Emme trotted down the stairs and turned. Clifton. She grabbed the railing. Why was he here? *Hide,* she told herself, but her body remained immobile. She felt a heat burn her face as if slapped.

Had he discovered she was the one who tossed chocolate on his fiancée? Did he think she dumped the sauce on purpose? Would he refuse to pay for the dinner decorations? Her lips moved. No sound came out.

"Mary Elaine." Her name rolled from Clifton's lips and lay suspended in the space between them.

Emme, suddenly aware she needed to breathe, sucked in air, then said softly, "Hello, Clifton." Her heart banged against her rib cage, and when she spoke, a tremor shook her voice. "You drop in as easily as you drop out of someone's life." She took a step toward the counter where he stood. Seeing him now chilled her insides, and her voice came out cool. "Are you my noon appointment?"

The shoulders that once rippled beneath her touch sagged. He nodded. "You own this florist business?"

She nodded.

"But the account is—"

"Emme Matthews. The name comes from my initials. You know—M ... E."

"Oh ... yeah ... I see." He lifted his shoulders and took a deep breath. "Have you ... I mean ... Why did you—"

"Why did I take on the dinner party at the plantation?" Tense muscles constricted her throat. She kept her words brief. "Simple economics." She willed her feet to move toward the counter where he stood.

The sun's rays sent a shaft of light, highlighting the green in Clifton's eyes—eyes that pierced deeply into her soul. Those were the eyes she had fallen in love with when she first stepped off the Christmas train over fifteen years ago. And the man behind those same eyes, with a few creases added at the corners, convinced her he wanted to marry her by giving her a ring.

"I ... uh ... always wondered what happened to you," he said.

A hummingbird darted into view at her window feeder then disappeared. "Did you?" Her response cool—a sardonic statement, not really inviting a response.

"It was shameful what I did. The least I could do was honor your request to never see you again."

His argument was disarming and tugged on her emotions, like the dangerous undertow at the beach. *Heart, don't go there.* "Your decision to go to Europe is in the past now, and I've moved on. Apparently, so have you."

He dropped his gaze, his hands clasped, white knuckled. "There's a problem."

"So I heard."

"You heard?"

"Something about bigamy?" Emme raised her chin. "You make a habit of loving and leaving?"

"A habit?" He studied her a long moment. "It was you last night ... the chocolate sauce."

"Mama?" Richie called from the stairs. Emme jumped.

"Don't interrupt, baby." Mellie Tidwell hurried down the stairs behind Richie and held up a ball. "I'm sorry. We wanted to know if it was okay to play some kickball in the park before nap time."

"Sure. You can go for a little while."

"Oh. boy." Richie clamored down the steps with Mellie close behind.

"Bye, Mama." Richie spoke louder than necessary.

"Let's be quiet; Mama's busy." Mellie said, sending Emme a "sorry, I tried look" as she closed the back door.

"You're married?" Clifton asked.

Emme's jaw tightened as she returned her attention to Clifton. "And how does that concern you?" She leaned into the counter, hands on hips. "Clifton, why are you here?"

Clifton stood. "I'm here because your marriage does concern me."

"What are you talking about?"

"We're married."

"Wha—" Her breath caught.

He pushed his hands against the counter and focused on her eyes. "The sociology assignment. The papers got filed. We're legally married."

"But ... how did that happen?"

"I had the same question. I talked to Carlton. He said he left the paperwork in a pile to be shredded in his father's office. He figures the secretary must have thought they were in the wrong pile and filed them. So, you see, if you're married—"

"I'd be a bigamist." Emme sat heavily on the stool behind the counter. She shook her head. "No, my being married is not an issue."

Only a few people were aware that Richie was not her natural child. She had her reasons to keep it that way. Being a single parent—widowed, divorced, or unwed—was common, and she just let people think what they wanted. She'd let Clifton do the same.

Better that than have him know the pitiful truth. Somewhere deep inside she'd held a foolish fantasy that Clifton would return for her, no matter what his mother thought, no matter if she had a child. Best he believed she'd moved on, because he obviously had.

"When I heard they'd discovered you were married I thought—"

"That I made a habit of loving and leaving women?" His eyes went dark.

Emme looked away. "We're really married?" Her voice was weak. Hurt, denial, anger, and need to do life on her own melded into one huge glob inside. She'd been through all the grieving stages in the death of their relationship. All this time they were married?

She faced him again. "Married." The word fell flat.

His jaw clenched.

"What now?"

"Would you agree to sign annulment papers?"

She felt a sting behind her eyes. Cry? No way. She gripped the edge of the counter and blinked the moisture away.

"Ironic the marriage your mother tried to prevent happened anyhow."

"About that—"

"Please, let's don't go there."

She glanced at the book of photos for special occasions—reminders of dreams they once shared. The very things Emme wanted to forget were closing in. Her plan to steer clear of Clifton and his mother, dashed.

But she'd dealt with disappointment before. If she had learned anything in coming to grips with her own dysfunctional family background, it was to shelter Richie and depend on no one but herself.

She straightened her posture. "Is your mother aware that I'm the florist?"

"No. I only just found out myself."

"I was told by the event planner that the Flower Cottage would be offered the contract for your wedding. Will that offer still stand?"

"Certainly, if you want the job. But it's probably best not to mention—"

"That the florist is the one you married by mistake?"

"I wouldn't say mistake is the right word." He sought her eyes and she couldn't look away. Did he want her to rescue him? Let him unburden his soul?

"Don't worry. I don't want my involvement known either. It will be easier for both of us if my identity is kept under wraps. Who does know?"

"Just the PI who found you, and me right now."

"I will sign—with the understanding I have the wedding contract and my identity remains secret. My assistant, Izzie, will handle any face-to-face contact with you and your family. Agreed?"

"Of course."

Emme raised a brow. "Congratulations, by the way, on your engagement."

He gave her a wavering smile. "After last night, that's questionable, but maybe things will work out. By the way, the decorations, the flag—you did an outstanding job."

"Thank you." Stiff, noncommittal words, so foreign to all they once had together.

He nodded his head toward the photo on the counter. "You have a little boy. A lot has happened in four years."

Emme heaved a heavy sigh. "It has. Do you have the papers to sign?"

He started to say something, but pressed his lips together instead, fished in his pocket, pulled out a business card and laid it on the counter. "Papers have been prepared at the attorney's office. The signatures need to be witnessed and notarized."

She picked up the card and ran her fingers over the embossed gray print of Horowitz & Tillman. "I'll take care of signing."

"I can't begin to tell you how sorry—"

She held up her hand, "Then please don't."

Emme noticed movement outside. Someone was hurrying toward her shop. She stepped from behind the counter and walked to the front door as Margaret Meadows, Mellie's sister, arrived on the front porch with a Yorkshire terrier in hand.

"It's Richie. He's hurt."

Chapter 7

Shrieks came from the park. Emme scrambled down the steps and ran.

Mellie sat on a park bench, cradling Richie in her arms. Emme struggled to catch her breath. Her heart sent pulses of fear pounding in her head. She lost all peripheral vision as she tunneled in on the red stain spreading onto Mellie's shirt.

Richie, red-faced, wailed louder and reached for Emme. She scooped Richie into her arms. Tears trickled down Mellie's cheeks.

"What happened?"

"He was running after the ball … oh, it happened so fast. He tripped on that tree root and went flying head first into the base of the tree."

Richie smelled of earth, tree bark, and blood. Warm blood from the gash on his head dampened her skin.

"Put pressure on the cut to curb the bleeding," a male voice advised.

Emme jerked her head around to see Clifton behind her.

"Here, use my handkerchief."

Emme pressed the handkerchief to Richie's head.

Mellie sniffed. "I got to him as quickly as I could but—"

"Accidents happen. Don't blame yourself," Emme said.

Richie's crying slowed with intermittent breaks to gulp in hiccups of air.

Clifton reached down, lifted the boy's chin and studied his eyes.

Emme stiffened. What was he doing?

"His pupils are equal, round, and he blinked at the sunlight. Good signs." Clifton pressed two fingers against Richie's wrist. "His pulse is rapid but steady."

Emme's tension eased as Clifton looked Richie over. He seemed to know what to check.

He carefully lifted the handkerchief and examined the wound. "I believe he's going to need stitches." He fixed his eyes on Emme. "My car is right here. I'll drive you to the emergency room."

Emme hesitated. Should she call 911? That would take longer, and Izzie had the van delivering the guest baskets.

Mellie said, "You go. I can watch the shop."

Emme looked at her son's flushed, tear-stained face. His wellbeing came first. "Thank you. I'll need my purse."

"I'll get your purse," Margaret said. Still holding the Yorkie, she rushed across the street to the flower shop.

Clifton pulled keys from his pocket. Putting his hand on her back, he guided her to his car.

Emme hugged Richie close to her, his mussed hair brushed her chin. Clifton opened the front passenger door, helped them in the front seat and hurried to get in the driver's seat. Margaret arrived and handed Emme her purse through the car window.

"Izzie should be back shortly," Emme said.

"Mellie and I can take care of things here. You just take care of Richie." She reached in the car and patted Richie's arm. "Keep us updated."

Clifton pulled away from the curb. Emme wiped tears from Richie's face with her free hand while continuing to hold Clifton's handkerchief over the gash. "It's okay," she told Richie, "we'll get you all patched up."

For Richie's sake, Emme struggled to display confidence, but head wounds could be serious. What if she were to lose him?

Clifton looked over. "You're doing fine, just maintain light pressure." His voice was soothing, comforting.

Emme gently rocked Richie. "Do you have some sort of medical training?"

"I do. Actually, thanks to your father."

"My father?"

"You remember when I was cutting that Christmas tree and almost chopped off my leg?"

Emme nodded. "I ran to Daddy for help."

"When he took care of me, that's the day I decided to be a doctor."

Richie sniffled and turned his eyes to Clifton. "Are you a doctor?"

Clifton smiled, "No. But I took a course in emergency medicine when I was in Europe."

"EMT. That's the training Daddy had," Emme said.

She patted Richie's back. Nearly four years had passed since she'd last seen Clifton but sitting next to him now seemed … right. Like parents taking their injured child to the doctor. The scenario, a picture of how their relationship could have been. But life changed course when Clifton went overseas.

"Strange how certain events make our lives take a different turn," Clifton said.

"True." Emme stroked Richie's tear-stained cheek.

What course would life have taken if Emme's father had not died, and her mother had not married Frank? What if there had never been a horrible plane crash that wiped out her cousin's family, leaving Richie behind?

Clifton came to a stop sign. She watched his hands turning the steering wheel. The green arrow turn light blinked on the dash, pointing to a new direction.

Even driving to the hospital emergency room, having Mary Elaine beside him again seemed natural, right. His heart went out to the injured boy. As a youngster, he had learned what it was like to be hurting and at the mercy of others.

Carlos had sent him to cut a Christmas tree. He'd been watching Mary Elaine weave through the trees during her family's once-a-year visit. Distracted, the axe bit into his leg, just above the ankle.

"Yow!" Blood quickly soaked the leg of his jeans. He slumped to the ground.

Mary Elaine rushed to him. "Don't move. I'll get my daddy."

The shock of the blow wore off and pain set in. He sucked in air through clinched teeth. He was nine years old and intent on keeping a brave face, but tears burned his eyes and trailed down his cheeks.

Mary Elaine's father crouched at his side. He pulled out a pocket knife, cut the leg of Clifton's jeans, tore off a strip, and bound the gash to stop the bleeding.

Mary Elaine patted his shoulder and brushed a tear from his cheek, just as she did now with her son.

Being close to her again brought on more feelings than the remembrance of a cut leg. She carried the familiar scent of lavender. He wished he could hold and comfort her, meet her needs, but he'd foolishly given up that right.

The sign for the emergency room directed them to a circular drive and glass sliding-door entry. Clifton braked to an abrupt stop, tires screeching. He hurried to open the passenger door to assist Mary Elaine and her whimpering son out of the car. At the check-in desk inside, Mary Elaine answered basic questions. Name: Richard Matthews. Age: Almost three. Date of Birth: March 31, 2012.

"Go through the double doors on your right, and we'll take a look," the intake nurse said.

Should he follow her? "Is there anyone I can call for you?" Clifton asked.

"Please." She pulled her phone from her pocket and thrust it in his hand. "Could you call my mom and let her know what's happened? Number three on speed dial.

"Nan and Frank right?"

"Right. Nan and Frank Bruckman."

"I'll call them for you."

Clifton watched as she went through the doors, and they closed behind her. Then he speed-dialed number three.

"Emme, I was just going to call."

"Mrs. Bruckman?"

"Who is this?"

"Clifton Davenport."

"Clifton? Why—"

Clifton explained the situation, leaving out the part about the surprise marriage. That was way more information than she needed right now. She was shocked enough to hear from him.

"Tell her I'll be there as soon as possible."

He clutched her phone and wondered what to do next. Should he leave or stay? Richie's wound did not appear life threatening, but head trauma could be tricky. First things first. He'd park his car and then make sure the boy was all right.

After he parked his car, Clifton checked for messages on his cell, then walked from the parking lot back to emergency. At least there were no missed calls or texts to add to the swirl of questions in his head.

Who was Richie's father? The boy was born in March. A quick math check put him born right at nine months after he left for Europe. No wonder she quit taking his calls. Had he meant that little to her? She said she wasn't married. The boy's name was Matthews. A rebound relationship? Could she have been divorced and taken back her maiden name? She spoke of notifying Izzie, but what about the boy's father? She'd indicated her marital status was none of his business.

The emergency room doors whooshed open and the nurse at intake automatically motioned to the big double doors on her right. "Room two."

When Mary Elaine saw him through the partially closed curtain, she motioned for him to come in. "I appreciate your staying."

"Of course. Your mother said she'd be here as soon as possible." He handed her phone back. "How is he?"

"They cleaned the wound. I'm waiting for the doctor."

She pushed a strand of hair back revealing the gulf-water blue eyes that had captivated him when they reconnected in college.

The nurse returned. Behind her, a doctor wearing green surgical garb entered the room. "I'm Dr. Scott," he said. "I understand you have a big ouchy, young man."

Richie's eyes grew large and he nodded slowly. The doctor inspected and cleaned the wound with a saline solution. "We'll fix you up good as new. Step over here, Mom and Dad. Everything will work better with a familiar hand to hold."

"I'm Mom. He is a … uh … friend."

"I can wait outside."

"Stay … please?" Richie held out his hand to Clifton, his eyes pleading.

Clifton turned to Mary Elaine. She nodded and bit at her lower lip.

He stood to Richie's left—the boy's grip tight. Mary Elaine stood to the right and took his other hand.

"Richie, you'll feel a pinch that will help stop any hurting," Dr. Scott said.

Clifton's training kicked in. "Hang on tight now."

The doctor inserted a short needle around the wound, while the nurse steadied Richie's head. Mary Elaine looked away. Richie whined, then gave a full out wail.

"You're doing great, Richie. The worst is behind you." Clifton patted the child's shoulder.

"He's right." The doctor pushed Richie's blond hair aside, dabbed the injury with a clean towel and cleaned around the gash again.

"Do you have to shave his head?" Emme asked.

"No. We've found there is less chance of infection by not shaving and just pushing the hair aside."

The doctor spoke to Richie. "I'm going to close up your injury, and you'll be good as new."

Richie looked at his mother, lips and chin trembling.

Mary Elaine glanced at Clifton and swallowed hard. He gave her a reassuring nod and spoke to Richie. "You'll feel some pressure and a click. Just hang on." Richie squeezed his hand.

Dr. Scott held the stapler in a vertical position. Each staple went in with a firm press and a click. "Five should give good closure," he said as the pressed in the last staple.

The doctor pulled off his surgical gloves with a snap and disposed of them. "There should be no noticeable scar." He shook hands with Clifton. "You've handled sutures before?"

"Some. I've had emergency medical training."

"Appreciate the help."

He turned to Mary Elaine, still holding Richie's hand and helping him sit up. "The nurse will bring follow-up instructions." Dr. Scott patted Richie's knee and said in parting, "An ice cream treat for bravery for this fella might be warranted."

"How about that for doctor's orders?" Clifton grinned at Richie.

Mary Elaine stepped aside to speak to Clifton. "Mom should be here shortly. It will be less complicated if you don't mention ..." She looked at Richie.

"The papers to sign?"

"Right."

Clifton shoved his hands in his pockets. A long dormant emptiness filled his heart, begging for Mary Elaine's smile. How could he stop the memories? His heart still responded to her, and the revelation rocked Clifton's entire being.

Mary Elaine lifted her chin. "Look, you go ahead. Call me later, and we'll work something out on getting the papers signed."

Their eyes held a long second. More memories threatened. He didn't want to leave her.

Clifton's phone sounded. "I'll call you."

He left her in the curtained room. He wanted to take her in his arms, be there for her. Crazy. His phone persisted. Stepping into a side hall, he swiped his screen. "Hello, Ms. Peacock."

"Clifton, I need your signature on last month's delayed checks. To avoid late fees, I need to send them out today."

Mailing late was part of a strategy he'd devised to help with cash flow. "I'll get there as soon as I can." As he headed to the parking lot, another call rang in.

"Hello?"

"Holton Horowitz here. I heard Spencer located the girl. I have the annulment papers ready and a judge lined up to sign them. Any progress?"

"Yes and no." Clifton saw Mary Elaine's mother had arrived.

"What does that mean?" Horowitz's voice took an upswing.

"Yes, I found her, and she agreed to sign, but—"

"Let me guess," he said with a hint of sarcasm. "She wants a pay-off."

"No. No way. She's not like that." He surprised himself with his curt reply. "Her son was injured after she agreed to sign. He's in the emergency room."

"She has a son? If she's married, we've got more problems—"

"I guess she's divorced. She said it was not an issue. I really don't know. Everything happened so quickly." Clifton pressed the open button on his car remote.

"Well, if she's divorced, that's good. Best get the papers signed ASAP while she's willing." Horowitz never was big on mincing words.

"I understand."

Clifton punched the end button, then jabbed the key in the ignition. The greatest favor he could do for Mary Elaine was to get the annulment finalized, but he couldn't be so crass as to push for her signature with her son lying in a hospital emergency room.

He checked his watch. He should call Renata, so she wouldn't worry. He headed in the direction of the plantation and called her cell phone.

After several rings, Gavin answered.

"Cliff, hey. Renata asked if you'd called. Did you get the papers signed?"

"I thought I dialed Renata's phone."

"You did. We came to check out the shooting houses on the hunting acreage and decided to zero in our guns. She's gone to check out her shooting target. She's a good shot."

"I know. Not my thing, so I'm glad you were able to take her. Tell her we found Mary Elaine, and she agreed to the annulment."

"Where did you find her?"

"She, uh … works in a business in downtown Hamilton Harbor."

"That's handy. Here's Renata. You can tell her."

Clifton could hear some of Renata's words in the background. "Gavin … adjustment … tight pattern … good coach—"

"Clifton, for you," Gavin said.

"Oh … Clifton, hi," her voice clear now.

"I wanted you to know I talked to Mary Elaine, and she's agreed to an annulment."

"Good." The volume of her voice lowered, "Gavin, you were right."

"What was Gavin right about?"

"He assured me that you would find her and take care of the problem."

"I'm glad to hear he was so confident."

"Well, he's kept me from becoming a basket case. Finding out you were married was a bit of a shock after all."

"I'm sorry." Sorry was his word of the day. "I appreciate you being so understanding."

"Gavin showed me how to adjust my sights. I just shot my best pattern ever."

"Save the target for me to see."

"He's an awesome coach." Muffled talk and then, "He's pinning up another target now."

Gavin was working overtime on smoothing things over with Renata.

"Well, I'll let you go."

"Can you join us at the range?"

"Afraid not. I've got business to take care of at the office."

"Okay. I'll see you later and bring my targets."

The call left Clifton staring at his phone. So much for Renata being worried. Good thing she wasn't jealous, right?

Chapter 8

Emme pulled Richie's fuzzy Spiderman blanket over his shoulders. A ray from the late afternoon sun peeked between the drawn curtains in his bedroom and spotlighted his eyelashes. They looked like golden threads fringing his closed eyes. What if he had been snatched from life as his family was?

The headline, "Tragedy Strikes Family," forever etched in her mind, rose to the forefront. The plane crash that took Richie's parents and grandparents had made the front page of the Atlanta newspaper. This precious child had been through a lot in his three years. Survived a plane crash in his mother's womb. Born to her cousin's wife, who had been kept alive by machines until the birth. And now a head injury.

Emme desperately wanted to shield him from any more hurt. She stroked his hand, still marked by the dimpled look of a baby. Clifton had held his little hand and comforted him with ease. She'd always suspected he'd make a good father. But ... no need to go there.

Emme smoothed a curl, pressed a kiss on Richie's forehead, and slipped out of his room. While rubbing the tense muscles in the back of her neck, the questions she'd shoved in the corners of her mind exposed themselves like discarded debris in a murky bog.

If the relationship with Clifton had continued, would he have agreed to be a father to Richie? Would his mother have accepted the child as her grandson?

Clifton's mother must have been ready to blow the roof clear off Colonnades when she heard Clifton was legally married to "that girl."

"We have to stop Clifton's ridiculous notion to marry that girl with the alcoholic stepfather." The words Mrs. Davenport spoke to her husband had been hushed, but clear.

"Now, Rosemary, you will only drive him away if you interfere. Besides you can't hold her responsible for her stepfather's actions. I think the girl is lovely."

"Lovely maybe, but lovely doesn't make her good marriage material for Clifton. She lived in the projects for heaven's sake. She'll be a black mark against our good name. Clifton needs someone who is not just nice, but extraordinary."

"In Clifton's eyes, she is extraordinary. You must accept that."

"Accept? I don't have to accept her."

Mrs. Davenport's words cut deep into her soul, opening old wounds from other words she had overheard years earlier.

"A pitiful sight when we adopted her." Learning she was adopted from a whispered conversation and knowing she had natural parents who didn't want her had crushed her spirit.

Then there was the muted talk and sideways glances in the school cafeteria. "I heard her stepfather shot a man and stole from him. I wonder if she got some of that money."

Girls she'd thought were her friends no longer welcomed her to sit with them. The tiny apartment they moved to after her stepfather lost his job at the police department had paper-thin walls. She had to muffle her sobs by burying her face in her pillow, damp and musty from crying herself to sleep at night.

Her back pressed against Richie's door, Emme lifted her head. She was determined to shield Richie from the kind of hurt she'd experienced. A clean break from Clifton was for the best. Emme would make sure Richie was never subjected to the rejection Mrs. Davenport could dish out.

Clifton needed the annulment papers signed so he could get married, and she needed his wedding to provide for her son. Emme sniffed at the irony.

Her cell phone sounded. Where did she leave it? She tracked the musical signal to her purse she'd tossed on the couch when her mom and Frank brought them home from the hospital. Retrieving her phone, she saw the call was from Izzie.

"Is Richie okay?"

"Thankfully, yes. He's resting right now." Emme put her phone on speaker, laid it on the kitchen counter and pulled a soda from the refrigerator.

"Good. Mellie said a handsome customer drove you to the hospital. I'm dying to hear what's happening. So spill, who is the mystery person?"

Emme popped the lid. The cold liquid soothed her parched throat. "Clifton Davenport."

Silence.

"You still there?"

"I'm waiting for you to tell me you're kidding. What was he doing there?"

"Telling me we are legally married."

The bomb exploded. "Marr ... Waaait ... a ... minute. You're the other woman?"

"It seems the papers for the pretend marriage we enacted for our college sociology assignment were filed by mistake. Clifton and I are legally married."

"Hold the phone ... now what?"

Emme traced an 'X' in the moisture on the side of the drink can. "Annulment."

"So did you sign papers?"

"No time. Richie got hurt. But I will."

"I'm finishing up the interior design consult at Appleberry's Furniture. I'll be there shortly. Don't you dare go anywhere. I want to know every last detail."

The phone call ended. For the first time since rushing Richie to the hospital and returning home, her tumble of concerns rolled into one thought. Married. Four years, they'd been married. Unbelievable. Her eyes moved to the built-in book shelving in the living room.

Drawn to the shelves, she removed a large book on the far left of the second shelf. In the exposed area, she pressed a spot inlaid in the wood and heard the metallic click of a concealed spring lock. She tugged on the side of the shelving that swung open to reveal a hidden compartment about three feet square. Mellie had shown her this special feature of the cottage. Emme lifted precious photo CDs and set aside other important paper files until she found the navy-blue folder.

Running her fingers over the smooth surface, she opened the file with a tinge of apprehension. On top lay her copy of the sociology term paper and group project. Listed on the cover page were the names Clifton R. Davenport, Carlton Gadsden, Jr., and Mary Elaine Matthews. She flipped to the back of the folder, reached in the pocket and pulled out a small plastic bag. Inside lay two objects, a faded red rose petal she'd saved from the broken branch of the rose bush Clifton fell on when they were ten years old, and the engagement ring Clifton told her to keep. The two items added up to hope-filled dreams and broken promises.

Emme lifted the rose petal out of the bag. Once a brilliant red, the delicate flower petal lay feather light in the palm of her hand. Carefully, she pulled out the ring. A platinum circle encrusted with diamonds and deep red rubies. The stones were meant to be an expression of love but in her case had become a token of a falsely spoken marriage proposal.

"I couldn't reach you, and I had to leave in a whirlwind rush." Clifton had called her from the airport. "Mother learned I was selected for the overseas master's program and surprised me with bags packed and a boarding pass. Hard to believe, but here I am in New York."

"You jumped on a plane without talking with me?"

"I told you. There was no time. Mother had the boarding pass—"

"My point exactly. There was no time because your mother wanted the time period to be short."

"You're wrong. She knew I wanted to talk to you. She said we could talk on the phone and if our relationship is right, it will all work out."

"*If* the relationship is right? See?"

"See what?"

Emme's heart had crashed to her toes. Her rational mind told her not to accuse, but her emotions wouldn't hold back.

"She's hoping you'll realize our engagement is wrong. She thinks the likes of me and my stepfather will disgrace your family name."

"Who told you that?"

"I overheard her talking—"

"You were eavesdropping?"

"Not exactly ... I—"

"And you didn't talk to me?"

"I didn't talk to you? What about you sitting in New York leaving on a one-year program without talking to me?"

"Listen. If you care about us, you'll support me."

"Your mother told you that, didn't she?"

"Frankly, yes."

"She's smart. She arranged circumstances, so I'd look bad if I didn't support you."

"You're demonizing her. Can't you just be happy for me? We can talk every day."

"You know what? Don't bother calling. If you really loved me, you wouldn't have left like you did."

"If you loved me, you'd be excited for me."

"That's not the real issue. Your mother thinks I'm not good enough for you. She wins."

"How can you say that? My going overseas isn't a win or lose situation."

"Oh, but it is. And your jumping at the chance, with no hesitation, is a double win for her because you can't see you're being manipulated."

"I think we'd better end this conversation. We'll talk later."

"Later won't change your mother. Don't bother calling. I won't answer."

Silence.

"I'll see that you get the ring back."

"No. No, you keep the ring I just ... I ... you need to understand that getting this study opportunity will be good for us down the road."

She had understood. He'd been hasty in offering her a ring. His mother saw a chance to get them apart, and he went along with her plan. Her first love, crashed.

Emme opened her eyes to reality. She studied the petal that was once a vibrant red, now dull and fragile.

A thickness swelled in her throat. Clifton's demeanor today marked him as a good potential father. For those brief moments in the emergency room, the marriage she never had the opportunity to experience seemed real. Stop. Where was she going with that fruitless line of thinking? Straight to a dead end.

Clifton left her behind long ago. All he needed from her was a signature on annulment papers and one more thing. She lifted the ring from the bag. She'd had four years to come to grips with Clifton's abrupt departure. Now was the time to return the ring.

Emme heard the rumble of Izzie's Suburban pulling into the back parking lot. She flipped the folder closed making the lightweight petal fly up in the air and float to a landing on the inside corner of the hidden storage space. As she reached for the dried rose petal, she noticed the folded edge of a paper wedged in the corner. *Must belong to Mellie,* she thought.

She carefully placed the petal back in the folder and dropped the ring and the folded paper inside her pocket. She'd give the paper to Mellie later. She pushed the shelving back in place, and went downstairs to greet her friend.

Izzie's footsteps pounded quick thuds on the back deck. Bouncing through the back door, she let loose with a barrage of questions. "How did he find you? What happened when you saw him? What did he say?"

Emme raised her arms and pushed her palms against the air. "Hold up. One question at a time."

"Heart be still," Izzie said, and slumped on a stool. "Okay, so how did he find you?"

Emme rubbed her forehead, warding off a headache. "The call I received asking if I was Mary Elaine Matthews was a private investigator." She picked up a pencil by the phone and pressed it against the message pad, snapping the point. "The noon appointment was Clifton."

"What in the world did you say to him?"

"Oh, I don't know." Emme tossed the pencil that hit the bottom of the trash can with a clink. "My first thought was he figured out I dumped the chocolate sauce on his girlfriend. Then he wanted to know if I was married and I said it was none of his business. That's when he told me we were married." She left out the part she couldn't put into words. The part about how it felt to have him at her side when Richie was hurt. Feelings that were pointless—futile.

"Well knock me over with a feather ... and now he wants an annulment?" Izzie pressed her hands on her hips. "If the bum is marrying that girl, the least he can do is let us have the wedding flower contract."

"I told him Pam had suggested we might have the contract. He was in favor, but we agreed it would be best to keep my identity under wraps.

"The nerve—"

Emme shook her head. "Staying under the radar was my idea."

"Girl, you realize you've got the makings of a brand-new soap opera."

"Speaking of soap, did you get the dress from the cleaners?"

Izzie scrunched her face. "I did, and they couldn't get all the chocolate stain out."

"Great. Now I've got to come up with two hundred to cover that dress."

"Correction. *We* will come up with money for that dress."

"Oh, Izzie. If things weren't so tight with business start-up costs, I'd argue with you. Maybe if I delay paying the electric bill."

"Listen to you, Miss Do-It-Yourself. You're weaving that web again."

"I know. I know," Emme scolded herself.

"Better to lean on the one who made us."

Emme's head felt like a giant weight perched on top of her shoulders. "It's so hard."

Izzie held out her hands. "Loads are lighter when we share them with God."

Emme nodded, straightened her back and joined hands with Izzie, who prayed a fervent prayer that sent Emme's focus heavenward and helped release some tension. Her prayer covered Richie's healing, peace in her situation with Clifton, and help with finances.

Just as Izzie said, "amen," Emme's cell phone sounded upstairs. She took the steps two at time to answer.

"Emme, Mom. How's Richie?"

"He's fine, resting."

"With all the excitement, I forgot to tell you. I have a check made out to you from Frank's boss for the decorating you did for his son's graduation."

"I offered to help. I didn't expect pay."

"He knows, but you are a talented decorator, and he appreciated your hard work."

Her mother told her the amount.

Emme dropped onto her overstuffed couch and let her mom's words and the idea of a fast-answered prayer envelop her. Two hundred dollars.

The fax machine, printing an incoming order, hummed. Old accounts were updated, new orders were entered, checks were signed, and Ms. Peacock was gone for the day. A melting pot of emotions had been brewing inside Clifton for several days, ever since leaving Emme and her son at the hospital.

Emme had moved on. So had he. But seeing her again, standing by her side at the hospital as a father and husband might, reignited a smoldering spark in the recesses of his soul that he was trying to ignore. He rifled through a credenza drawer behind his desk, hoping to find another stray roll of antacids.

He moved a box of paperclips.

"Ah, pay dirt."

He needed to put Rolaids on his office supply list. When he picked up the roll, he noticed a small box wedged in the back of the drawer.

He crunched a couple of chalky tablets and opened the box. Inside was the small notebook labeled "Christmas Tree Biznes," printed in his seven-year-old hand where he used to keep track of the trees he helped sell and load for a dollar commission. He gently lifted the book his dad had chosen to keep. Underneath lay another surprise, the WWJD bracelet given to him by Mary Elaine the last time she came to the Christmas tree farm with her family. He touched the soft blue-and-white threads. The smooth, lettered beads blurred—a memory tugged his heart.

"Are those your initials?" Clifton had asked her when he saw the bracelet.

"No." Mary Elaine giggled and slipped the bracelet from her wrist for him to see. "WWJD stands for 'what would Jesus do.' I made it for you."

"Is that what Jesus would do? Give the bracelet away?"

"Yes, I believe he would," she had said, placing the hand-woven beaded band around his wrist.

Clifton stroked the lettered beads and slipped the bracelet into his pocket. Mary Elaine might want the keepsake for her son.

His footsteps on the hardwood floor pierced the quiet as he crossed the room and studied his father's portrait. *Dad, why did you keep these items?* An ache antacid couldn't touch gripped his chest. "I could use your advice right now," he whispered. "The confidence you had in me was misplaced."

Clifton looked into his dad's kind eyes, but the memory of his father's face in pain surfaced. While cancer ravaged his body, his dad had spoken to his sons.

"Clifton, you have God-given instincts and business smarts." He patted Clifton's hand, his touch weak and fingers cold. "You just need to learn to trust your instincts and look to God for right timing."

Clifton, his vision clouded, looked across the bed at Gavin who was in the same tearful condition. His father turned his attention to his brother, and with labored breathing said, "God has blessed you with a green thumb. You continue learning all you can about horticulture. I have great hopes for you two. You're both young, you'll make mistakes, but learn from them. I know you will make me proud."

Mistakes. That was an understatement. Gavin had done well with the horticulture part of the operation, but Clifton's choice of a business manager was a fiasco that landed them deep in debt. A poor excuse, but in fact, his decision had been made in haste, just as his father had warned against.

"If you're planning on seeing Mary Elaine again, I think you ought to know she has a baby," his mother announced when he returned for his father's funeral.

"She got married?"

"I don't know if she's married, but she has a baby that's about two months old. Tell me the truth, could that be your baby?"

"We never ... no. How do you know she has a baby?"

"I saw her with a baby in a stroller outside the beauty shop in Tallahassee. The girl that does my hair said the baby was Mary Elaine's. Honestly, can you see now she was not right for you? She had to have been pregnant while she was seeing you and been looking for a father for her child."

Had she been seeing someone else? Was that the real reason she was so upset when she learned he was going to be gone a year? He'd seen her with a university campus policeman she knew from high school. Was he more than just a friend?

Clifton heaved a sigh. His foggy thinking had led to his appointing Bolton Nix to take over operations while he ran away from hurt to business opportunities in Brazil—and ultimately, Renata.

She seemed to have walked into his life at just the right time. When they met, both had lost a parent to cancer and they formed an immediate bond that didn't go unnoticed by Renata's father.

"My boy," Mendes had said, "my girl's happiness is my first priority." Mendes had invited Clifton to dinner for two at the Coach House, a converted barn dating back to Tallahassee's horse and buggy days. The restaurant offered five-star-rated dinners in private dining rooms. "I see you have eyes for each other."

A waiter arrived with freshly baked bread on a wooden cutting board. Rather than cutting the bread, Mendes broke the bread and offered a chunk to Clifton. The yeast aroma was inviting, but he had little appetite. Mendes took a bite and continued.

"Renata loves your plantation and wants to stay in America—too many hurtful memories in Brazil since her mother died. I've done some checking, and I know you owe back taxes and have financial need."

"Yes, sir. But I have plans to—"

"Let me finish. What I propose is a coalition. I will purchase the acreage used for hunting, and you can use the cash to get out of debt. When you and Renata marry, I'll gift the property back as long as I retain hunting rights for me and my friends."

The coalition seemed more a command than a proposal.

"She will be happy, and I can see her often."

"But you don't need to buy the property to see her."

Mendes held up a beefy hand, bearing a glittering gold ring on his little finger. "Everyone needs a hand up at times, especially in business." He pushed the butter closer to Clifton, motioning for him to try some of the bread. "I want my daughter taken care of."

He never dreamed the answer to his financial woes might come from Renata's father.

Clifton had worked on a plan to get out of debt that would have required filing Chapter 11 bankruptcy to allow for reorganization. His instincts cautioned him about going into business with relatives-to-be, but the solution seemed to have dropped from heaven. Mendes's plan could be an easy, expedient way out of debt.

But now, he questioned his own motives. Was he really captivated by Renata or the business deal? Did she really care for him or just the idea of living on an American plantation and planning a wedding, no matter who the groom? What would his relationship be with Mary Elaine if his mother hadn't pulled strings to get him in the study program abroad?

"Would the agreement with Mendes have been your choice, Dad?" Clifton asked, staring at the eyes of the man he'd idolized since childhood. "Renata's a great girl—more understanding than I deserve under the circumstances. So, our marriage must be right." The words coming from his mouth rang true, but he had trouble convincing his insides. His shoulders went slack, and he shoved his hands in his pockets.

The soft threads of the bracelet fashioned by Mary Elaine met his fingers. Stop over-thinking. The twists and turns in his life had changed matters of love. Though his heart still leaped at the thought of Mary Elaine, there was no gain in dwelling on the old memories. After all, she did have a child, not his, who'd emerged from some kind of relationship. Clifton glanced at his watch and steeled his resolve.

The time had arrived to meet Horowitz's secretary at the Flower Cottage and sign the annulment papers.

Chapter 9

Where on earth could the ring be? Her pocket? The folder? Emme retraced her moves from five days earlier. She searched every inch of the hidden space in the wall, flipping through the pages of the books that might hold the ring captive. When she checked her pocket, she found a small hole in the seam.

Using a flashlight, she scanned the baseboard. Carefully, on hands and knees, she tracked through the deep pile carpet leading to her desk where she had put the note she had found and given to Mellie the next day. She vacuumed the carpet and examined the dust and dirt in the vacuum bag. Her search recovered a button, two bobby pins, and popcorn kernels. The ring had to be somewhere inside the cottage, either up or downstairs. She hadn't worn those slacks outside, or had she?

Would Clifton believe the engagement ring she'd kept safe these four years had just disappeared? She was not so sure she would if the tables were turned. She shook her head in frustration and went to check on Richie.

He'd contracted a little cold and was napping late. With his stuffy head, he slept mouth open, sprawled on his Thomas the Tank Engine pillow. Emme stacked the books she'd read to him for naptime on his bedside table and snugged his blanket about his shoulders. Storytime had been longer and naps a little later since his fall.

She smiled at the row of stuffed animals perched on his headboard, all with bandaged heads. Richie insisted each animal be doctored and inspected like "the nice man who took him to the hospital." She pinched the bridge of her nose and imperceptibly rocked to the click-click of the ceiling fan. *Oh, sweet boy, that nice man could have been a daddy to you.*

She walked to the window and pulled the curtain back. The sky was gray and overcast. The change in barometric pressure dampened her mood, though in her heart she knew the weather wasn't the only factor dulling her spirits. Today, her shocker marriage to Clifton was to officially end.

Emme pressed her palms against her temples and let the curtain drop back into place. Moving away from the window, she bent to pick up Troublesome Engines off the floor and placed the stray book beside the others.

The crunch of tires sounded on the gravel lot. Emme glanced at her watch. Her heartbeat sped up and throat tightened, the same feelings she had when death was overtaking her dad. Clifton's arrival signaled a different kind of death. The death of their relationship.

She reached the landing at the bottom of the stairs and saw Clifton approaching the back door with hurried steps. All at once, he became the young boy in the red-and-green knit cap fourteen years earlier, rushing to meet the Christmas train. Oh God, please stop the memories. *He's engaged to a Brazilian fashion plate!*

Emme opened the door before he had a chance to knock.

"Mary Elaine, you startled me." Frown lines creased his forehead.

"I was expecting you, remember?"

"Yeah ... uh ... I mean Emme. I guess you go by that now."

"I answer to both." Keep the meeting businesslike. She gave him a reserved smile and glanced behind him. "Where is the attorney's secretary?"

"Ms. Dinkins will be here soon. I just called to let her know I was here."

Emme stepped aside and motioned for him to enter. "Thanks for making arrangements to sign the papers here. Richie has been napping later and longer since his injury."

"Of course. No need to explain. How is he?"

"He has a bit of a cold, but he gets the staples out in two days."

"Speaking of staples ..." Clifton held up a paper sack from Publix. "For Richie's bravery. I hope he likes chocolate."

"He does." Emme accepted the bag, peeked in and grinned. "Doctor's orders?"

"Right. Since you liked ice cream bars, I thought he might too."

"Who doesn't?" Emme pulled the box of ice cream bars from the bag. "He'll be thrilled." Emme placed them in the small freezer of the under-counter refrigerator in the work area.

"Remember, they are for him."

Emme turned to face him. "Hey, and what might you be implying?"

Clifton lifted a brow. He was the college student teasing her when they went for a late-night ice cream treat, and she managed to eat hers and most of his. "I think you know what I mean."

"Yeah, well ... some old habits change with responsibility."

Clifton pressed his lips together and nodded.

"Speaking of chocolate." Emme motioned to the lavender dress in the plastic cleaners bag hanging from the overhead door jam in the work room. "The dry cleaner couldn't get the stain out completely. "I've attached two hundred dollars to the dress that should cover the cost."

"I hate your having to pay. I feel at fault too for startling you—"

"No. Izzie and I believe giving her cash is the best thing to do, and ..." She turned to face him. "I can't find the ring." She blurted her confession and locked gazes with him.

His brows knit in a frown. "The ring?"

"Your grandmother's ring. The one you gave me." Emme flung her hands outward. "I had the ring in a place for safekeeping. The night Richie got hurt, I retrieved the ring to return to you. But now I can't find it. I've checked the folder, the wall safe, the slacks I was wearing. I discovered a hole in the pocket—"

"I'm sure the ring will turn up."

"I've looked everywhere. I am so sorry."

"Look things happen. I'm in no position to complain. I hope I haven't put you in a bad spot."

"No," she responded simply. Her chest throbbed. She knew he was fishing for an explanation about Richie's father, but she wasn't ready to broach that subject. Signing these papers should give him what he truly needed. Make small talk. Don't show the wound bound tightly on her heart. Keep the conversation light.

"How do you like my place?" she asked.

"I think it looks like your dream come true. You used to talk about owning your own business in marketing class."

"And you talked of selling Christmas trees to retail stores all over north Florida."

Clifton took a seat at the customer counter, his hazel eyes trained on her. "As a matter of fact, I'm working on a proposal for Dollar Mart ... and it's probably a foolish notion, but I'd like to get the Christmas train running—"

"Foolish? No, no. Never give up on your dreams."

"I suppose I shouldn't." He scanned the shop surroundings. "You got the cottage surrounded by flowers you wanted."

Emme met his gaze. They had done a lot of dream sharing, laughing—and kissing—after the classes they took together. "You remembered."

"I remember a lot."

Her heartbeat thundered in her ears. Keep the conversation casual. Do not ask him what he remembered, she told herself as she said, "Like what?"

"Like laying eyes on you after eight years when I first walked into that sociology class, and Christmas visits with your family when we were youngsters."

Emme stared at her hands instead of his eyes. He continued.

"Me thinking your initials were WWJD." He paused and pulled something from his pocket.

Emme lifted her eyes as Clifton placed the bracelet of blue and white on the counter, straightening the beads to lie flat. "I … uh … thought you might like to have the bracelet for Richie."

A warm sensation reached clear down to her toes. "You kept the bracelet?" Emme reached for the bracelet and ran her fingers over the smooth threads. "All these years." She felt the sting of tears behind her eyes. She mustn't cry. She mustn't care.

"I just discovered my dad had kept my old box of Christmas tree sales records. I found the bracelet tucked underneath the paperwork."

She took a deep breath, shook her head, and pushed the bracelet back toward him, hoping he hadn't seen the tears threatening to spill. "The bracelet is yours," she said, clearing her throat. "So you partnered with your dad selling the trees?"

Clifton slipped the bracelet in his pocket. "My dad paid me a dollar for every tree I helped sell and load."

"Ah, so you helping us find a tree each year wasn't totally altruistic?"

He shook his head. "Guess not."

Good. Keep the conversation light, but … No, he owed her some answers. She raised her head. "So, did you find the business help you were hoping for overseas?"

Immediately, Emme wished she could withdraw the question. Why inquire about the obvious?

Clifton's answer came slowly. "My only intent was to take advantage of a one-time opportunity."

She had touched a nerve. Emme bit at her lower lip. Why torment him?

"I can relate. I thought living in a big city would be wonderful. Exciting, more opportunities. After you left, I moved to Atlanta and added floral design to my business degree. That's where I met Izzie. She's from Hamilton Harbor, and she told me about this shop coming available."

Clifton's brows pressed together. His clasped hands on the counter tightened, then relaxed as though coming to terms with opposing forces. "I'm glad to see you are doing so well. I ... I need to tell you something."

"I'm listening."

"I just found out you were right. My mother was behind my overseas opportunity and my quick departure."

Emme's stomach jolted. "You just figured that out?"

"I guess I was too intent on believing I'd earned a spot in the class. Then you wouldn't take my calls."

Emme had made it plain she didn't want to hear from him. She had hoped he'd see things her way if she held out. That strategy backfired. Learning he finally discovered she was right about his mother gave her no satisfaction.

"I'm sorry we ..." He looked at the picture of Richie. "Our friendship was ruined, but ..."

Was he going to pose the question about her marital status again? He tapped the wedding photo book on the counter. "Interesting that we both wound up working with plants and flowers."

Emme's tightened nerves relaxed. Get off the subject that could only open old wounds. The old Clifton she used to chat with had returned. "Flowers and major events go together." She motioned to the photos of baby, wedding, and funeral arrangements on the front cover. "Keeps us both in business, I guess."

"Business. Right." Clifton pressed the palms of his hands against his knees and exhaled heavily.

"Speaking of," Emme nodded toward the front window where she could see a woman getting out of a car. "The secretary from your attorney's office?"

Clifton turned. "Yes, that's her."

Clifton stood while Emme went to open the door.

"Mary Elaine Matthews?"

"Hello, Ms. Dinkins," Clifton joined Emme. "You're in the right place." Clifton made introductions, and Emme directed her to a stool at the front counter.

"Mr. Horowitz has everything prepared. The judge said he would sign these first thing in the morning, and then, I'll get them filed. All I need are your signatures in the places indicated."

Ms. Dinkins slid a paper in front of Emme. The bright red fingernail on her index finger pointed like a beacon to the line requiring her signature. Above the line were the words, I DO NOT CONTEST THIS ACTION. She did not want to think. She signed, each letter swirling from her pen eradicating what might have been. Her unworthy connection to the Davenport name officially removed. Their marriage with an unknown beginning and no middle, now had an end.

The paperwork finished, and Ms. Dinkins gone, Emme walked behind Clifton to the rear of her shop. He turned before opening the door, reached for Emme's hand, and gave a gentle tug. His touch sent a shockwave traveling from her fingertips directly into her soul.

"Thank you for signing. I want you to know that I thought of you often, but I didn't want to make a pest of myself when you asked me to quit calling. I couldn't blame you for wanting me out of your life after leaving like I did."

His expression poked more holes in the shield protecting her heart. The dry cleaners' bag behind him framed his image. "Wait." Emme walked over and lifted the dress from the door frame. "Don't forget Renata's dress."

The plastic crinkled as he placed the bagged dress over his arm. An awkward silence hung heavy in the room.

Four years evaporated as she breathed in the same light woodsy scent Clifton had worn when they dated. Her knees turned to gelatin. He leaned toward her. The green in his eyes penetrated her heart. Did his chin tremble?

Rattling sounded as his hand, like a separate third party in the room, fumbled for the doorknob.

His words tumbled out. "Thank you. I'll uh ... see you around?"

"Sure." Her answer came out in a squeak, sounding like it came from someone else. With shaky hands, Emme shut the door behind Clifton. Her chest heaved, trying to breathe, as she leaned against the door. She closed her eyes and inhaled his scent—a lingering ghost from their past.

Clifton's footsteps fell heavy on the wood deck behind the Flower Cottage. When he reached his car, he was almost running.

He slammed the car door closed, started the engine, and put the car in gear. But where was he going? He'd wanted to kiss her. What on earth was he thinking? Kiss her a fond farewell? Part ways on good terms? Which way should he turn?

His office work was completed, the annulment signed, now what? He couldn't just sit in Emme's parking lot. He opted to turn toward the downtown marina. He drove past the day trip fishing boats and leisure boats rocking lazily, their weight buoyed by the bay waters. He could use something to lighten the burden settling on his shoulders.

He parked his car at the dead end where the concrete seawall and metal railing was all that separated firm ground from the seawater. Clifton stepped out of his car. The wind slapped at his shirt and slacks. He sucked in the salty air, then got a whiff of a decaying fish head covered by flies.

The contrast of fresh and rotten heightened the division warring inside him. Was he in the midst of a conspiracy? The professor of his college sociology class—the same class where he and Mary Elaine "got married"—would make an interesting hypothetical study of the opposing forces.

Clifton sunk his hand in his pocket, touching the bracelet Emme wanted him to keep. He freed the bracelet and touched the lettered beads—WWJD. What would Jesus do? Would he caution Clifton about focusing on the hugs and kisses they called homework for the mock wedding? Limit thinking about long talks over ice cream? Forget joking about getting busted by a campus cop for jaywalking? Clifton leaned against the railing and stared at the huge barnacle- crusted pylons lining the seawall. *Lord, what would you do? I need some direction.* He stared at the rolling and restless bay water beneath him.

Clifton closed his eyes and let the sea breezes envelop him. He drew the purifying sensation deep into his lungs. Could the salt air cleanse the worries and give fresh perspective? Would the annulment provide the clean break he needed?

Be about your father's business. His eyes popped open. His father's business? A knowing entered his spirit as he looked across the bay to

Beachcomber Island—covered in trees. Trees were the main-stay of his earthly father's business. The answer was right before his eyes. Amazing. He was to be about his father's business. A wave of purpose washed over him.

He would double check with Carlos about the number of Christmas trees available in November and make sure he had accurate profit projections. If his figures were correct, obtaining a contract with Dollar Mart would give him the funds to buy back the Davenport property and free him from dependence on Mendes.

As he started back to his car, his phone sounded. Gavin. "Hello, brother."

"What happened with the annulment? We're waiting to hear. Renata called me so she wouldn't bother you. Her father is bugging her."

"The annulment is signed. I was just going to call."

"Remember, we're supposed to meet Mendes to show him your plans for the new watering system."

Mendes. He was grateful for the help yet plagued by his close examination of the plantation operation.

He'd returned to his car … and the bad odor. He flicked the fish head into the water and watched as scavenger fish ganged up to feast on the remains.

"Mr. Mendes bought tickets to a United Way fundraiser and mother, me, Renata, and you are expected to attend."

Clifton watched the water settle, the fish head devoured. "I'll be there in thirty minutes."

He fingered the WWJD bracelet. Never give up on your dreams.

More than ever, he had to be about his father's business.
***

Emme slid into the driver's seat of the van. Izzie slammed the rear doors and walked to the open window on the driver's side.

"You're cleared for take-off." She handed Emme a slip of paper. "When you deliver the flowers to the high school, give this information to Laura Lee in the principal's office. She wanted the website address where I buy most of my earrings."

Today, Izzie's ear lobes were decorated with dangling feathered earrings that could help her take flight if she got caught in a wind storm.

"Sure you want competition for your unique 'Izzie' look?" Emme teased.

"Unique? I just wear earrings to go with my outfits. Seems normal to me." Izzie stepped back and held out her arms to show off her bright, neon yellow top, gathered in the front and worn over a long circular skirt with multiple colorfully patterned panels that would fit right in at a quilt show.

"That's because you're you. Trust me, your dress is very unique. Thanks for helping me with the morning's orders." Emme cranked the engine and started to back out of the flower shop's rear lot. "Good luck on your beach consult this afternoon. I'm glad your interior design business is gaining ground."

"Word is spreading, but I'll still be on your team awhile yet."

"Good. I don't know what I'd do without you."

Emme truly didn't know what she would have done over the past few months if Izzie hadn't been there. She relied on her, not only for creative talent but moral support, especially the day Aurora Kemp stepped out of her shiny black Mercedes and into the flower shop. Dressed in a pale blue, sleeveless dress, auburn hair with precision highlights, and the figure of a person who employed a physical trainer, she was magazine cover perfect.

"You're Mary Elaine?"

She used her given name. Did she know her?

"Yes."

"I'm Aurora Kemp, Richie's aunt."

"Kimberly's sister?" She nodded. Emme hurried around the counter and went for a hug, but Aurora held out her well-manicured hand instead.

Emme shook her hand and took a step back. "So good to meet you at last. You've been so kind to send gifts on Richie's birthdays and Christmas."

Aurora scrutinized the shop's interior. "Of course. And you have been so kind to take care of Richie while I was tied up in Europe."

Tied up? Emme understood she had shed well-heeled husband number two and had been preoccupied with landing rich husband number three. "Richie is a blessing," she said.

"My husband and I have moved back to the States. I think it's time the boy came to live with me," Aurora said.

She might as well have balled up her fist and slugged Emme in the stomach. Emme tried to speak. "You're not serious ..." Words caught in her throat.

Before she could muster more words, Aurora lifted her head and sniffed as though smelling something distasteful. "You have him living at a business where people come and go. You never know who might walk in. The neighborhood is a ghost town with all those empty, run-down houses, and he has no one to play with."

She made what had seemed charming and full of potential to Emme sound like a slum. "He has the park to play in across the street and friends at school."

"You call that sandy lot with moss covered trees a park?" Her tone dripped sarcasm.

"The town is undergoing revitalization. The city has plans to improve the park soon."

A car door slammed. The clunky sound of the Richie's boots announced his arrival. Richie burst through the back door.

"Mama, look." Richie held up a small pottery flower pot, filled with dirt. "We planted flower seeds. You can sell them when they get big enough." His trusting eyes sparkled.

Emme squeezed Richie tightly. The idea he could be taken from her shot chills throughout her body. She was his mother. He knew no different. What would happen to him if he was taken from her?

Was she selfish to keep the knowledge of his real mother and father from him? The decision came from her own insecurities as a youngster, after she learned she was adopted. She remembered thinking she was being raised by kind strangers. Her mother and dad thought they were doing the right thing by telling her, but their honesty always left a big question inside her. Her childhood was filled with wondering about her real parents. Was she not good enough to keep? Would life be better or worse if she lived with them? The questions fed her insecurities, and she didn't want Richie to experience those feelings in his young life. Not until he was older and able to understand. But she had to deal with the reality of Aurora standing there and pray she said nothing to upset him.

"Richie, we have a surprise visitor. Say hello to your Aunt Aurora, who always sends you gifts for birthday and Christmas."

Richie pulled from Emme and rushed to Aurora, his little boots clicking on the wooden floor. Pride mixed with unease warred within at the out-stretched-arms-welcoming he gave his aunt. Was there something about being of the same blood? Could Richie's mother have been jealous of her sister and wrong about her suitability to raise Richie?

Aurora patted Richie's back and peeled his arms, held in a tight embrace, from around her neck. She stood and smoothed her dress. "Richie, I brought you something."

Of course she did. That's all she'd ever done for him.

She reached in her purse and pulled out a hand-held digital game player, the exact kind of toy Emme could not afford and didn't want Richie to get hooked on.

"And here's a set of games to go with the player. I didn't know what games you might like, so I bought all I could find."

"Neat." He flung his arms around her neck again and planted a kiss on her cheek, just as he had Emme's when he got home. Emme felt a pain in her jaw and tightness in her stomach.

"It turns on right here."

"Cool. Can I play with it now?"

"Of course."

Richie ran to the child-sized table in the play area.

Emme realized Mellie, who had picked Richie up for her, still stood by the back door. "Mellie, I'm sorry, meet Aurora Kemp, Richie's aunt." They exchanged pleasantries.

"Mellie, could you take Richie upstairs for a snack. I have cut-up apples in the fridge."

Richie thanked Aurora again and went upstairs with Mellie, still clutching his new game player.

"Nice young man."

Young man? He was her sweet, dimple-cheeked boy.

"You do see he deserves better than you can offer. You'll be hearing from me." With that bombshell, she'd turned and left, leaving the scent of expensive perfume mingling with the earthy smells of the flower shop.

Two weeks later, Emme did hear from Aurora by way of a process server who presented her with a notice of a custody hearing.

Emme clenched the van steering wheel tighter to stop her hands from shaking at the thought of that hearing. She couldn't give Richie the advantages Aurora could. Was she wrong to want to keep him while she struggled to make ends meet?

She traveled the short block from her shop and turned onto Main Street. Her flower cargo scented the air as she rolled past old storefronts. The once thriving downtown went dormant when the mall opened north of the city, but the Downtown Reconstruction Board with a Main Street Revitalization grant was helping attract new businesses. Among those reopened were a real estate office, once a dress shop; Margaret's dog grooming in an old beauty shop; and Appleberry's Furniture, housed in the old dime store. An antique shop had recently opened in the old bank building with the original teller cages.

Emme rolled past Larry's Low-Price Autos where he'd added one of those blow-up figures that popped about and waved to get the attention of passers-by—victims might be the better word. At least, he did offer her a balloon note that stopped monthly payments. She'd be able to pay off the entire note after the Mendes-Davenport wedding. The jittery pop-up man's gestures replicated her insides whenever she thought of Clifton and her need to profit from his marriage.

As Emme turned in to her first delivery place, A Peaceful Rest Funeral Home, her cell phone jingled. Pam.

"I'm calling to let you know the Mendes-Davenport wedding date has been changed. I just got a call from Mrs. Davenport. The Mendes family will be in Brazil longer than expected and requested the date be changed from June to August. Of course, I told her we would work on the necessary changes. I was worried about getting the Gulf Haven reservations changed, but somebody in the great upstairs smiled down on us. They had an August cancellation, and I snapped it up."

Emme's heart rate accelerated. She had been counting on the one blessing she could eke out of Clifton's June wedding. Money. The finances she needed to pay off the van by August 13 and show the judge she could support Richie at the hearing on August 14.

"What date in August?" If the wedding was set for early August, maybe if ...

"August twenty second."

Emme's stomach did a somersault. Words escaped her.

"Emme, you there?"

"Yes. Yes. I ... uh ... I don't suppose Mendes has changed his stand on making final payment for the flowers after the wedding? I should think he'd understand about up-front expenses on perishables."

"Since they changed the date, I can ask, but he was quick to lecture me on how you can't survive in business by paying before a job is finished."

"Can you try?"

"Will do. I have to call and tell him I was able to get Gulf Haven reserved. Maybe that will soften him up?" The question in her voice let Emme know she held little hope.

Emme parked under the portico of the funeral home and pulled two arrangements from the rear of the van. She'd started for the front entrance when a man's voice called out.

"Ma'am, you can't leave your van there."

"Oh, but I'll be right back. My hands are full. Would you mind opening the door for me?"

"You're asking a police officer to aid and abet in a parking violation?"

Emme stopped. She knew that voice.

"Tony?" She turned to see Tony Duncan, a wide grin spread on his face. "You scoundrel. What are you doing here?"

"I work here. Well, not here exactly. For the police department. I'm on a funeral detail today."

Emme set down the arrangements. "Give me a hug, you." She hung her arms around his neck and squeezed.

"Take it easy. I might get you for assaulting an officer."

"Well deserved, sneaking up on me like that. What a surprise. When did you come to Hamilton Harbor?"

"I asked Elaine's husband, Jeff, to give me a call if there were any openings. He called and here I am."

"Who would have thought Elaine would help you get a job after you cited her for jaywalking on campus."

"Rules are rules."

"Yeah, but at midnight, leaving a study session and no cars in sight?"

"Except my police cruiser. Two sides to all stories, remember?" Tony grinned and picked up the funeral sprays, "How about you open the door for me so I can salvage my reputation."

Emme led the way and Tony followed. They had first met at the children's home where Emme stayed so she wouldn't have to leave her high school when Frank got a job that required a move.

After delivering the flowers, the two took a few minutes to catch up on news since college.

"We've come a long way from the children's home and playing clowns at birthday parties," Tony said.

"Don't forget our role as detectives in our Bee Line Detective Agency."

"From kids to Seminoles and beyond. Pray for Jeff. He has to train me, so you know he'll have his hands full."

Emme snickered. "After we had to rescue you when you got stuck in that swamp bog, I'd never dream you'd be our protector."

"No one's more surprised than me. Elaine tells me you're busy with a three-year-old and your florist shop."

"I am. My world is flowers and Richie right now."

"And Clifton?"

Emme sighed. "No longer an item. He's getting married. My consolation is getting to do the wedding flowers."

"Sorry things didn't work out for you. I always thought you made a good couple."

"Yeah well, things aren't always what they seem."

Emme's phone sounded. Pam again. "I need to take this call. Join us at church in the old downtown theater. It's a good way to meet people." She spoke quickly, waved and answered the call on the way to her van.

"Hi, Pam."

"Mendes was not moved by the fact that flower expense is normally paid two weeks before the wedding. He just said, 'I pay when the job is done' and hung up."

With Emme's plan A down the tubes, she needed to move to plan B—as soon as she had a plan B.

Chapter 10

Clifton double checked the numbers on the order entries for August before hitting the enter key. Another item he could check off his long Monday list. With elbows on his desk, he rested his forehead on his fists and contemplated which tasks could be completed before he had to leave for the airport.

He was scheduled to pick up Renata and her party at the airport at three o'clock and deliver them to Gulf Haven, the twenty-room beach mansion reserved for two weeks of pre-wedding events, culminating in their sunset nuptials a week from Saturday.

"Earth to Cliff."

"Gavin. I didn't hear you come in." Clifton rubbed his temples with his fingers. "Keeping our good earth producing is heavy on my brain right now. Aging equipment is putting a squeeze on our profit margin."

His brother stood before him, a bouquet of buttercups in hand.

"What are the flowers for?"

"Renata. They're some of her favorites. Thought you might like to take them to her. You did remember she's arriving on an afternoon flight?"

"I'm not that far gone yet."

"Right." Gavin said, returning a hesitant nod. He reached in his pocket. "By the way, here's your personal Renata phone. I can still check your email, but you need to be answering her texts. She's all yours now."

With the four-hour time difference in Brazil and problems with reception, he and Renata constantly missed half of what was being said. Texting and emails seemed the perfect answer, especially when Gavin took over.

"I'm forever indebted to you for taking my personal phone and handling correspondence for me." Clifton tapped the paperwork on his desk with his pen. "No way I'd have been able to put together these business proposals I hope will get us out of debt if I had to read and answer all Renata's chit chat and questions about wedding details these past few weeks. I have to ask your advice on everything anyhow. You're better at that stuff."

"My pleasure, big brother." He held the direct line to Renata an extra moment before releasing the phone into Clifton's hand. "Glad I could help, except you're missing all of what she says if you don't start reviewing the copies of emails and texts I've sent you." Gavin started for the break room, then added, "I wrapped the flower stems in wet paper toweling. I'll put them in the fridge to keep them cool 'til you're ready to go."

Buttercups. An uncomfortable burning gnawed at Clifton's throat. Gavin did know more little things about Renata than he could ever remember. Renata's penchant for details about colors, dresses, sunset timing, and on and on, seemed endless.

Having Gavin handle her electronic messaging seemed a win-win at the time, but with Renata's arrival just hours away, his deception might not have been so wise. Gavin kept him posted on their communications. He even made hard copies but retaining all they said—that just didn't happen.

Gavin walked back out of the break room. "Renata's plane arrives at three o'clock. Between her and those traveling with her, they'll probably have a lot of luggage, so I put a handcart in your car to help unload baggage when you get to Gulf Haven."

Clifton's brows knit together. "How do you think of all these niceties?"

With a shake of his head, Gavin started to leave, then turned back.

"The wedding party had a long layover in Atlanta. Renata texted that her phone was running down and the battery charger was in her checked luggage, so you probably won't hear from her until they arrive. Unless, of course, she borrows someone else's phone."

"Thanks for the warning."

Gavin tilted his head. "Warning?"

Clifton looked up from the cost spreadsheet he'd been going over. "You know, warning me that I'll be stretched more for time dealing with messages."

"After six weeks I'd think you'd be happy to be with her again."

"Of course. I'm just referring to the tedium of typing the texts and emails we had to resort to because of the time difference and bad phone connections."

Gavin seemed okay with that explanation and left. But why did Clifton feel compelled to explain himself to him?

After returning a few phone calls and talking to Carlos about meeting an afternoon shipment, he checked his list again and glanced at his watch, 12:30. He'd grab his leftover sub sandwich for lunch, stop and drop off the fertilizer injector parts for Henry, change clothes and be on his way.

Clifton turned onto Highway 73 from the plantation. Davenport Community Church stood ahead on the left with a sign boasting Sunday services since 1890. Drawn to the little church, he left the confines of his list, wheeled into the gravel lot, and parked in front of the sanctuary.

He had worked on curtailing his spur-of-the-moment behavior since college days, but he wasn't totally free yet. Besides, hadn't impulsivity been endorsed when his mother surprised him at the last minute with a year-long sabbatical? Facing challenges from moment to moment had been his hallmark, so he should be inspired to step up to the plate and make his marriage to Renata work.

He climbed the concrete steps, worn down over the years by the feet of many parishioners, including his family. Using the key always kept on a ledge over the entry, he let himself in.

The afternoon sun penetrated the stained-glass windows, giving the wooden pews in the sanctuary a cozy, comfortable glow. In this place, like no other, he could connect with the Lord.

His footsteps on the wooden floor echoed around the room as he made his way to the altar and knelt.

Clifton prayed silently. *Lord, life seems to be closing in on me. Marriage to Renata seems so ... logical. Right for Mendes's business objectives. The natural next step in our relationship. So why doesn't the marriage feel right? Is this normal pre-wedding nerves?* He pressed his clasped hands against his bowed forehead. "I need your peace, your assurance," he whispered.

Clifton allowed the quiet to soak in. Gradually, he became aware of the scar on his leg from the axe mishap. His perpetual reminder of Mary Elaine—Emme.

He continued praying aloud. "And Lord I can't seem to get Emme out of my mind." He couldn't help questioning her story about losing the ring, especially since his mother was all over the loss when he told her.

"I'll bet she or that stepfather of hers sold the ring," she had said.

Could she have sold the ring or was the heirloom lost? Maybe she threw the ring away to get back at him. Saying she lost it would be easier.

But he couldn't see Emme as vindictive. Izzie said she had been working hard behind the scenes to meet all the wedding decor requests.

With eyes closed, he could see Emme's expression when they repeated their marriage vows during the staged wedding ceremony four years ago. His knees nearly buckled when she said, "I do." Signing annulment papers did nothing to rid him of that vision.

Back on the road after his church visit, he picked up speed. With the windows down and the fresh air washing over him, his sagging spirits were rejuvenated. But the revival was interrupted when his phone sounded.

Clifton answered with the Bluetooth connection. "Hi, brother, what's up?"

"Are you on the way to the airport?"

"Check."

"Good, do you have the flowers?"

"I do." Clifton tilted his rear-view mirror to double check. They were there all right. The wind yanked at the petals, one landing in his lap. Clifton pushed the buttons to close the windows and flipped on the air conditioner.

"Keep the buttercups upright and cool. The petals are fragile."

"I know." Clifton said and brushed the petal off his pants. *Lord help me through this day.* "Any other tips, Mr. Etiquette?"

"A few. Be sure to tell Mendes he's raised a wonderful daughter."

"That seems a bit contrived."

"Listen, I've worked as a guide on his hunting trips long enough to know what he likes to hear."

"I've said nice things about her to him before."

"Well, say nice things again."

"Okay. Anything else?"

"No. Just talk to her about things that interest her."

"What things interest her besides wedding plans?"

"Have you been reading my emails?"

"Yes ... sort of, but there are so many. Did you have to write so much?"

"Look, you asked me to take care of details with Renata for you—"

"I know. I know ... sorry. It's just so much material. I've been trying to catch up."

"Let me give you the basics. Then you'll need to turn on the charm to make your little reunion work."

"Charm? I've been accused of a lot of things, but charming isn't one of them."

"Well, use your Davenport business sense. Look at the situation like a marketing campaign where you're selling a product, namely you, to a customer, namely Renata's father. Put on your best salesman smile coupled with Davenport pride, and there's your results—charm."

"Boy, you make charisma sound easy." Regrettably, Gavin was right. He did need to keep Renata's father happy, and the weight of that need pushed against him, making his head hurt. The only reason Leonardo Mendes made the property purchase and then wedding gift offer was to please his daughter. If not for her, Mendes never would have considered a deal.

"Remember, her father first, then focus on Renata. I rented a full-size SUV, which should take care of Mendes and the rest of today's arrivals. Renata will ride with you, of course."

"How did I ever get dressed today without your advice?"

"What are you wearing?"

"Gavin!" His brother had in-bred style and social skills, but there was a limit.

"Just kidding ... sort of."

"How many am I meeting at the airport anyway?"

"Seriously?"

"Yes, or I wouldn't have asked." Clifton bested Gavin by a year and a half, but Gavin made him feel like the little brother.

Gavin sighed. "Let's see ... there's her Aunt Sofia and Uncle Jorge; Father Cardoso, the priest; Maria Mendes, her granny; four bridesmaids plus her maid of honor, Bianca; and of course, Mr. Mendes and Renata. That should be eleven."

"Bianca lives in Tallahassee. Why is she flying in from Brazil?"

"Oh, boy. You've got a lot of catching up to do. She flew over to Brazil two weeks ago to help Renata with wedding preparations."

"That's right. Jason called accusing me of sabotaging his marriage. He said she switched from preoccupation with their wedding to ours."

"Brides and weddings. It's in their DNA, bro."

"That's fine, but I never could have taken a steady diet of wedding talk with a nursery business to salvage." His stomach growled, protesting the leftover sub sandwich he'd wolfed down. "Turning communication with Renata over to you has probably helped me maintain my sanity."

"You do realize you're getting a great girl, don't you?"

Gavin's wistful question reminded him of Renata's lively, upbeat personality that lit up the room. Maybe the saying opposites attract was true, but would their differences make a good marriage? They had to, for all involved. "I do indeed."

"Good. Drive carefully."

Drive carefully was all he could do. Clifton rolled to a stop. Cars were at a standstill on the two-lane highway. He pulled his car to the center line, trying to see what was holding up the traffic. Blue lights flashed about a quarter of a mile up the road. Probably an accident. He looked at the clock on the dash. Two-ten and he still had another thirteen miles to go.

Clifton flipped on the radio and caught the end of a program. "Second Corinthians 4:8 tells us that we are troubled on every side, yet not distressed; we are perplexed, but not in despair. Remember these things and hold them in your heart. Until next time, this is Pastor Hank Hailey, encouraging you to keep the faith."

As the program broke to a commercial, the words "perplexed but not in despair" nudged his heart. *Lord, if marriage to Renata is the right thing, give me a heart to love and cherish her. I don't want our union to be just a business arrangement.*

The clock on the dash flipped to 2:25 p.m.

His cell phone sounded. Clifton punched the button to receive the call. With no salutation his mother said, "Mary Lou at the hairdresser's showed me how you can track a flight. Renata's plane just landed."

"Great. My luck to have her plane arrive early. Who ever heard of that?"

"You're not there yet?"

"No. Traffic is backed up. Car wreck, I guess."

"Is there any other way you could go?"

"Afraid not. I'm sandwiched in."

"I'm under a hair dryer, so I can't help. What about Gavin?"

"He's at the plantation. Don't worry. They'll have time to stretch their legs."

"Hurry when you can. Mr. Mendes won't take kindly to no one being there to greet them."

"I'll get there when I get there. He'll have to understand." Why he thought that feasible was a mystery. Understanding wasn't a big part of Mendes's repertoire.

Clifton turned up the song on the radio—"Tryin' to Get That Feeling Again."

Traffic began to move at a crawl as Barry Manilow crooned. The song lyrics reached out and took hold of him. Was Carlos right when he referred to Mary Elaine as Clifton's first love? No question he had a crush on her that still held a special place in his heart, but couldn't that same sensation repeat itself? There was hope for a spark to ignite between Renata and him. Right? Those questions would soon be answered.

Clifton rolled down his windows and tugged at his collar hoping the outside air might refresh his spirit. Instead, he was greeted by exhaust fumes swirling through the hot, humid air.

Emme shoved the case of water forward in the back of the van to make room for the flat tire. The cars whizzing by added some breeze to temper the heat radiating off the Highway 98 pavement.

She tried not to disturb the Mendes-Davenport welcome bags and boxed flower arrangements any more than they were already after the bumpy ride on the shoulder of the road. Emme and Izzie each grabbed hold and hoisted the deflated tire into the van.

"Life happens between the bumps in the road," Izzie said, as the jack clinked against the metal van floor.

"Sounds like perfect insight for a poster. But whatever the quote means, I have to tell you I'm not too inspired in one-hundred-degree weather."

"Think about the words. Life moves us from situation to situation, each with its own challenges. We tend to think we'll start living when we get a handle on all our problems, but new ones always crop up."

"And that's when life happens … between the crop-ups?"

"And during." Izzie brushed her dirty hands together. "I'll get the jack back in the compartment for you later."

"That's fine. I'm glad we left early, and you knew what to do."

"My mom made me change a tire before I went off to college. She said I was getting a highfalutin' education in college, but she wanted me to have a practical education too."

"Thank the Lord for your mom's wisdom." A jab of loss touched her heart. She not only lost her dad who would have shown her how to change a tire but in effect, her mother when she married Frank. His contribution was to put a strain on family finances and leave her to self-fund college.

She slammed the rear doors shut. "If left up to me, we'd still be waiting for help." Emme shook the sand from her shoes and climbed into the van.

"That flat tire episode has put us an hour behind." Izzie cleaned her hands with the wet wipes Emme offered. "It's a good thing how we look doesn't matter." She pulled on her multicolor over-blouse to cover her dirt-smudged shell and dabbed at the dirt on the knees of her yellow leggings. Large yellow daisy earrings accented her ears.

"I had hoped to get everything set up in the guest rooms and be out of the mansion by one o'clock," Emme said. "And I wanted to talk last minute plans with Chef as well."

Since the "chocolate incident" at Colonnades, Pam Boswick, Chef Ormond, Izzie, and Emme had worked the Azalea Festival, three graduation parties, two weddings, and a bank dinner party. They seemed almost a team, having one another on speed dial. Chef had even braved using Izzie and Emme as servers again, and the extra cash had become her plan B.

"Did Pam give you the flight arrival time?" Izzie asked.

"Three. Pam wanted everything in place by two. But with the flat tire, we'll need to hustle to get in and out before the wedding party arrives."

The Mendes-Davenport nuptials now included not only wedding flowers, but two weeks of planned events prior. A twinge of doubt nudged at Emme. Was she really ready to tackle an exclusive wedding? Mrs. Davenport's words had seared a brand on her heart—"Clifton needs someone who is not just nice, but extraordinary."

Emme set her jaw and tightened her grip on the steering wheel. "But hustle we will."

With every creative bone in her body, she determined to make the Davenport wedding job extraordinary.

"You sure you're not ready to reveal yourself to Ms. D? With Pam's backing, I don't see her pulling you off the job."

"No need to muddy the water. Besides, keeping my identity hidden is the agreement I made with Clifton."

"Like he's someone who honors his commitments?"

"How about we leave the past in the past. I'm trying to look at this job as an opportunity to give us a step up. I could use a little help here."

"Sorry. You know me. Ever the one with good ideas for what I think everyone else should do."

Emme glanced at her friend and smiled her appreciation. No more need for words on a subject she'd put to rest. Questions like what if Clifton had honored their engagement, and this was their wedding week? Would they have chosen a sunset beach wedding behind Gulf Haven with two weeks of wedding events? Not likely.

Crossing the bridge joining Hamilton Harbor to Harbor Beach, Emme rolled down the van windows and took in the clean air blowing over the bay waters. The beach side of the bridge led to the clear, green Gulf waters and white sand beaches of northwest Florida. Though close by, she hadn't even seen the beach of late. She'd been holed up at the flower shop, busy with everyday deliveries along with preparations for the Mendes-Davenport wedding festivities.

"If I get no other benefit," Izzie said, "seeing Gulf Haven will make our venture worthwhile."

"I understand the place is fabulous. And I wouldn't mind getting a fabulous compliment on our work from Mrs. Davenport. If we didn't need the money, that would be the only reward I'd need. However—"

"We do need the money," Izzie said. "I've always heard that the wealthy are the hardest to get money from. Mendes must fall in that category."

"Indeed."

"Any news on your request to delay the custody hearing?"

"No. But your idea to have a father figure for Richie is working out. Tony has been approved for the Big Brother program, and he and Richie meet officially on Thursday."

Izzie shrugged. "Tony will be a good Big Brother, but I actually had Frank in mind. Besides, you know he and Nan can help financially—"

"I will handle my debts on my own."

"Press on, oh 'weaver of the web,'" Izzie muttered.

"I just ... it's important to me to handle my own expenses. Clifton's wedding is my ticket ..." Emme spotted the stately entry to Gulf Haven. She had always wondered what was behind those walls of decorative stone. "And here we are."

Emme pulled to a stop. An inauspicious plaque surrounded by trimmed ivy identified Gulf Haven. "Call Pam and let her know we're here." She pulled up to the black iron gate and pressed the call button.

"May I help you?"

"The Flower Cottage for the Mendes-Davenport wedding. I should be on your list."

"One moment."

With no further word, the huge gate began to swing open. Emme drove the van to the entrance marked for deliveries and parked.

Pam, dressed in a white blouse and tailored blue skirt, joined them at the rear of the van. "You changed a flat tire? I'm impressed."

"Izzie gets the credit."

"Joint effort. You handed me the tools and lug nuts."

Emme opened the rear van doors. "Wha—?"

"Tell me I'm not seeing a flood in the back of the van," Izzie said.

All three stood and stared as water ran out on the ground.

Izzie reached over the jack and pulled the case of water toward her, exposing the point of an X-ACTO® knife. "The knife must have fallen from a supply bin and cut into the bottles when I pushed the case against the point." Emme said.

Water continued to seep from the slits in the water bottles.

"The bags! Hurry, let's get them out." Emme ran and opened the side door.

Working quickly, the three pulled out the specially sewn canvas welcome bags of sunset colors that doubled as beach bags. All with soaked bottoms.

Emme began assessing the damage. "Labels on the sparkling juice are stained."

"Wet colored tissue paper bled onto all the labels in this bag," Pam said.

Izzie unpacked another wet bag. "The event plans, maps, tags—all messed up."

"It's right at noon. Any way you can get these fixed and back here by three?" Pam asked.

"We will, or my name isn't Isabella Elena Rapunzel Ketterling."

"Rapunzel?" Pam crooked a brow. "You're kidding."

"Maybe, but impressive don't you think?" Izzie winked.

"Impressive is what we are going to show you, Pam," Emme said.

"Oh, I'm impressed already." Pam had been intrigued to learn of Emme's need to stay out of the client's sight. "Working undercover adds an exciting dimension," she had said.

"The guest room flowers are okay," Izzie said.

"Unload them, and I'll put them out while you're gone."

They quickly pulled the boxes holding the guest room arrangements from the van and set them by the side entry.

Emme climbed in the driver's seat and cranked the van. Pam closed the door for Izzie on the passenger side and stepped away from the van. "Be careful, but if you expect to stay undercover, you had better hurry."

Chapter 11

Clifton pulled his car into the rental car parking at the airport. If he could expedite baggage loading for the Brazilian entourage, the gesture might make up for arriving late. Stepping out of his car, he pushed the lock button on the remote, turned to hurry to the terminal, then stopped. "The flowers."

He retrieved the wind-blown bouquet from his back seat and went to the nearest trash bin.

The roar of a jet's engines lifting off the runway served as a noisy backdrop and created an invisible whirlwind that tugged at the yellow blooms. He cast off the ragged, wind-blown petals.

If only he could cast off thoughts of Mary Elaine that plagued him as easily.

Perplexed but not in despair. The words of the radio preacher he'd heard earlier tumbled across his thoughts like the discarded gum wrapper wind-dancing at his feet. He shouldn't despair. What would his dad say? Look at the bright side. He was a guy blessed with a beautiful fiancée who had just arrived at the airport after a two-month separation.

Clutching his meager offering after he weeded out the damaged flowers, his heels clicked a steady beat against the concrete walkway leading to baggage claim. The automatic doors slid open at his approach, and before him stood the group of eleven, huddled around no fewer than thirty bags. He needed to add Gavin to his blessings list for thinking of the handcart.

"Clifton, over here." Renata called out. A solemn-faced father stood beside her, staring at him.

Clifton put on what he hoped was his brightest smile and walked over to the group. "So sorry I'm late. An accident had traffic backed up." He gave Renata a quick welcome kiss and handed her his offering. "For you Mary ... uh ... I mean ... happy. Happy you're back."

Renata wrinkled her brow. Could he have bungled his greeting any worse? He had to get Mary Elaine wiped from his brain.

"You remembered I love buttercups." Renata reached up and hugged him. Her sweet scent evoked pleasant memories of dancing and holding her close at parties in Brazil. Comfortable there, but here, not so much. The song lyrics he'd just heard hit him. But the shiver that tingled through him and his knees that started to quiver came more from the heavy, snort-like breathing of Mr. Mendes, than from feelings evoked by seeing Renata. Not exactly what he or Barry Manilow had in mind.

"Mr. Mendes, so good to see you." Clifton pumped his hand. The man's tense jawline relaxed enough to speak his name.

"Clifton. Glad you finally arrived."

Framed in monotone, Mendes hung his words, laced with displeasure, in the air between them. His attitude bore little resemblance to the man who insisted he wanted to give the Davenport plantation a helping hand with his investment. He'd better add being late on his list of "things not to do" with his father-in-law to be.

"Oh, Papa, lighten up. You heard him say there was a traffic jam."

"Right. I'm really sorry to be late." Clifton was grateful for Renata's quick reprieve as she began introducing her companions.

"Clifton, this is my Aunt Sofia. You know Uncle Jorge." The couple stood erect with little facial expression but did nod their heads and shake his offered hand. "Meet Granny, Papa's mother." The elder woman held out her hand. Clifton wasn't sure whether to kiss, shake, or take her hand and bow. He opted for a light squeeze of her fragile hand. She nodded graciously.

"And our neighborhood priest, Father Cardoso." He offered Clifton a warm smile and handshake.

"Did you enjoy your flight?" Clifton asked, then wondered if the priest spoke English.

"Long, but quite comfortable."

He understood. Relish the small things. *Thank you, Lord.*

Renata steered him to her girlfriends who ranged from tall to short, skinny to hefty—all had dark hair and olive skin. Renata inhaled and named her friends in one breath. "Meet Ana, Larissa, Camilla, Marina, and of course, Bianca."

Clifton tried to remember the first couple of names then gave up. "Please don't take offense if I can't remember your names. Just know I am very glad you're here." The girls giggled.

Bianca opened her arms to Clifton. "Not long now and you'll be married just like Jason and me. Aren't you excited?" Clifton leaned down to hug his fraternity brother's new wife. Jason had joined him on business in Brazil where they were both drawn to Renata and Bianca with their good English skills. The two girls, both graduates of the University of Tennessee, had become welcome tour guides.

"Sure am. What do you hear from Jason?"

"The usual. He's tired of wedding talk and can't wait to get you married off."

"Tell him he started the ball rolling when he proposed to you."

Bianca grinned—her curly hair slicked back in a ponytail showcased her pretty, round face. She spoke as if sharing a confidence, but all could hear. "When Renata first laid eyes on you, she'd already set a goal to find her prince charming, marry, and settle in the States. You were a marked man. I'm just happy to be here and witness her success."

"I know someone named Bianca who set that goal too," Renata said.

"True. Jason is marked with a wedding band now." Bianca waggled her left-hand ring finger, making her diamond shimmer in the airport lighting.

"And I'm proud to be following your example." Renata grasped Clifton's arm.

Should he paw the ground with his hoof? Clifton Davenport, the prize horse?

"We'll have such fun together." Renata let loose with her characteristic cackle that any horse might envy.

Clifton had almost forgotten her laugh-snorts he'd once thought endearing. Did he have any irritating habits?

While Renata rummaged in her carry-on bag, Mr. Mendes drew closer to him. "In business you must allow for the unexpected. Always make a point to allow extra time. Besides, you would think on such an important occasion—"

"Now, Papa," Renata pulled out her sunglasses and stuck them on her head. "No lectures right now." She steered Clifton toward the rental car counters. "You made arrangements for a van?"

With paperwork filled out, luggage loaded, and Renata's companions situated in the rental van, Clifton opened the passenger door of his Mercedes and helped Renata in. He slipped into the driver's side and glanced in her direction. She was gorgeous, smart, witty, and optimistic. What was not to like about Renata? But was her beauty and positive attitude enough to build a life and future on? Were these the normal questions that gave brides and grooms proverbial cold feet?

"A penny for your thoughts," she said, meeting his eyes then glancing downward, "or in my country a centavo."

Was she as uncomfortable as he? "I was just thinking how beautiful you are and—"

She smiled and coaxed, "And?"

"And how lucky I am that you want to leave your country and start a new life here."

"Umm … I believe our communication during these few weeks of separation has brought us closer."

Clifton's heart took a deep dive into his stomach. What if she knew the closeness she felt was to Gavin, not him? She placed her hand on his. "We have the wedding, then, as you said, like grafting a flower, we'll have the rest of our lives to grow together."

"I said that?"

"Of course, silly," she said and squeezed his arm.

He cleared his throat and wished Gavin weren't so eloquent. "I … uh … guess I forgot."

"Bianca was right. Beginning a new life in the States is fulfilling a dream for me."

Clifton smiled, put his car in reverse and began to back up. A horn sounded behind him.

He slammed on brakes stopping just short of ramming the side of Mr. Mendes in the rental van. Clifton pulled forward, thrust his car into park and hurried to apologize.

"I'm so sorry. I didn't see you."

"No worry. You're just captivated by my girl, eh?"

Now, that was a response he hadn't expected "I uh … I guess so." Clifton felt as though his face and ears had been stuck under a heat lamp. "If you'll just follow me."

"Sure, sure. Keep your eyes on the road." The man actually gave him a bit of a wink and rolled up his window.

Clifton relaxed a bit. If he cared for Mendes's daughter and made her happy, things might just work out for everyone involved.

Renata sat quiet while Clifton steered through the airport parking lot's maze of turns and onto the highway. She broke the silence. "You called me Mary."

"Mary?"

"You started to call me Mary when you gave me these flowers." She touched the petals lightly.

His blunder didn't fool her. "Uh ... must have been a name I heard on the radio coming here," he lied. "I'm really sorry." How many times had he apologized since he arrived at the airport? "What a terrible way to greet you."

"That's okay. Just don't let that slip-up happen again."

She poked him in the ribs and let out a hoot that was somewhere between a donkey hee-haw and a giggle. Clifton tightened his grip on the steering wheel.

On the way back to town, Emme and Izzie worked out their rescue plan. Izzie would be responsible for getting the items out of the bags, drying the bags in the clothes dryer, and gathering new tissue paper, maps, attraction brochures, and event lists. Emme would rerun computer generated tags and labels.

With the bags dry, they worked as a team to reattach the labels. Emme handled the "Blinded by Love" for heart-shaped sunglasses, "You Give Me Fever" on hand-sewn palmetto leaf fans, and "A Splash of Love" on local Econfina water bottles, while Izzie repacked "Renata's favorites" on bags of Hershey's chocolate kisses, "Clifton's favorites" on bags of black jelly beans, and "You Light Up My life" on sunblock. When they finished inserting the sparkling juice bottles tagged with "Love Sparks Romance," they were back on the road.

Arriving at Gulf Haven at 3:30, Emme screeched to a halt, and spoke to the man in the box who reopened the gate.

"We're thirty minutes off Pam's timetable," Emme said, as the van's digital clock added another minute.

Izzie called Pam on speaker phone. "I guess I'll have to drop Rapunzel from my name, but we're back."

"Thank goodness. I'll meet you at the service entrance."

Emme followed the bricked drive that wound through thick hedges of Ligustrum bordered by scores of bright yellow day lilies. Arriving at the covered side entry, Pam burst out the door and started talking as Emme braked to a stop. "Ladies, I just talked to Mrs. Davenport. The flight came in early. Let's roll."

Roll they did. Each grabbed a guest bag and followed Pam's lead. They charged through a supply room and laundry room, down a hallway, then detoured through a billiard room and vast library. Passing through a huge carved door they entered a bright circular atrium with a magnificent glass-domed ceiling, exposing the sky. To their left was a massive, columned front entry. Directly across and rising to the second floor was a curved staircase of stone with open grill work railings. Pam dashed toward the stairs.

"There are twelve bedrooms upstairs. They are using ten. I've put their supply requests in each room—things they couldn't bring on their flight. I placed the flower arrangements in each room, but you may want to straighten them. They got jostled a bit."

At the top of the stairs, Emme paused to catch her breath. The second level was open to the atrium below. The tops of palm trees reaching to the sky were at eyelevel here. The rooms were all situated to the left and on a curve that wrapped around the atrium. Exquisite.

"The end rooms will be unoccupied. I selected the rooms with the best ocean view. I'll place the bags; you two do the arranging."

"Izzie, take the first five. I'll start at the other end," Emme directed.

Pam deposited guest bags while Emme and Izzie went to work on last-minute staging. The rush allowed for only quick glimpses of the view of the Gulf's green waters. Emme varied the display in each room. Fresh flowers on the nightstand in one with the welcome bag monogrammed with Renata and Clifton's initials on the bed facing the door. In another room, the dresser provided a better place to spotlight the welcome bag with the flowers on an accent table in a small seating area.

The next room she entered was labeled for Renata. Positioned on the dresser were nail polish and nail polish remover, two large bottles of Aussie shampoo and conditioner, and a one-ounce bottle of an expensive Paris perfume.

Emme raised her brows. Definitely out of her league. The best scent she could manage came from lavender-fragranced bath soap. She glanced at her unadorned fingernails. "No way a florist can keep on nail polish," she mumbled. Working quickly, Emme straightened the welcome bouquet of flowers and placed them on a table across from the entry door to highlight the room's amazing view of green waves rolling onto the white sand beaches.

In the last room, Emme made a final adjustment to a wire-rimmed bow on a vase of bright yellow, red, and orange zinnias. She heard a car door slam and then others. Her heart jumped with each door closure. She sprinted from the bedroom colliding with Pam. Both wound up on the oriental carpet runner outside the bedrooms. Amid a tangle of arms, legs and panicked laughter, Izzie reached to help them up.

"How do we get out of here?" Emme asked.

"Go back the way we came in," Pam said. "When you get to the bottom of the stairs double back behind the atrium to the utility area. I'll run interference."

There was a click at the front door. Giggling, chatter.

"Now or never, ladies. Go." Pam led the way, forging ahead down the stone staircase, Emme and Izzie fitted to her back like a glove. At the bottom of the stairs, Pam called out, "Welcome, welcome." Emme and Izzie skirted behind huge pots of bougainvillea surrounding the open garden entry, while Pam intercepted the group filing in the front door. "So glad you are here."

Emme stubbed her toe on the threshold entering the library, the sound echoing through the atrium. Izzie bumped into her and both skidded on the polished hardwood floor. A heavy library table stopped their skid. Emme held her breath and closed her eyes. She had longed to see inside this place. Now, she only wanted to see it from the outside.

A loud noise echoed throughout Gulf Haven's massive domed entry as Pam greeted Clifton and the entourage. But the sound was lost in Renata and her bridesmaids' shrieks of excitement at the sight of the garden entry lined with pots of fuchsia bougainvillea and massive palm trees. Clifton had only seen pictures of the inside of the imposing beach retreat built in the 1930s for an heir of the Bentley automobile fortune. The reality was impressive with its staircase carved from Florida's native limestone and huge columns covered in clipped ivy surrounding a fountain. A butler in formal attire had probably greeted guests in the past, but Clifton was glad to see the event planner handling pleasantries instead.

"I'll get the luggage." Clifton said, thankful Gavin thought of the baggage carrier.

After the bags and people were safely nestled in their rooms, Clifton and Renata made their way back down the mansion's stone staircase, their footsteps echoing across the open expanse. The fountain splashed water into a pool surrounded by dense philodendron, parlor palms, and other plants Gavin most likely could identify by their scientific botanical names.

He stopped at the foot of the stairs. "The luggage has been delivered to the rooms. Is there anything else you need right now?"

"I can't think of a thing. Everything is perfect. Beautiful ocean view, rooms with fresh flowers and amazing welcome bags—complete with my favorite chocolate kisses. And I didn't even know you liked black jelly beans. You are full of surprises."

"There's black jelly beans in the guest bags?"

"You didn't know? They're tagged Clifton's favorites."

Mary Elaine. She knew of his love for the sweet licorice-flavored candies. He used to rifle through her jelly bean stash and pick them out when they studied together. "No. You don't think grooms are consulted on such matters, do you?"

"They should be." Renata grabbed and squeezed his hand as they walked to the stone bench encircling the fountain. She pointed to the bougainvillea sprouting from huge pots stationed around the archways leading to different sections of the downstairs. "These flowers remind me of something you said in those premarital course questions."

Great. Was he in for more Gavin intrusion? He didn't remember saying anything remotely flowery when he answered questions on the form Gavin made sure he filled out. "What do you mean?"

"You know, your comments about looking at love as a growing process. What were your words?"

Beads of sweat popped out on Clifton's brow. The water flowing into the pool disturbed his ability to think. The premarital course was only required in Florida if you married the same day the marriage license was issued. Bianca and Jason had taken the course and convinced Renata that she and Clifton should follow suit.

"Love as a growing process?" He loosened his collar. "Are you sure I said that?" He'd answered the questions one afternoon between a phone conference and checking an equipment shipment and given them to Gavin to send. He never read Renata's responses. He swallowed the taste of regret.

"You forgot what you wrote already?"

Clifton clenched his hands on his knees. "I suppose."

"You said ... let me see ... a really good marriage is like growing a beautiful, exotic flower that blooms only when nurtured with needed love and care."

A Gavinism—Clifton's new word for Gavin's embellishments. He must have felt compelled to make Clifton's simple responses look better. He forced a grin, placed his hand on Renata's, and looked into her eyes. "Pretty good sentiment, even if I did forget the exact words."

He searched her deep brown eyes, willing a spark to ignite. Leaning in, their lips touched, eyes closed. Not even a glowing ember. Was the feeling mutual? What happened to the easy way he felt with her when they first met? These surroundings, the mansion, gigantic trees inside the house, the fountain waters crashing into the pool—he was out of his element here. They'd been apart two months. Perhaps they needed time to rekindle their relationship.

She patted his hand "There were a lot of questions to answer, but I committed that one to memory."

Renata stood and twirled about. "You have good taste."

"It is a nice place, but Gulf Haven was Gavin's idea."

"Gavin? I thought you said you found the perfect place in your email."

"Oh ... well ... I approved the location at Gavin's suggestion." He had to study those emails.

"I thank you both then." She tipped her head and bobbed a curtsy to him.

"You are welcome." Her hand touched his, soft and warm, but the warmth didn't make it to his uneasy heart. Wasn't separation supposed to make the heart's affection stronger? He gave her a quick glance, turned to face her and took her other hand in his.

She looked down.

Awkward. His actions were affecting her too. They had been an item for two years since meeting at her father's offices in Brazil and subsequent hunting trips at the Davenport plantation. They had spent a lot of time together. But now alone—they just needed to get reacquainted.

"Lemonade and iced tea is available on the terrace." Pam appeared from one of the arched doorways. "I thought you might want to watch the sunset. A preview for your wedding?"

"Sounds good." Clifton rubbed the clammy palms of his hands against his slacks, grateful for the save. "Renata, you want to let the others know?"

"Of course."

"I also ordered a buffet dinner to be ready when you are. After a long travel day, I imagine everyone will want to retire early."

"Perfect." Clifton spoke to Pam. "Could dinner be ready after sunset?"

"Consider your request done. I'll alert Chef Ormond."

Renata patted his hand, stood on tiptoe to raise her five-feet-two-inch height closer to his six feet, and kissed him on the cheek. "I'll get the others to come down."

The idea of having others join them seemed strangely comforting. Come to think of it, their relationship had always included others. Renata's sweet perfume lingered. Clifton needed fresh air. The fragrance not unpleasant, but the strain of the day's activity left him feeling … what? Boxed in?

Renata's shrill laughter rode the air waves down the ornate staircase, past the spattering fountain and lodged in his ears. Would a sunset and ocean breezes be enough to relieve his unease?

Chapter 12

"I wonder if Gulf Haven's sun room ever looked so … sunny?" Emme posed the question and stepped back to admire the décor she and Izzie had labored over. Arrangements of golden jonquils, buttercups, and sweet pea turned the sun room, overlooking the Gulf's green waters, into a yellow fantasia for the ladies' luncheon.

Emme had cracked the sliding door leading to the patio while they worked. The crush of waves breaking on the shoreline and squeals of circling seagulls lent a musical backdrop that had to take a back seat when Izzie broke out in song: "Sun-ny, thank you for the sun-shine bou-quet." Her quick shuffle steps sent the tassels swaying on her pink lace-up sandals.

Emme kept rhythm as she straightened the parchment scrolls, featuring the Davenport coat of arms tied with yellow ribbon, at each place setting. She had taken extra pains at the library to research the family emblem's design and meaning. Izzie continued to hum the "Sunny" song and flitted about—a colorfully patterned butterfly in her purple-and-pink geometric-print dress—working her final magic on the flower baskets for each guest.

Satisfied with their work, they packed supplies and returned to the kitchen. Chef's clinking pans and the aroma of fresh rolls prompted Emme and Izzie to shift gears. Attached to the kitchen were three one-room efficiencies for the help. Emme and Izzie used one to change into white shirts and black slacks to take on another role as Chef Ormond's helpers.

Emme pointed at Izzie's reflection. "I always have a hard time adjusting to seeing you in simple posts for earrings."

"I can do boring when necessary." Izzie presented a cockeyed grin and buttoned the cuffs of her long-sleeved shirt.

"Putting these clothes on makes me feel like a criminal returning to the scene of the crime," Emme said as she pulled her hair back and fluffed her ponytail.

"Yeah, well. Let's pray we can stay under the radar this time." Izzie tucked her shirt into her black slacks. "At least we've had no mishaps at any of the other events Chef's used us for."

"Yes, but on those assignments, I didn't have to hide in the kitchen when guests arrived. He's brave to hire us for this luncheon." Emme picked up the slacks and knit top she'd shed in a crumpled heap and folded them. She was thankful for the extra jobs with Chef, but the work took time away from Richie. He was always excited to have Mellie or her mother stay with him, but what if the judge at the custody hearing didn't agree?

"Hey, we're a team." Izzie said. "Once we get ol' Clifton married off, you can get some financial relief and come out of the shadows. The wedding will be history and Mrs. 'D' will know you're magnificent."

The idea of Mrs. Davenport learning she was the wedding florist made Emme's stomach flip and her knees go limp.

"Wouldn't you love to see the look on her face when she realizes you're the florist?"

"Not really. I'd just as soon remain 'generic florist' as far as she's concerned."

"Ladies, you ready?" Chef called. Emme and Izzie joined him in the kitchen where his assistant was stirring something on the gas stove, and Chef was arranging cheese-filled crepes in large skillets.

"Reporting for service. We took off our florist hats and ... POOF ..." Izzie spread out her fingers for emphasis. "... changed into your worker bees."

"Very good." Chef responded with little expression. The man was all business when presented with a French knife and a cutting board. "I need you to put out the tableware and condiments. As usual, the table setting is sketched for you on the service cart."

Dutifully, Izzie gathered flatware; Emme, the glassware.

"Your individual flower baskets on the sunny yellow table linens ..." Chef's brows shot upward, "the perfect accent for my fruited cheese blintzes."

It was a compliment to treasure.

"Thanks," Emme said. "Just so there's no chocolate sauce to serve. We can't afford to buy another dress."

"That had to hurt your profits." Chef said. Reducing a stalk of celery to tiny pieces in seconds, he scraped them from the cutting board into a bowl.

"It would be nice if I had profits to cut into right now," Emme added.

When service began, Emme helped arrange the watercress salad and fresh croissants on luncheon plates. Izzie returned with her first report. "Guess who's thrilled with the table setting?"

"The bride?"

"Well, yeah, she took pictures on her phone and sent them to Clifton. But Mrs. D said the decorations were beautiful."

"Really?"

"And then she poured glory water on Renata, saying she stood out like a jewel in a sea of yellow." Izzie rambled on while she and Emme placed the prepared plates of cheese blintzes and steamed vegetables on a serving tray. "Renata is wearing a yellow sundress, and I have to admit, with her dark skin and hair, she does stand out."

Emme brushed at a strand of hair hanging limp from the heat of the dish water.

"Maybe she has ugly insides," Izzie added in a whisper that made Emme giggle.

Izzie returned periodically with general eye-witness accounts, but after the eight-layer mango cake and coffee service, Izzie returned to the kitchen in a flurry. "Wait 'til you hear. Renata just cornered me."

"Why?"

"To thank us for being so generous by giving her cash to cover the dress expense."

"Good. I was afraid she might say two hundred wasn't enough."

"No, no. To the contrary." Izzie shoved her hand in her pocket and pulled out a roll of cash. "She gave the money back. Said she couldn't accept the money."

"What?"

Izzie nodded. "She said she got the dress on sale, and two hundred was way too much."

Emme stared at the cash. "But she might not find a sale again."

"That's what I said, but she said all the repayment she wanted was for me to take a group picture. So, I've got to get back in there. By the way, she said the dress is fine—she has a shawl that will cover the stain."

So much for ugly insides. The girl was pretty and nice.

Emme busied herself scraping and rinsing the lunch dishes. She was only half aware of Chef and his assistant packing some of the washed items and taking them outside to load in the van. With each crystal glass she dipped into the sudsy water, she wondered which one might have been held by the beautiful Renata.

Then Izzie returned with a tray of used coffee cups and the latest news.

"Gavin's arrived, and Renata included him in one of the group shots. I'm telling you, she's going to make a mighty attentive sister-in-law."

"What are you talking about?"

"If I didn't know better, I'd believe he was the groom. They were standing so close, you'd think they were posing for the wedding cake topper. After the photo session, she got a text from Clifton and read the message out loud—some kind of trouble in the greenhouses. He wanted Gavin to escort the girls on the afternoon shopping trip."

Izzie leaned in closer as she removed cups from the tray. "And here is an interesting tidbit. When she asked Gavin if that was okay, he put his hand on Renata's shoulder and said, 'I would do anything for you,' and ran his hand right down her arm."

Emme cut her eyes to take in Izzie's tipped head and wrinkled brow as she added, "And what say you about the fondness going on between Renata and Gavin?"

Emme shrugged. "I didn't see them. Couldn't their affection be like brother and sister? They are going to be family."

"I've seen brotherly and sisterly love, but sibling fondness isn't electric. I'm telling you, the look on his face when he put his hand on her shoulder and said he'd do anything for her had enough power to run Richie's model train right off its tracks."

Raising her right hand, Izzie added, "I kid you not. They didn't act like they knew there was anyone else in the room."

Emme finished washing the last of the crystal and started work on the coffee cups, glad for sturdier items she could put some muscle behind. "So what's your point?"

"Me-thinks she's not too upset Clifton can't join them."

Carlos stood on a ladder in the chrysanthemum greenhouse—bare-chested, he used his shirt to dam up water from the latest broken pipe catastrophe.

Clifton's feet sunk into the soupy earthen floor. "You can relax now. I've got the main water valve shut off." Clifton scrubbed his hands through his hair, then rested them on his hips to survey the damage.

Carlos released his grip. The pipes sagged, releasing the remaining water. "It's a good thing the black cloth was suspended over the growing tables, or the water would have crushed these plants even worse."

"What a mess." Clifton picked up a chrysanthemum stem with three yellow buds that would never mature and let the broken flower drop back to the floor. The force of water from the broken pipes had filled the containers of chrysanthemums, washing out the carefully balanced fertilizer and potting soil. Dripping water from the pots and plant tables slowed to erratic plinks on the muddy floor. The greenhouse smelled of wet earth mixed with the strong, sweet odor of battered plants.

Holding his waterlogged shirt, Carlos stepped down from the ladder. "These plants were at just the right stage for the fall shipment."

"I know. The one crop we count on to help the bottom line at the end of the year." The soggy mess mirrored his insides. "So much for my goal of proactive maintenance."

Carlos twisted his shirt, wringing out the excess water. "Your plan to gradually replace the worn pipe lines in each greenhouse was a good one."

"But the plan needed to start a year ago." Clifton tipped one of the potted plants with broken leaves sideways. The water drained out and splashed at his feet muddying his khaki pants. "Good thought, but wrong timing—the story of my life." Projecting a heavy sigh, he asked, "Do you think we can salvage any of these plants?"

Carlos looked about him, slung the wet shirt over his shoulder and made a decisive nod. "With manpower and fresh potting mix. I'll get Eduardo in from pruning and bring in a load of mix. The two of us can handle the repotting. The process will just take some time. You need to focus on your wedding."

From the looks of the photos at the ladies' luncheon sent by Renata, the wedding festivities were running smoothly. Besides, sloshing around in the muddy greenhouse was preferable to the dreaded shopping trip with Renata and her girlfriends. "No, the three of us will handle repotting these plants." Clifton sent a quick text to Renata, explaining the situation. "I'll go change clothes and call Henry again for repairs. He warned me the last patch might not last long."

As Clifton climbed into the ATV, and ground the vehicle into gear, his phone sounded.

"What's happened?" Gavin asked his brother.

"Apparently the pipes in all the old greenhouses have decided to wear out at the same time. The plants are a disaster." His personal phone beeped. "Hold on. I'm getting a message from Renata." He put Gavin on speaker and turned off the ATV to handle his "Renata" phone. The incoming photo uploaded to display a smiling group of girls gathered around Renata, Gavin close at her side.

"Looks like you are in the midst of a happy harem."

Gavin chuckled. "I think they all enjoyed lunch. Table decorations were first-rate." Clifton's heart skipped. He'd zoomed in on the table setting with the individual baskets of bright yellow blooms in the first batch of photos Renata had sent. What if Gavin and the ladies knew the girl who arranged them was the one he'd been married to?

His thoughts went fuzzy. "I don't guess I have to respond to her photo." The words fell dry from his mouth.

"You ought to comment on how nice everyone looks and tell her you hope she had a good time at the luncheon."

Clifton hit reply and began punching in letters. He kept hitting the wrong keys, creating words that made no sense. He jabbed the correction button repeatedly until his attempt at a message disappeared. Renata didn't need his reply.

"You'd best start handling communication on your own. Little brother won't be around to take care of texts on your honeymoon."

"Yeah, well ..." He suddenly tasted the bagel he had for breakfast which wasn't so good the second time around. "After Saturday, we'll be together, and they'll be no need for texting."

"Uh ... maybe." Gavin's reply was not reassuring.

"Listen, are you okay with taking them to the shopping outlet? This greenhouse disaster has to be handled."

"I can take them shopping, but are you sure you don't need me back at the plantation?"

"Handling that bunch of women will help me the most right now."

The "Renata" phone chimed. "I'm getting another message."

Clifton read the text for Gavin to hear. "Your mother planned a lovely luncheon. You're so sweet to let her know my favorite color."

He grimaced and shook his head. "More like my little brother told mother Renata's favorite color. Planner extraordinaire, you give me brownie points I don't deserve. You've got Renata thinking I'm some kind of thoughtful romantic."

"Is that so bad?"

"I guess not, but she's going to wonder what happened to Romeo when she gets stuck with me."

"You did ask me to handle communications with her."

"True. But you didn't have to go overboard. I'm still trying to wade through the copious mound of emails you two exchanged."

"I've got faith in you big brother."

"Next time you see her, smile a lot and listen. Talk about what she did today, so you don't have to worry about prior conversations. Relax. You're getting a great girl."

"I know," Clifton looked down at his dirt smeared hands and muddied pants. "but I'm more worried about what she's getting in return."

"Quit worrying. Listen, the girls are eying me, I'd better run." Clifton heard Renata's cackle in the background.

Pressing the end button on his phone. Clifton's muscles eased a fraction of their tension. At least, he didn't have to go on the shopping trip. The idea of changing into work clothes and repotting plants made the chrysanthemum disaster seem a welcome diversion from the pressures of keeping up with wedding events.

As he restarted the ATV, his work phone sounded.

"Clifton." His mother spoke in a hushed voice. I'm still at the mansion. "I heard there's a problem at one of the greenhouses?"

"Yes, but it's under control now." His dad always handled the business, and his mother managed the household and community affairs. Sound logic. If his mother knew all the current financial issues, there would be little peace at the office.

"I wish you could have come to the mansion." She gave him no break in conversation for a reply. "The table design was perfect for the sun porch with a beautiful centerpiece spray running the length of the table and individual baskets of flowers with the Davenport coat of arms and history on cute little scrolls. Pam's florist choice has been a good one."

Clifton smiled and thought of the extra time and research Emme must have put in. Would his mother speak in such glowing terms if she knew the florist was his surprise ex-wife? "Renata sent a photo."

"I just went to compliment Chef Ormond on last night's buffet dinner and today's luncheon. Do you know that Mendes is holding back payment to the florist until after the wedding? Chef says his refusal to pay in advance has put the florist in a financial bind."

Clifton pulled the ATV to a stop in front of Colonnades. "Mendes has some bullish ways."

"I suppose. But I thought a nice gesture would be to pay her right away for today's work. The luncheon was an add-on."

"How much?" he asked, resigned to dealing with the payment or keep hearing about her request.

"How much what?"

"How much do we owe her?"

"Three hundred."

Clifton winced. Three hundred would put their reserve funds dangerously low. Crossing the columned porch and entering the house, Clifton calculated expenses in his head. With fewer plants to ship out and the cost of repairs, cash flow was tight. Emme and he had one more thing in common.

"I'll have Ms. Peacock cut a check tomorrow. I need to handle the mess in the greenhouse now."

Lord, a soaked greenhouse and nuptials tied to Mendes's offers of capital improvement—is this your way of showing me this marriage is right?

Chapter 13

The kitchen at Gulf Haven buzzed with the hum of a mixer and a whirring food processor. The rolling handcart Emme pushed rumbled across the tiled floor, adding to the noise. "Mmm, cinnamon and apples— the start of your all-American apple pie?"

"Right." Chef Ormond stopped the processor and mixer and poured dough onto a flour-dusted work surface.

"You're torturing my taste buds," Izzie said.

She walked in the kitchen holding an arrangement of red roses, blue-tinted carnations, and white gladiolas, styled for the mantle in the mansion's banquet hall. The team of Emme, Izzie, Chef, and Pam had come together in a quick planning session. Mrs. Davenport had decided after yesterday's luncheon to entertain the Brazilian wedding guests with an American-themed dinner.

"Nice job, ladies, with the star-spangled colors."

"If you think the flowers look good now, wait 'til we add the finishing touches," Izzie said.

"We've had fun coming up with a classic American theme." Emme pointed to the cart laden with flowers, ribbon, streamers, glittery floral picks, and greenery.

Pam rushed through the kitchen entry. "Listen up everyone." Dressed in a fitted white collared blouse and trim tan skirt, her shiny black hair bounced as she walked. "Dina Waddell, the food editor for *Hamilton Harbor News*, called. She just talked to Rosemary Davenport and is going to cover this evening's dinner with a feature in the food section."

"You didn't happen to have anything to do with connecting them, did you?" Emme asked, raising a brow.

"Let's just say we're doing favors for each other. Dina has been clamoring for a wedding exclusive and we get free publicity." Her black-rimmed glasses caught the light, shooting a gleaming star at her cohorts. "Chef, you'll have the chance to shine with your all-American menu. And ladies, you will have a grand opportunity to promote the Flower Cottage."

"I'm liking being a part of your mutual favors," Chef Ormond said beaming.

Izzie eyed Emme, prodding her. "Tell them your idea."

"You have something special in mind?" Pam asked.

"Well. You said Mrs. Davenport likes unique ideas, but I'm not sure how this idea will work."

"So spill. Remember, we agreed no idea is too trivial or dumb to consider," Pam said.

"A model train for the centerpiece."

"Train?"

"Wait until you hear all of the inspiration. The idea is genius." Izzie pulled a stool over for Pam. Chef listened as he rolled pastry into large flat circles.

Emme continued. "There used to be a Davenport Express train that took families to pick out Christmas trees at the plantation. I have a model freight train at my shop that we can label the Davenport Express to highlight the part Davenports have played as a special part of America's heritage."

Chef's eyebrows knit together. "Will the train be just a display or actually run?"

"We can set the model to run with a remote."

Pam stared at Emme. "I've never seen anything like that done on a dinner table before."

"Well, that's why I was a little concerned about bringing up the idea."

"Wait a minute. That's precisely why I enjoy working with you two. Your fresh ideas. We need to try new things."

"Hold up." Chef's eyes were bright. "How about adding classic American individual packets of condiments for the hamburgers and hot dogs on the menu ... and ..." He held up his index finger. "... tuck them into the freight cars."

Emme caught the vision. "And deliver the packets by the Davenport Express—like a lazy Susan."

"Oh, how fun." Izzie clasped her hands together, a delighted kid.

"Cute idea. Not sure Mrs. Davenport will go for the lazy Susan turntable idea, but she should appreciate the Davenport heritage connection. You haven't failed me yet. Go for it girls."

Emme examined the long table centerpiece, highlighted with swirls of red, white, and blue ribbon woven among the blossoms, making sure everything was in order. She added a few more glitter picks for sparkle and pizzazz. Lemon leaf garlands freshened the air. The floral arrangement of roses and carnations graced the fireplace mantle, and sprays of red and white dahlias with blue forget-me-nots accented the archways and dining table. Outlining the centerpiece in a tight ellipse were the tracks ready for the model train experiment. Could tonight's dinner décor be special enough to elicit the extraordinary response she'd like to hear from Rosemary Davenport?

Izzie brought in the last of the boxes with the train accessories. "I had to pinkie swear with Richie that his train would be back unscathed tomorrow."

"Good. He respects the pinkie promise you taught him."

"Chef offered the flameless votive candles left from last night's activities to help with lighting if you want."

"Good. I'll go get them."

Emme made her way from the dining room through a formal living area to the French doors leading to the terrace. She saw the votive candles scattered around the terrace, some on tables others on ledges or the wet bar.

"Clifton, over here," a girl's voice called out.

Curiosity made Emme look toward the beach. A volleyball game was in full swing beyond the sea oats and sand dunes surrounding the terrace. A wooden walkway led to the beach.

Clifton played opposite Gavin, and both had all girl teammates. The sight of Clifton's lean muscular body made Emme's heart leap, frog-like. What was she doing? Get a grip, Mary Elaine Matthews. But her heart defied all reason.

She located a tray behind the bar, scooped up two battery-operated votive candles and placed them on the tray. The gleeful chatter coming from the beach game continued. Don't look back. Emme closed her eyes, but the sight of Clifton jumping to return a shot lingered. They'd once laughed in the same way while enjoying a warm Sunday afternoon playing ultimate Frisbee on Landis Green at FSU.

"Emme?"

Emme jumped and twirled about. "Izzie, you scared me."

"Sorry. You left your phone in the dining room." She held up the phone, her hand over the microphone. "You've got a call from your favorite car dealer."

Emme rolled her eyes and accepted the phone.

"Hello?"

"Larry, at Low-Price. Just a reminder. The note on the van is due tomorrow. You know I don't have to remind you, but I like to go the extra mile for my customers."

Emme let her attention go back to the volleyball game. Clifton made a slam dunk return at the net.

"The extra mile—right." More like putting in extra time needling customers crazy enough to take out a loan with him. Emme's stomach hurt and her head throbbed. She didn't want to say things couldn't get worse for fear they might. The van note for five thousand dollars was due tomorrow. She'd struggled to save three thousand. Where would she get an extra two thousand? Maybe she could convince Larry to take the three and hold a note on the rest. Maybe Mendes could be convinced to pay up before the wedding. Maybe birds would fly north instead of south in the winter. She was trying to take one day at a time. Deal with the van Thursday and the custody hearing Friday.

"Thanks for the reminder. I *will* see you then."

She jabbed at her phone ending the call.

"Now what?"

"Same old *friendly* reminder." Emme shoved her phone in her back pocket and glanced at the merriment on the beach. "I might not have the full amount scraped together, but I'll see him without fail."

"Don't you think you should take your mom and stepdad's offer to help? We're not meant to shoulder all troubles on our own." Izzie shifted her attention to the volleyball game. "Ah ... doesn't help that Clifton looks right nice without clothes ... I mean ... in a swim suit."

Emme kicked at a clump of wet sand that had gathered on the terrace. Her usual tendency to argue drained out of her like outgoing tidewaters. She drew in one last deep breath of sea air, a healing balm to set her thinking straight. "Come on, let's resurrect the Davenport Express."

Emme finished the connections and added the engine and cars. "Cross your fingers." Emme pressed the remote button.

Nothing.

"Great. The train always worked perfectly at the shop."

"Have you ladies taken to playing with model trains in your spare time?"

Emme whirled about. Clifton. "What are you ... are you with ..."

"Relax. The group decided to go shelling along the beach. I have to get back to the plantation. What's with the train?"

"I'm afraid it's a silly idea I had for your all-American dinner that we may have to rethink," Emme said.

"It's a great idea," Izzie said. "We just need to get the thing working. You wouldn't happen to know anything about model trains, would you?"

"Some." He stepped over to take a closer look. "I used to have a similar Lionel set." Clifton answered Izzie's question but locked eyes with Emme. She remembered his comment about having a train room at Colonnades before his mother turned the space into a sitting room.

"Good. Put your expertise to work." Izzie checked the time. "I hate to run out on you, Emme, but I don't want to be late for my interior design appointment."

"You go ahead."

"At least the consult is on the beach. I'll be back as soon as I can."

"Clifton, I don't want to tie you up—"

"No, no. Let me take a look. The wheels might not be aligned." Clifton reached for the engine, then stopped. "Davenport Express," he said, reading the sign Emme had made for the train. "This is the Christmas train?"

Emme nodded. "I thought the train would be a way to tie the all-American theme to the Davenport Plantation."

"Ah. I see." He took in the decorations on the table and around the doors and mantle. "You do incredible work." His eyes came back to the centerpiece and Emme. "Eerie."

"Eerie? How so?" Emme's stomach was doing a weird, skittery thing. He was still in a swimsuit, a T-shirt covering his bare chest. His nearness seemed to radiate the beach sun he'd been soaking in.

"My head has been immersed in reviving the Christmas train."

"You're moving on your idea to restart the train?" She gave him a high-five. Their hands popped together, sending nostalgic warm fuzzies all over her. "Fantastic."

"I've been pouring over stats, rail beds, and train crossing permits for a few weeks. Here, let's try taking the cars apart and realigning them on the track, one at a time."

Emme helped remove the cars. Working side by side seemed normal, instinctive.

"The greenery even looks like the Christmas tree farm."

"Gold star." Emme beamed. "I wanted to portray the countryside where the train traveled." She envisioned the train rumbling on the tracks, slowing, horn blowing to announce its arrival, and Clifton's red nose and cheeks from the cold—adorable. She felt heat rising in her own cheeks. Change the subject.

"So how long will it take to restore train service to the plantation?"

"Not sure. I've made a proposal to reopen the train spur. I haven't gotten word from Coast Line on the feasibility from their end yet."

"My stepfather handles security for Coast Line. Maybe he could be of some help with contacts."

"Really? So how is his—"

"Drinking problem?" Clifton knew better than anyone the hurts caused by Frank's drinking problems. "Actually, he's been doing well, clean over a year now, but—"

"Still hard to completely trust?" He could still finish her sentences. Did he have to send her that lopsided grin?

"Yes," Emme said, steering clear of the sentiments. Holding up a train car, she asked, "So ... the train?"

"Of course ... the train." Clifton picked up the engine, then set it down. "Check all the track connections first. Give them a good push."

Emme worked one side of the track while Clifton checked the other, bringing them back together. Too close for comfort. Talk business. "Your Dollar Mart proposal. Will trees cost more at the store than those bought at the farm by train customers?"

"I'd sell wholesale at both places. Dollar Mart would add their percentage."

"And where will you sell the train tickets and promote the Christmas train?"

"Newspaper and brochures with sales at the train depot."

"What if—"

"Uh-oh. I hear wheels turning."

"Shush or I might lose the idea."

Clifton pressed his lips together. She used to touch her finger to his lips to quiet him during their brainstorming sessions for marketing class, and he'd kiss her fingers. He was too close for comfort. She stepped back, seeking safety in distance.

"What if you combine your proposals? Dollar Mart would not only handle your trees but also ticket sales for the Christmas train."

"Why would they sell tickets that would curtail tree sales at the store?"

"Offer Dollar Mart a percentage of the ticket sales to offset the loss of a tree sale. Coming there for a ticket puts a customer in their store who will likely buy more than the train ticket. You get another sales outlet, free advertising. The customer has the choice of selecting their tree at the plantation plus the train ride or paying less overall for a tree at the store. Win, win for everybody."

"You might have something there. I wish we had more time to talk ideas like we—"

"Used to? Don't go there."

"I miss those times we used to bounce ideas off each other."

"And times have changed." Was her lip quivering? She swallowed and the lump in her throat felt like a freight train car had lodged there. "What next for the train?"

Clifton sighed heavily and picked up the engine. "The engine carries the load." He placed the engine on the track, carefully aligning the wheels on the rails. "I remember my dad always rolled the train cars forward and back to get them lined up right."

The little boy in Clifton, for Emme's eyes only, emerged.

"Okay. Let's test our work."

Emme pressed the button on the remote. The light came on and the engine took off, making a tinny sound as it ground along the track.

"Oh my gosh! You did it." She grabbed his arm, and they watched as the engine rounded the track.

"Now add one car at a time. Run the car forward and back." He demonstrated. "Then attach it to the one in front."

Emme followed his instruction. Like old times. They stood shoulder to shoulder.

"Ready to try it again?" he asked.

Emme looked up at him. His words struck her with double meaning. But a do-over of their relationship was impossible.

"The train?" she asked.

He nodded.

The air between them thinned. Her surroundings switched to slow-motion. Emme gradually became aware of the remote in her hand. She had to will her finger to press the button.

The engine moved, pulling its freight cars behind. The power-driven train slid along the tracks and electrified the air surrounding them. They watched in silence until the engine returned.

Emme set down the remote and stepped back from the table. "Looks like the Davenport train is moving."

"Yes." They held eye contact a few seconds longer than normal. "To a different time and place." Clifton stepped toward her, startling her with the intensity of his eyes searching hers. He pressed his lips together, ran his hands through his short hair, then patted the table.

"Mission accomplished. I'd better be going."

"Thank you."

Then, just as forcefully as his gaze had penetrated hers, he turned and hurried from the room.

Emme stared after him. She heard laughter, accented by one high-pitched cackle coming from the beach. Clifton Davenport had been tempted to kiss her. She was certain he'd considered it. And she was even more certain that she'd have let him.

What on earth was he thinking? Clifton was scrubbed free of beach sand and suntan lotion, but soap and water couldn't wash away the memory of Emme's azure eyes reaching deep into his soul. His feelings for Emme had returned. Or had they ever left? Was he reliving a first love fantasy for Mary Elaine? Or was genuine love hidden beneath the surface of his senses?

Her nearness, her light lavender scent, her ability to finish his thoughts before he spoke—all produced a desire he had hoped would develop with Renata. He couldn't think rationally when he was around Emme. Was it the draw of forbidden fruit? The yearning for a last fling before settling down? Or the fact that she was his first love and his emotions were stuck in the past? Whatever the reason, he needed to stay clear of her.

Clifton had changed into khakis and a sport shirt at Colonnades. His assigned duty tonight was to pick up Pastor Hanover at the parsonage. Gavin's assignment was to pick up their mother where her car was being serviced. The plan was for all to converge at Gulf Haven for the evening's dinner.

The pastor's house, built from plantation timber, was tucked in a grove of pines behind the church. Already outside, Pastor Hanover waved from the front porch and made his way down the front steps. Clifton stepped out of his car to open the passenger door. A sense of belonging wrapped around him like a father's hug. These church grounds were an integral part of his family heritage. Getting married in this little church would have suited him, but the bride's wishes took precedence.

An Abe Lincoln look-alike with his lanky, six-foot frame, Pastor was dressed in cowboy boots, jeans, and a blue check shirt.

"I like your outfit. I see you got word about Mother's American theme and casual dress.

"I aim to please. Especially when I get explicit instructions from your mother." Pastor smiled and added a wink.

Clifton got back in the car, wishing he could absorb some of his pastor's wisdom and compassion. Pastor Hanover, whose deep voice needed no amplification in the sanctuary, asked, "How are you holding up with all the wedding excitement?"

Clifton started the car. "Pretty good." Turning to look behind him before backing out, he caught Pastor Hanover's gaze. "I suppose."

Pastor's bushy white brows shot upward. "Problems?"

"No ... yes ..." He shoved the gear shift back into park. "I don't know."

Pastor Hanover waited.

Clifton decided spilling his thoughts to his pastor had to be more fruitful than talking to his father's portrait. His one-sided conversations with the wall had become more frequent of late. "Arranged marriages are scriptural, right?"

"They are." He turned to Clifton, gently resting his hand on his shoulder. "Do you consider your marriage to Renata arranged?"

Clifton squeezed his lips together. "The marriage has ended up involving her father and finances."

"How so?"

"Mendes purchased a large portion of Davenport land to help out financially when we were in danger of bankruptcy. Renata and I had dated for some time and engagement seemed the next step, when her father proposed to gift the property back to Davenport ownership if we married."

Pastor Hanover puzzled over his statement. "Would you have married Renata without his offer?"

"I … I think so. Our relationship was headed in that direction."

Pastor Hanover gave a nod of understanding that Clifton desperately wanted. "But logical thinking doesn't always work in affairs of the heart. How does Renata feel about her father's property gift?"

"Happy. And she thinks I should be too."

Checking the time, Pastor said, "We don't want to be late. Go ahead. We can talk on the way."

Clifton put the car in reverse and began to back out again.

"First, I see you're experiencing normal role expectations. You need to be the provider, and Renata has need for protection."

"Makes sense. And she is accustomed to her father's protection."

"Right. And to answer your question, there were arranged marriages in the Bible. The idea was to join couples with the same religious and cultural beliefs in order to pass those principles to future generations."

Clifton stopped again before pulling out on the road. "We're from different denominations, but both Christian."

"And that gives you common ground. Have you and Renata spoken about spiritual matters?"

Had they? He could think of no conversation with her about anything spiritual. "We wrote some responses about religious beliefs on a premarital correspondence course. I believe her catechism classes were important to her." Hadn't he read that? He had been in the middle of negotiating prices with a vendor when Gavin reminded him to answer his questions, so he could send them.

"You two have differences to overcome, but the fact that I will be meeting with the two of you and her priest after dinner tonight is an important step."

"I hope we have the common ground you're talking about." Clifton sighed heavily as he pulled from the lot onto the road. "Both of us losing a parent to cancer is one thing we have in common, for sure."

"But you need the assurance this is God's will for the two of you to marry."

Clifton rubbed a fingertip between his brows as if he could erase the frown line. "I guess so."

"Let's pray about the situation," Pastor said.

"Isn't that a little late with the wedding set for a week from Saturday?"

Pastor chuckled. "Not with God."

Clifton continued driving, listening intently to his Pastor's prayer.

"Lord, you know the situation. Should Clifton take Renata as his wife, postpone this marriage, break his engagement, or tell his fiancée his concerns, so they can make their decision together. Please make your will obvious to Clifton."

Yes, Lord, really obvious.

Chapter 14

Emme stood in the Gulf Haven cook's quarters with Izzie. She could almost feel the knots in her stomach. To most, the strong smell of seasoned hot dogs and hamburgers, ready to cook on the inside kitchen grill, would be inviting, but the smell added to her uneasiness. She had just returned from her quick journey back to the shop to check on Richie and Mellie. After changing into her standard black slacks with a white shirt, she tucked in her shirt and began working on her tie.

Izzie had finally taught her the tying technique, but her trembling hands wouldn't cooperate tonight.

"Can you help me fix this tie? I'm having an awful time."

"It's no wonder. Your hands are shaking like you've been watching a horror movie."

Her hands were trembling—not from a fearful sight, but from the scary emotions that had overtaken her.

She hadn't told Izzie what happened before Clifton left. She wasn't sure what happened herself. How could she share something so impossible to define?

Old feelings for Clifton had rushed over her like the miniature engine that scurried around the tracks. And then, as suddenly as the train stopped when it lost power, Clifton had left.

Emme couldn't afford to get sidetracked. Too much was riding on the evening's success—a custody fight and a van she could lose if she didn't come up with two thousand dollars. She had to get hold of herself.

"I ... uh ... guess I'm worried about how the model train idea is going to be received."

The two, now dressed to help Chef Ormond, entered the kitchen.

"Chef, tell Emme she's worrying for nothing."

"Why are you worried?"

"The more I think about the train, the more I believe Mrs. Davenport will either love the idea or hate it. No in-between. And the food editor may see the centerpiece as clever but could just as easily bill the train as cheesy. And what if the thing quits?" The image of Clifton helping her get the train running sent an electric shock through her again.

"Would you stop," Izzie said. "Mrs. D loved the Davenport coat of arms. The Davenport Express spotlights the Davenport name. She'll be blown away."

"It is a most impressive centerpiece, sure to bring smiles." Chef made an exaggerated smiley face that made Emme laugh.

"Okay, then, I see you've been busy dirtying pots for me. I'd better get busy." Izzie got to work on the place settings in the dining hall.

Moonlighting with Chef Ormond over the last weeks, she'd learned to anticipate his routine. She concentrated on keeping his cookware washed and work areas clean as he produced culinary creations that satisfied his client's taste buds. Even though tonight's menu was something one might pick up at the ball park, he gave the preparation of the all-American meal as much care and attention as he would a complicated French cuisine.

But the soft thud of pots in the sink of sudsy water yielded abruptly to a demanding Mrs. Davenport bursting through the kitchen door.

"Who is responsible for that toy train?" Her words hit hard on the T's leaving little doubt that Mrs. Davenport did not care for the train idea. "We'll be a laughing stock."

Emme froze, her hands grasping a sauce pan in the hot soapy water.

"We thought the train would go well with the American food theme," Chef said.

"That's right," Izzie chimed in, "and it represents the Davenport Express."

"But it's juvenile!" she shot back, her pitch shrill. "We can't have a train on the table with a newspaper reporter coming. I'm shocked … I … I'll deal with you later."

A searing heat flushed over Emme; her heart thumped hard against her chest. She heard Mrs. Davenport push back through the kitchen door, calling out, "Gavin, let me have your phone."

Emme grabbed a dish towel and turned around.

"Emme, no."

Pushing past Izzie's protests, Emme rushed into the dining room and planted herself in front of an astonished Mrs. Davenport. "Please, don't blame them. The train was my idea."

Rosemary Davenport literally took a step back. "Mary Elaine? What ..."

"I thought the model train would be unique."

Mrs. Davenport fisted her hips and raised her eyebrows. "Uniquely awful. What are you doing here?" She turned to Izzie who had followed behind Emme. "Why would you consult with a ..." She looked at the towel in Emme's hand. "A dishwasher." She hit heavy on the dishwasher word.

Emme held up a hand. She realized a group of people had gathered across the room, but she had to handle the question. "I am working as a dishwasher tonight, but I own the Flower Cottage and take full responsibility for the decorations."

"You ... are the florist? Hiding back there?" The grim set of her mouth turned to a lopsided smirk. "Well, doesn't this explain a lot—the trumped-up marriage to Clifton, the chocolate poured on Renata, but never would I have believed even you would stoop so low as to sabotage our dinner to get back at Clifton for dumping you."

The stares from the guests' curious eyes closed in on Emme. She didn't want to get into a debate about past hurts that would only muddy the matter at hand. "Please believe me, I never intended to hurt anyone. It's true. I did hide. But only because I wanted the chance to do a good job for you."

Mrs. Davenport stiffened, her eyes wide. "Well you didn't do a good job. And you can consider yourself off this one. You're fired."

"Clifton, thank heaven you're here."

Renata rushed toward Clifton and Pastor Hanover as soon as they stepped into the garden foyer at Gulf Haven. The fountain shot up streams of water that fell back down and tackled the pool's surface.

"What's going on?"

"It's so awful." Her voice carried a tense edge as she steered them into the dining hall. "Your old girlfriend was here and tried to ruin the dinner. Your mother ordered her to leave."

Across the room, Clifton's mother waved her arms in expressive gestures while she spoke on the phone just outside the kitchen door. She reminded him of a squawking chicken with ruffled feathers.

Mendes stood with the other guests, chattering in their native Portuguese and eying the dining table as though it was laden with dangerous explosives.

What on earth? He switched to automatic "rapid repair" mode—a technique the deteriorating water lines in the greenhouses had taught him. Clifton patted Renata's hand. "Assure your family and friends that everything will be okay."

He strode to his mother as she was saying, "Pam, you can't bring that food editor here, something dreadful has happened—"

Reaching over her shoulder and retrieving the phone, Clifton said, "Pam? Clifton here. Just a little mix-up. Come on as planned."

"Are you sure?" Pam asked while his mother railed in the background. "I just arrived at the guard gate."

"Yes. Everything will be fine."

"Okay. We'll be there shortly."

Ending the call, Clifton pocketed the phone.

"Have you lost your senses? That girl you wanted to marry, Mary Elaine, was here intent on embarrassing us. We can't have the food editor see this ... this ..." She motioned at the banquet table with the centerpiece of greenery interwoven with flowers and red, white, and blue ribbons, encircled by the model train.

"Classic American train that depicts the old Davenport Express? Of course we can. I helped her set it up."

"You what?" His mother's jaw went slack; her shoulders sagged.

"The food editor will be intrigued. Watch. Gavin, step around on the other side of the table."

"Sure." Gavin walked around the table. The Brazilian guests gathered in.

"I'll pass you the salt," Clifton said.

"Clifton, for heaven's sake, what are you doing?" His mother's tone was a hopeless whine.

Clifton lifted the remote that Emme had left by his seat and pressed the button. The engine took off. The tiny wheels trilled on the track, pulling the load of packaged condiments. When the railcar, carrying the salt packets, reached Gavin, he took his finger off the control. "There you go."

Renata's girlfriends giggled. Mr. Mendes said something in Portuguese to Uncle Jorge; both men cracked approving smiles.

Gavin grinned and picked up a salt packet from the train car. "Thank you for the delivery."

A camera flash brightened Gavin's beaming face as he stood in front of the group from Brazil.

"Perfect." A small-framed woman with long brown hair commented on the picture in her 35mm camera viewer screen. The dinner guests were so engrossed in the demonstration, Pam's entrance with the food editor had gone unnoticed.

Miraculously recovering her composure, Rosemary Davenport swooped over to welcome the food editor. "Ms. Waddell, thank you for coming. We are so privileged to have you join our little dinner party."

Chapter 15

Emme sat in her shop in the dark. The leaky faucet in the work sink plinked water into a cup, stirring up the smell of stale coffee. Mixed in were the musky odors emitted by discarded flower trimmings.

After Mrs. Davenport's dramatic firing, Emme had managed to make it as far as her work table before the tears came. Salty streams streaked her face and ran into her mouth. Her head rested on the flower stem clippings. Pieces of red, white, and blue ribbon lay scattered on the work table and at her feet. With Richie spending the night with Mellie, only the hum of the florist cooler disturbed the quiet.

She was left to replay the scene with Mrs. Davenport over and over. Each time the result the same. If only she were a movie producer who could hit a rewind button and tape a do-over. In the new scene, she'd stick to the original decoration plans, delete the idiotic notion of the Davenport express, and erase the shot of Clifton helping get the train running and sending exasperating vibrations to her heart.

But there would be no makeover. The scene had been live. There was nothing she could rewind and tape over. She couldn't make Mrs. Davenport's "fired" disappear any more than she could the stack of unpaid bills accumulating in the basket under the front counter. Not to mention the letter summoning her to court for the custody hearing day after tomorrow.

Emme's arms and legs felt numb, immovable, like Richie's toy duck that needed to be rewound after running down.

A sweep of headlights temporarily illuminated the room. Emme stood and peered out the window over the work sink. Izzie. She unlocked the back door and flicked on the lights.

"Have you been sitting in the dark?" Izzie had reprimand in her voice. She stopped and stared. "What happened to your forehead?"

"I don't know." Emme touched her head and reached in her purse for her cosmetic mirror. What looked like a V was carved in the middle of her forehead. She pointed to the stems she hadn't bothered to move when she put her head down.

"Sitting head down in the dark won't get it, girlfriend."

"Sitting under lights won't *get it* either," Emme said after seeing her smudged eye mascara and streaked makeup.

"That V may stand for victory. Ms. D may have fired you, but you get the last laugh."

"What are you talking about?"

"Clifton arrived and acted like everything was going according to plan. He demoed running the train to pass salt to Gavin. Everyone, especially the newspaper lady, loved the novelty. She took lots of pictures. Mrs. D was forced to act like she liked the idea."

The clipped flower stems plunked into the wastebasket as Emme brushed them off the table. "I'm glad everyone liked the train, but I'm still just as fired.

"The point is, you are talented, and the fact is indisputable. Who cares what Mrs. D thinks? Having her jump on you is just a minor setback."

"Minor? Without this wedding job, I'm all but guaranteed to lose the van. Not to mention the shop and Rich … She choked on his name as his little trusting face smiled at her from the photo on the client counter. "There's no way, I can handle—"

"Stop right there. Pastor Creighton says more is accomplished by folding your hands in prayer than wringing them."

"Prayer is fine but won't take away the fact that I'll never be good enough to handle the Davenport's upscale functions. The train apparently proved that to her."

"Who knows? When Clifton saw what happened, he stepped in like a champ. I'm thinking there is an outside chance they could keep you on the wedding. Especially since you've got all the flowers ordered and designs completed."

"Which is another not so minor setback. Cash flow is tied up in that wedding order. Since Mendes doesn't believe in paying before services are rendered, I'm stuck."

"Therefore …" Izzie began.

"Therefore, I'll use the talents God entrusted to me." Emme brushed more debris on the worktable into a pile.

"Look at me." Izzie snapped her fingers.

"So you're in a raging sea and calling for help. You're about to go under. You open your mouth to scream and a wave hits. You suck in water and sputter. Then a helicopter thunders overhead creating a wind. A rope is dropped from the copter right over your head. What are you supposed to do?"

"Oh, Izzie. I don't need a helicopter unless it's dropping money."

"Just answer the question. What are you supposed to do?"

Emme shrugged an "I give up" gesture. "Grab hold?"

"Bingo. Now who has offered a lifeline?"

"I know where you're going with your line of thinking ... but—"

"Maybe getting fired is God's nudge to get you to talk to Frank and make amends. He and your mom have offered help in any way. What do you think?"

Emme had thought a lot about Frank over the past eight years, and most of the sentiments were not good. She'd begun to believe the change in her stepfather's alcohol addiction was genuine, but past hurts were so hard to erase. There was one thing Mrs. Davenport's "not good enough" judgment had done. The label gave her a perspective on the anguish Frank must have experienced when falsely accused, humiliated, and forced to resign from the police force.

At fifteen, she was too absorbed in her own self-pity. Charges against Frank were highly publicized and an embarrassment to her at school. When Frank started drinking, all she could see was fault. Only in the past year, when Pastor Creighton spoke on forgiveness, had heart tugs started to push her toward some kind of reconciliation. She had allowed Frank to be around Richie more, and Richie adored him.

"I'll give talking to mom and Frank some thought."

"Good. I believe God can intervene in your situation directly, but I also think He likes working through other people."

Emme had to agree. "Like Tony volunteering to be Big Brother to Richie?"

"Right. See? If you hadn't shared your need in Sunday school, Tony might not have known how he could help. Listen, your mom and Frank have been there for you, as much as you would allow. Admit your need. God may show up in ways that surprise you."

Had she been brought to the point of accepting help for a purpose? Was Tony's ending up in Hamilton Harbor a coincidence? He had been like a big brother to her at the children's home. Or had some angelic ground work been laid ahead of time? Frank had humbled himself and asked forgiveness for embarrassing her and taking her college fund. Was it her turn to humble herself?

He was suffocating. Clifton struggled for air as he pushed the pillow off his head and awoke from a fitful night of dozing in the west wing bedroom at Colonnades. On any other day, the aroma of coffee and his mother's fresh baked orange sweet rolls would have coaxed him out of bed. Instead, fresh paint fumes—the reason for the pillow over his face—overpowered the enticing smells.

The green color for the bedroom walls was a much-belabored email topic. Renata had thought she was discussing the subject with him instead of Gavin. One more deception to add to the others. He had labored to stay awake and read the discussion of tints and hues in the emails. The exchange must have contributed to his vision of submerging himself in the blue depths of Mary Elaine's eyes.

Now he wished he could pull the sheet over his head and erase the image of signed annulment papers that put a final stake in the relationship traded for his adventures in Europe and South America. But bed covers couldn't hide the hurt he'd caused or delay the day's activities.

Beside his bed was the check for the luncheon his mother had wanted him to deliver to "the florist." Of course, that was before she knew the florist was Mary Elaine, alias Emme. He'd also picked out a Lionel car from his old train set for Richie to thank him for the loan of his train. He would have to fit a trip to the Flower Cottage into the pre-planned schedule that ruled his life these days. Getting the check to Emme was the least he could do to apologize for his mother's rash decision to fire her.

He needed air. Getting out of bed, Clifton ambled to French doors that opened onto a balcony. He held up his arms to get a good stretch, then rolled his shoulders to relax the tension.

Pastor Hanover had prayed for God to make it clear if marrying Renata was right. Mendes's investment interest in the plantation and finding Mary Elaine for the annulment—positive signs. Weren't they?

But finding Mary Elaine had also served to stir unrest in his spirit and resurrected a longing in his soul for the girl who captured his heart the moment she arrived on the Christmas train years ago. When she walked back into his life at the university and they locked gazes, a spark re-ignited.

Now his brain was moving to overload—his stomach was queasy from paint fumes. "Mary Elaine and I were actually married," he whispered and closed his eyes. What kind of life could they have made together? Could they have worked through her concern about being accepted by his mother?

"Your mother finally did it," she had said.

"Did what?"

"Found a way to separate us."

He had stood in the air terminal, a hastily packed carry-on at his feet. "Do you have to read something personal into everything my mother does?"

"You can seriously say that, when she made sure you didn't even have time to say goodbye?"

"She wanted the trip to be a surprise. I only had time to grab the bags she'd packed and get to the airport."

"Don't you see? Your mother carefully planned your departure, so you'd have no time for me to change your mind."

"Don't be that way. I'm the one who applied for the study program. I figured being selected would be a long shot ... not to mention an honor."

"She has connections. I'll guarantee you she pushed for you to get the appointment to keep you away from me."

"You don't think I could have gotten the appointment on my own merit?"

"Well, yes, but—"

"Can't you see what a great opportunity this will be for me and our future? If we were married ... I couldn't go."

"I guess I'm just a hindrance to you. Clifton, why did you give me your grandmother's ring?"

Then came the words he wished he could take back. "My going overseas is not all about you. You're being selfish."

Silence.

"I have to go. I'll call you later when you can be more reasonable."

"Don't bother, I won't be answering."

Clifton opened his eyes. Was replaying the memory he could never undo some type of penance? Suffering he must endure over and over for his wrongdoing?

Mary Elaine had been right. His mother did use her influence to get him into the study program, and she basically admitted she hoped the result would drive them apart.

He pressed his hands against the railing and took in the hilltop panorama selected by his ancestors for Colonnades. The green expanse of lawn was bordered by a wooded section of oak trees. That was the view he'd share with Renata. He closed his eyes to envision her standing beside him on the balcony—her dark hair stirring in the breeze.

But shutting his eyes only served as a backdrop to his past with Mary Elaine—holding hands at the class project wedding ceremony, tear-filled elation as she accepted his grandmother's ring, hurt in her voice when he called to tell her he'd be gone for a year. The encounters hung like dark storm clouds in his head.

His mother had seized on his impulsive ways, using his flaw for her own agenda. His consolation? She truly believed her meddling was for his own good. He wished he could have a do-over, but that opportunity left when he stepped on the plane in New York headed for Europe, leaving Mary Elaine behind.

He took a last deep breath and stepped back into the bedroom, but the lingering paint smell made his head hurt. He needed an aspirin and a shower. He walked to the closet and pulled out clothes. Should he move back into his old room and give the newly painted room a chance to air out?

The plan for Colonnades put his mother in the main house, Gavin in the east wing where the family had most recently lived, and Clifton and Renata in the west wing, once occupied by servants.

Clifton checked the time and the wedding event list Gavin left beside his bed. The morning's schedule dictated breakfast and a tour of the plantation for the Brazilian wedding party.

He stepped into the bathroom, flipped on the light and flinched at the sight of the huge palm frond print wallpaper. Another Renata-Gavin collaboration. Showered and dressed, he emerged from the bathroom jungle, scanned the list of bridesmaid's names again, and trotted downstairs to face the day.

"Mom, you've got the house smelling good."

"I hope so. Our guests should be here soon."

The doorbell chimed. "Soon is right."

Clifton strode to the front door as Gavin came downstairs. "Mornin' big brother. All ready for the tour?"

"As I'll ever be." Clifton reached for the front door knob, his hand shaky. What was wrong with him? He grasped the handle firmly to steady his hand and opened the Colonnades' heavy cypress front door.

"Good morning," Renata stood in front of her entourage. She was dressed in jeans and a white blouse that made her dark hair and eyes dazzle in contrast. Everyone was smiling except Mr. Mendes and his sidekick, Uncle Jorge. The two presented somber faces—a permanent state?

Clifton's mother joined them, "Please, everyone come into the dining room. All is ready."

After a lavish buffet breakfast, the guests lingered over cups of hot coffee and tea.

"Mrs. Davenport, the breakfast was delicious," Renata said. "I'm going to need your sweet roll recipe."

"Of course, dear. With you and Clifton in the west wing, we'll have to cook together often."

Through the dining room window, Clifton caught a glimpse of Carlos arriving on one of the properties' green all-terrain vehicles.

Gavin stood. "Our transportation has arrived."

Clifton appreciated his brother's efficiency in planning the tour. The quicker they got ready to go, the quicker he could check off another wedding event on the list. Outside, other workers had arrived, driving three more ATVs for the group to use.

"There's room for everyone," Gavin said.

"You young people go. Have a good time," Aunt Sophia said. She and Granny Mendes elected to stay at Colonnades with Clifton's mother. The "young people" included Mr. Mendes and Uncle Jorge who, along with Clifton and Gavin, were selected to drive the vehicles. Mendes took the vehicle right behind Clifton's.

The idea of Renata's father scrutinizing his every move from the rear churned the food lying heavy on his stomach. He had already endured the penetrating eyes of Mendes and Uncle Jorge during breakfast. They seemed intent not to miss his next flaw or foul up.

Bianca joined Clifton and Renata, while the other bridesmaids found seats in the other vehicles.

Once situated, Gavin announced, "I hope y'all enjoyed breakfast and are ready for the grand tour. We'll start with the hunting reserve."

The group took off with Gavin in the lead. They soon reached wooded trails scented with a mixture of pine and scrub oaks. Gavin turned off at various spots to show strategically hidden shooting houses and fields of rye planted for deer in preparation for hunting in the cold months.

Next, they arrived at an open field surrounded by pines, used for quail hunts. This was what first attracted Mendes and his associates to the property in the States.

The fresh smell of pine straw filled the air as they motored over the dirt trails. The rush of fresh air rejuvenated Clifton's mind. Why didn't he roam the outdoors more often? The property's open, unfettered land was the core of his family's heritage. Did his ancestors consider the generations that would follow or whether the property would remain in the family? What about the generations that would follow him? Would he have children to receive the Davenport legacy?

The forested paths yielded to one hundred twenty acres of fields, planted with conical-shaped Christmas trees. Gavin stopped for the group to see samples of the Christmas tree varieties raised on the plantation. "Cliff, you want to share about the Christmas trees?"

Clifton slid out of the ATV and inhaled the tree fragrance. "I stay in the office too much. It's refreshing to get out here among the trees again. As a youngster, I used to help prune and prepare these trees for families that arrived on the Davenport Christmas train."

"Like the train at dinner last night?" Renata asked.

"Yes. The Davenport Express."

"Where train?" One of the girlfriends asked in her broken English.

"There is only a rail car remaining at the plantation entrance. The railroad closed the section of track that our spur ran from, which essentially stopped our cut-your-own business. Now we cut and ship orders—mostly to service groups for resale, but I'm working on a market expansion."

"What kind of trees are these?" Mendes asked. Was he checking his tree knowledge, or did he really want to know?

"We grow two types." He stepped over and touched the branch of the tree next to him. "The Sand Pine is our most popular and traditional-looking Florida Christmas tree." He pointed to a different row of trees. "The other variety we grow is the Red Cedar, which is actually a type of juniper."

"Seems a waste to cut them," Jorge Rodrigues interjected.

"Glad you mentioned that." Clifton found strength in his voice. Horticulture aptitude was Gavin's strong suit, but he knew Christmas trees. "Actually, Christmas tree harvesting doesn't upset the ecology."

Gavin approached Clifton. "Sorry to interrupt, but Eduardo has a question," he handed Clifton his phone.

"Excuse me." Clifton took Gavin's phone. "Can you fill them in on why cutting the trees doesn't hurt the environment?"

Clifton let Gavin take over while he moved back from the group. "Yes?"

"I hate to bother you, but we are at a standstill here without the PVC elbow couplings. I know you bought some, but where are they?"

Clifton told him where to find them, slipped Gavin's phone into his shirt pocket, and tuned in to Gavin's oration.

"… More trees are planted than harvested each year. The general rule is to plant two to three trees for every tree cut. While growing, these trees provide environmental benefits such as wildlife habitat and increased soil stability. He turned and pointed to a tree. "This Sand Pine grows up to two feet a year …"

Clifton's mind drifted as Gavin shared and fielded questions. He ran his fingers over the dark green foliage of the red cedar next to him. The leaves with saw tooth serrations were prickly to the touch, like the ache that pierced his heart at the thought of helping Mary Elaine and her family find a Christmas tree. He had gazed like a sick pup into her blue eyes years ago and then again when they reconnected in college.

"Cliff can tell you about the economics."

All eyes were on him. Waiting. He swallowed hard. Where did Gavin leave off? "Economics? Uh … sure."

He groped around his brain for some economic information and came up with something he'd heard his father proclaim many times. "From a business standpoint, a Florida family buying a homegrown Florida tree is good for the environment because less fuel is used in transportation.

Florida's economy gets a boost when its farmers are supported, not to mention the fun for the family to select and cut their own tree."

Mendes gave a barely perceived nod.

"Next stop, the greenhouses," Gavin said.

"Que tipo de vida selvagem?" Ana asked Gavin.

Gavin arched his brow in question, and Renata came to his rescue. "You said the trees provide a wildlife habitat. Ana wants to know what kind of wildlife?"

Gavin began explaining as he returned to his vehicle. Ana had been riding with him. Renata turned to Clifton and said, "Ana has some questions, I'll ride with Gavin and interpret."

"Fine. See you at the next stop."

The ground in the chrysanthemum greenhouse was still slippery slush. Boards had been placed strategically to get around. "You can see the waterline issue I had to deal with Tuesday," Clifton told the group. "We have a maintenance plan, but things are wearing out before the plan can be implemented."

Renata spoke up with a totally different train of thought. "Is this the trick house?"

"Trick?"

"Remember? I texted about unusually cool Brazil weather, and you said you could trick your plants?"

A bead of sweat trickled down his face. The warm temperature in the greenhouse wasn't the only thing making him perspire. This wasn't the first question Renata had posed that put him on the spot, requiring Gavin's intervention.

"Trick house is really a term my brother coined. Gavin, why don't you explain?"

Gavin began, "We use black cloth to shorten the days, tricking the plants ..."

Renata moved closer to Gavin to hear and had to cling to his arm to keep steady on the narrow board walkways. Renata's father lagged behind with Clifton.

"What is going to happen to the bottom line with all the extra water line expense?" Mendes asked. A legitimate question with Mendes's proposal to invest in the nursery business after he and Renata married.

"I'll have to redo my estimates because the water system is wearing out faster than the projected three years."

Mendes lifted his chin, looking down at Clifton. "And what happens if those estimates are wrong?"

"I'm bidding on the Christmas tree concessions for all of the Dollar Mart stores across north Florida. If I get the contract, the nursery business will be in good standing."

"If not?"

"I don't deny money will be tight ..."

"Hey, Cliff, you've still got my phone." Gavin raised his voice to be heard over the girls' chatter.

Clifton reached in his pants pocket and stepped along a narrow board toe to heel to hand the phone to his brother.

"Thanks. We're headed outside to see the landscape trees," Gavin said.

Clifton returned his attention to Mendes's money concerns. They left the greenhouse and walked behind the procession led by Gavin and Renata.

"Sorry. Like I was saying, the money will be tight with repair needs dipping into the regular expenses right now, but we are paying all our bills.

Gravel crunched under their shoes, like a horse with huge grinding teeth chomping on oats. The conversation, interspersed with the abrasive noise, left an unpleasant taste in Clifton's mouth.

The entourage plodded between greenhouses and entered an open stretch of heartier potted shrubs and trees that could handle the extremes of north Florida weather.

An early morning shower had left behind enough moisture to make the air hot and steamy. Renata slowed and waited for Clifton to catch up.

"Where is it? "Renata asked

"It?" They stood in the ornamental tree section surrounded by tall potted crepe myrtles and redbuds. His role switched from talking nursery operations he understood, to items Renata apparently had texted or emailed and Gavin had answered. What was she talking about now?

"The tree, you know, the special tree you told me about. Isn't it supposed to be here?"

"I bet she's talking about the grafted tree that's on the south side of greenhouse six," Gavin said, coming to his rescue once again.

"Oh, that tree. My brain is still with these potted trees," Clifton said trying to sound halfway intelligent.

"You find writing about plantation operations easier than explaining them in person?"

Clifton gave Gavin a quick glance, then returned his focus to Renata. Had she guessed their deception or was she just curious? Were her questions intended or unintended traps? He should have guessed awkward moments such as these would happen.

Turning the tedium of electronic correspondence over to Gavin was a relief, allowing him to concentrate on keeping the company afloat. He had put no thought to the repercussions. Renata was pleasant enough, but her father and his assistant didn't appear so forgiving of his blunders. The heat of their scrutiny bored into his back as they converged outside greenhouse six.

"Here's the mysterious tree you were asking about," Clifton said. "Gavin is quite adept at grafting and combined two favorites—the kumquat and tangerine. Both fruits grow on one tree."

"Fascinating. You are a man of amazing talent." Renata moved alongside Gavin and patted him on the arm.

The others crowded around the tree to hear Gavin's discourse on grafting. Bianca turned, her brow furrowed, and mouth drawn in a straight line. She clutched Clifton's arm, swapping places so he stood on the other side of Renata. "Join us. Can't leave you out."

Renata gave Clifton a quick smile, but her hand remained on his brother's arm.

When Gavin began explaining detailed cross pollination techniques, Clifton hung back to listen and noticed that Mr. Mendes and Uncle Jorge were studying the pair-up shift. Mr. Mendes, arms crossed, wore a disagreeable expression.

Clifton decided he'd best move back to the side of his bride-to-be. "Grafting is quite a science," he said. He took her arm to help her walk down the dirt pathway beside a row of shoulder high lime trees covered with dark green, golf ball-sized fruit.

Renata squeezed his arm. He placed his hand on the small of her back. He hoped the picture they presented would be more acceptable in the eyes of his future father-in-law.

"That concludes our tour," Gavin said. "We'll rejoin the ladies at Colonnades." To Clifton Gavin said, "I need to get back to the chrysanthemum greenhouse as soon as I drop off my riders." Renata returned to her seat beside Clifton for the return trip.

Granny Mendes and Sophia sat on rocking chairs on the Greek Revival front porch. Nettie Sue, their former housekeeper's daughter who helped at the plantation on special occasions, served minted iced lemonade. Clifton's mother greeted the group.

"The ladies have had a tour of Colonnades while you were gone." She glanced at the two sipping their lemonades and lowered her voice to Clifton. "We did a lot of pointing and smiling. Thank goodness Sophia knows some English."

"I like the verde ... uh, green ... bedroom." Sophia said. Granny added a snappy nod.

"I told them I stayed out of the decorating and you and Renata picked out the colors and furnishings." The need to impress the Brazilian guests by graciously welcoming Renata to the family was rubbing off on his mother.

"Might as well give Renata the decorating credit," Clifton said, "Decorating is not my strong suit."

"Clifton, you're too modest," Renata said. "You're the one who suggested the green." She punctuated her comment with her trademark high-pitched chortle.

Great. He was getting credit for another of Gavin's actions. Clifton forced a smile. "But you made the ultimate choice."

There must be an end to the nightmare he'd created. Clifton escorted Renata to a porch swing and picked up lemonades that Nettie Sue was pouring for the group. Once married, he and Renata would be together. No more go-betweens. They could make their own future and leave the one laid by Gavin behind ... couldn't they? What color would the room have been if Mary Elaine made the choice? And why did she have to pop into his thoughts right now?

"Surrounded by all these plants, you can have fresh flowers in your home every day," Bianca said, joining them. She ran her fingers along the side of her frosty glass of lemonade.

That remark unfortunately sparked another thought from Renata. "Oh, that reminds me," she said nudging Clifton with her elbow. "You not only recommended the gorgeous blue-gray bedspread for our room, but tell them about the flower you selected for the accent pillows."

"Flower?"

She gave him an odd look. "You know, the flower that grows wild around here."

A flower that grows wild. Think. Gavin told him something about pillows. What did he say? "Uh ... you mean clover?"

"No. You're kidding, right?"

"Uh ..." Clifton felt his phone vibrate against his chest and checked the screen. "Excuse me. I have a call buzzing in that I really need to take."

Clifton took the call while he hurried into the house. He stepped into the study to the right of the main hall. The scent of his father's sweet cherry pipe tobacco still lingered.

"Gavin?"

"No, Carlos, you've got Clifton."

"I thought I called Gavin."

Clifton looked at the phone in his hand. "Looks like my phone and Gavin's got switched when we were on tour. Something I can help you with?"

"Just checking to see if he picked up the part at the hardware store I ordered for the fruit tree watering system outside."

"I was just going to call Gavin. If he hasn't picked up your order, I'll get the part when I go to town."

"Thanks."

Clifton punched the number to ring his own phone. His eye went to the portrait of his brother and himself, hanging over the mantle. He was ten—Gavin, nine. Clifton, his thick hair straight and blond, much lighter than now, stood with his arm resting on Gavin's shoulder—a habit he needed to shake. Interesting that he still leaned on his little brother's shoulder.

"Hey," Gavin said, "looks like I'm getting a call from myself."

"I guess I messed up and handed you the wrong phone. Carlos called and wanted to know if you picked up the part for the outside water line."

"Not yet. I got preoccupied preparing for the morning tour."

"Don't worry. I can pick up the part. I have to go to town, anyhow."

"Sorry for the foul up."

"No worry—so goes my morning."

"What's wrong?"

"I've been stumbling through trick houses and grafted trees I know little about—"

"You grafted that rose bush."

"That was years ago, and Dad showed me how. But that's all beside the point. Now Renata's making me out to be some kind of interior decorator."

"Better than a serial killer."

"No time to kid. What is the wild flower on the pillows you ordered? I can't remember all these details."

"Phlox," Gavin said. "Lavender phlox."

Clifton's brain chased after a stray thought, clouding his concentration—a grafted rose. He repeated Gavin's word aloud and tried to refocus. "Phlox." One more item to clutter his burdened brain.

His gaze settled on himself as a ten-year old boy. That is what he looked like when he and his dad grafted the rose branch. He had clumsily broken it during what turned out to be Mary Elaine's last Christmas visit before her father died.

Since Clifton had seldom shown interest in plant propagation, his dad had taken great patience with him in grafting the rose and teaching him the process. "Son, splice the branch into a host, wrap the joint, and then wait."

"How long?"

"Until the time is right."

He had checked the host bush for months, until a red bud finally formed, and he rushed to tell his dad.

"Ah ... you see? The bud found its right time."

Advice his father had worked hard to instill in him. He kicked at some crumpled fringe on the edge of the oriental carpet but managed to rumple the rug even more.

"Clifton?"

He jumped and turned around, knocking a heavy dictionary off the desk. The book landed with a reverberating thud on the wood floor.

"Renata."

"Sorry. I didn't mean to startle you."

"No, no. Come in." Clifton stood behind the desk, a barrier between them. "I guess I was lost in thought trying to remember who those two fellows were." He motioned to the painting accented by an art light.

"I bet you kept your mom busy at that age."

"Busy along with anxious, frustrated, and lots of other adjectives."

Giving her a lopsided grin, he retrieved and returned the book to the desk. "I got a call from Carlos. He needs me to pick up a part for him in Hamilton Harbor. Do you mind?"

"Of course not. You do what you need to. Hanging out by the pool is the plan for the afternoon."

Clifton ventured from behind the desk, took Renata's hand and pressed his lips to her forehead. "You are a sweetheart. Have a relaxing afternoon, and I'll see you at the barbeque tonight."

She touched his chin. Was she inviting a kiss? Why was he so uncomfortable around her? Was the feeling mutual? She smiled and grasped his hand.

"Fine. Your mom said the chef was setting up on the back patio already."

She let go of his hand. They stepped out of the study. Shadows stretched their forms to the living room threshold across the hall, pointing to the place where he announced his engagement to Mary Elaine. If only he could erase the constant stream of memories flowing from his heart.

Emme met Mellie at the front door of the Flower Cottage. "Thanks for coming on short notice. Izzie got a last-minute home decoration call."

"My pleasure. Where's Richie?" As usual Mellie searched for Richie first thing when she came in the door.

"Upstairs. He wanted to color a picture of a policeman from his color book to give his new Big Brother. I appreciate your coming, so I can be with him for their first meeting."

"Glad to. A male influence should be good for Richie."

"I hope so." Male influence. How would life have been for Richie with Clifton as his male influence? The vision of Richie asking Clifton if he was a doctor and then doctoring all his stuffed animals pointed to a need Richie had that she could never fully meet. "His involvement in the program might help win the judge to my side at the custody hearing."

"You said an old friend volunteered?"

"My friend Tony, from my days at the children's home. He was like a big brother to me and it's amazing that he wound up here in Hamilton Harbor."

"Umm." Mellie paused on the way to the work area to admire a summer silk arrangement of golden daisies and black-eyed Susans. "Sometimes I wonder if things we label a coincidence might really be a God-directed incident."

Emme mulled over the idea, then Mellie asked, "Any orders I can help you with?"

"Sure. You can add red and black bows to these graduation party arrangements."

"Glad to." She picked up a roll of ribbon, "By the way, I've been meaning to tell you—since Margaret and I got back from our trip things have been hectic—that paper you found in the wall safe upstairs was some kind of map with a ring inside. I'm guessing the items may have belonged to Regina Hamilton, the original homeowner."

"A ring was with the map?"

"Why, yes. You didn't see it?"

"No." Emme's pulse rate jittered with hope. "Was the ring silver with diamonds and rubies?"

Mellie nodded. "How did you know?"

"Thank heaven. I've searched and searched. That's the Davenport family ring Clifton gave me. The ring must have gotten caught in the folds of that paper when I put it in the bag for you."

"Well. That solves the mystery. Margaret and I even sent the items to a family member of Regina Hamilton's to see what she might know."

"You sent the ring?"

"By registered mail, of course. Margaret and I went to school with Marigold Hamilton—she's the niece of Regina Hamilton. She had a little sister and we had some good times together."

Mellie had a way of making a long story longer.

"And did she remember the map ... or ring?"

"She had no recollection of the ring ... of course, we know why now ... and about the map ... her mother, she's ninety something in a nursing home, said the map was incomplete. Marigold made a copy of the map and returned it. She asked me to take it to the Historical Society and see what they might know. The society was in this house before it became the Flower Cottage."

Emme listened to Mellie's story that kept unraveling like pulling on a loose thread. Rude or not she had to interrupt.

"And does Marigold still have the ring?"

"Oh, no. Marigold returned the ring." Mellie opened her snap-top purse and pulled out a plastic bag. "I had it evaluated by an antique dealer friend of mine, and the ring is actually quite valuable." Mellie handed Emme the bag with a yellow tag attached that twirled about like an excited puppy.

"Oh, Mellie, what a relief. I've been agonizing over this ring." When the tag stopped turning, the amount stood out like a flashing neon sign. Emme blinked to make sure she'd read the tag right—$5000. "Valuable is an understatement."

Mellie returned a proud nod.

Emme fingered the piece of jewelry nestled in the bag. The gems caught the light and winked as if happy to see her again, but no happier than she was to have the ring and be able to return it to Clifton. But Richie and his new Big Brother had to come first right now.

"Richie," Emme called upstairs, "ready to meet your Big Brother?"

"Yes, ma'am." She could hear scrambling on the wooden floor above her.

"We need to go. Mellie, you're a lifesaver. I'm setting this ring right here for safekeeping. I don't want to lose it again." She placed the bag at the end of the counter by Richie's photo. Richie appeared with his coloring book paper in hand.

"Ready, mama."

For a moment, the sight of his smile warmed her heart melting away thoughts of rings, van payments, and court hearings. However, another strange coincidence niggled in the recesses of her mind as she took his hand and they walked out the front door. The ring was valued at the exact amount owed on her van.

Feldman Park needed some TLC. The scraggly grass, crisp underfoot, had fallen victim to little rain. But the sprawling oaks provided shade and made a welcome place to meet her old friend.

"Look." Richie clutched his paper and pointed at the black and white cruiser that pulled up and parked curbside. Tony, looking impressive dressed in his black uniform, got out.

Emme greeted Tony with a hug. "Richie has been really excited about meeting you."

Tony stooped down to Richie's level. "Same here."

Richie gave Tony the paper, then stuck out his chubby hand. The grown-up gesture tugged at Emme's insides. Tony accepted the paper and shook Richie's hand. Richie's eyes grew wide, scaling Tony as he straightened to his full, over six-foot height.

"A fine picture. Thank you."

"It's a policeman, like you," Richie said.

"I see. I'll keep this as a reminder of what I should look like. You know I'm new to town and I need someone to play ball with. Would you like to toss a ball with me?"

Richie grinned and nodded.

"I left a sack with some baseballs and a catcher's mitt by the car. Can you get the bag for me?"

Richie skipped away.

"You will be his hero, for sure. I appreciate your help," Emme said.

"Hey, I'd have been hurt if you had called on anyone else."

Tony removed his hat, exposing black hair and the fist-sized cowlick that had lovingly earned him the nickname "moo man" when they were teens.

"The department encourages donating lunchtime once a week to the Big Brother program. Your call came at a good time."

Tony watched as Richie reached his car. "You said the boy's aunt is trying to gain custody? I hope my working with him aids your cause."

"Me too." Emme bit at her lower lip. "Richie's mother pleaded with me before she died to take the baby and make sure Aurora didn't get him. I hope I've done the right thing, raising him as my own." Tony, more than anyone, could relate to the vacant place created by lack of parents. "I don't want him to know hurt—the kind many of us experienced when we ended up at the children's home."

Tony nodded. "You know I'll do what I can to help."

Richie returned, lugging the bag over his shoulder. Tony ushered Richie to an open space in the park.

Emme smiled after the two. Getting Tony's help, like the assistance she asked for from her mom and Frank, rendered another crack in her shell of independence. She settled on the wrought iron park bench, as hard as her morning visit with her mother and stepfather.

She had driven to their house in Melrose Beach, fifteen miles from Hamilton Harbor. She could count on her right hand and not use all the fingers, the number of times she'd visited their home since she'd moved from Atlanta.

"Whose house?" Richie had asked.

The question weighed heavy. A child should know when he's arrived at his grandparents' house.

Her mother and Frank had married three years after her father's heart attack. Frank was a dedicated policeman and nice enough until he shot a fleeing subject under questionable conditions. Tension tightened at her throat, remembering when the story hit the news and then went viral— *Money Missing, Arresting Officer Prime Suspect.*

The case was the beginning of his alcohol problem. Frank managed to drink up Emme's college savings. His betrayal drove a wedge between her and her mother, who kept giving him chances each time he messed up and begged to come back.

Her finger seemed detached from part of her body, drawing courage from an unknown source to press the doorbell button. She stood at the door, holding Riche's hand and staring at the welcome sign on the grapevine wreath. How many times had her mother claimed Frank had stopped drinking and welcomed him back? Even though he was finally cleared of the theft charge, alcohol held him hostage.

The door opened. "Emme." Frank's surprise was hard to miss. "And Richie. Come in please. Nan, we have company," he called out toward the kitchen.

Her mother rounded the corner to the foyer and clasped her throat. "Mary Elaine." Her given name came out on a whispered breath.

Frank stepped back while her mother rushed toward them with open arms. "What a wonderful surprise."

"I ... I need to talk to you."

"Why, of course. Come in. Richie, I have been collecting some things you might like to play with," she said, glancing at Emme with glistening eyes. "Just in case you came for a visit."

Her mother ushered Richie to a laundry basket filled with toys on the screened back porch.

In the living room, Frank motioned for Emme to have a seat on a side chair next to the window where she could watch Richie playing on the porch.

"Coffee or coke?" Frank offered.

"Nothing, thank you."

She took a seat. Her mother came in and sat on the couch next to her husband.

Get to the point, her dad used to say. Emme took a deep breath and came out with her request. "I hate to ask, but you did mention setting aside some money to repay my college fund."

Her mother nodded. "Eight thousand."

"Plus interest." Frank added. "Do you need money?"

"I have a van payment—a five-thousand-dollar balloon note—due today. I was counting on payment from the Davenport wedding, but—"

"You needn't explain. The money is yours," Frank said.

Her mom pushed forward on the couch, "Frank set up the account to require both of our signatures before a withdrawal can be made."

Thinking of Izzie's persistent urgings to talk to them, Emme marveled at their eagerness to rally around her.

Frank clasped his hands together. "I have to be at work at noon. A rail crossing is being redone about twenty miles out of town. But I'll take off long enough to meet you at 3:00, Nan, before the bank closes."

Emme's chin quivered. "You'd do that for me?"

Frank lowered his head. "I'd like to do more to make up for the hurts I've caused."

Before Emme knew what was happening, Frank's genuine desire to help propelled her out of her chair and into their embrace. A liberating force surged through Emme's body as the three wept and hugged. Pent-up resentment melted with the taste of salty tears. They had conversation—real conversation—for the first time in years.

Emme sat Indian-style on the floor. "It's like there's a thirsty spot in my soul that is never quite quenched. I set my sights on proving I could be a successful floral designer, especially in the eyes of Mrs. Davenport after she labeled me not good enough for Clifton." She snickered. "I guess she proved her point when she fired me. But being seen as worthy in her eyes is far less important than the upcoming custody hearing."

Emme's mother patted her hand—her fingers a soothing balm. "I believe we've all got an empty spot we search to fill. When knowing you are a child of God becomes real to you, I know that void will be filled. You'll see."

"Umm. True." Frank rested his elbows on his knees and steepled his hands. "You know if our value was dependent on what a certain person said about us, there would probably be a lot of let-down folks in the world. I've found our worth doesn't come from what others think of us, but in how we handle life's circumstances. I did a miserable job of handling my situation, but with the help of others, I've learned to trade my independent mind and look for God-directed victories."

Emme shifted on the hard bench in Feldman's Park and thought about Frank's comment. Certainly, meeting with her mother and Frank had been a God-directed victory, and now another was playing out before her as she watched Richie scrambling to retrieve a ball.

"You're doing great," Tony told Richie.

"Step back a few steps and keep your eye on the ball, not me, when I pitch it."

Richie was attentive and listened to Tony's instruction.

Emme pinched the bridge of her nose and closed her eyes. The Big Brother meeting, like the meeting this morning, revealed benefits in lowering her four walls of self-sufficiency. The walls she'd built had served to keep her safe and secure. One wall went up when her dad died. Another when her mother married Frank. She built a third fortification to guard against romance when Clifton walked out. And the fourth? That barricade was let down long enough to allow a sweet baby boy into her life—the one factor that kept her embittered heart from totally crusting over.

Now her self-constructed barriers were crumbling stone by stone. Clifton knocked the sign labeled "over" off the top of his wall when he gave Richie first aid. Learning that Clifton became an EMT due to her father's inspiration softened the hurt of her dad's death and his replacement by Frank. Turning loose of her self-sufficiency that had blocked a relationship with Frank and her mom helped push back all her walls. But would she be able to stand? Without her armor of independence, she'd be vulnerable and exposed.

"Join us." The words registered a split second after Tony sent a quick pitch her way. She raised her hand in reflex and caught the ball, surprising herself and delighting Richie.

"Throw it," Richie shouted, jumping in excitement.

Emme stood and tossed the ball to Tony.

"Aw, you throw like a girl," Tony said.

"What do you expect?"

Tony walked behind her, put one hand on her left shoulder, put the ball in her right hand then covered her hand guiding her through the proper arm movement and release technique.

Richie's giggles tickled Emme. She had to admit that opening up enough to share her need and getting involved with the Big Brother program was a good move.

Would these moves be enough to prove to the judge that she was worthy to remain Richie's mother?

Chapter 16

Renata lingered in the hall outside the study, watching as Clifton walked out the front door. He had called her "a sweetheart," not "my sweet" or "my love," but just "a sweetheart."

She had tugged at his chin to coax a kiss, willing a spark to ignite. Did he really love her? Did she really love him? Were these normal doubts creeping over her as their wedding day closed in? Admit it. Lips touching Clifton didn't produce the electric tremor that overtook her like a shock wave whenever Gavin came near.

She turned her attention back to the portrait in the study. Clifton held the grin of a strategist ready to tackle the world. Gavin, seated beside his brother, seemed to lend stability and support. The image gave more information to the insight she'd been gathering on the brothers.

Clifton, the tactician, came to Brazil to negotiate business opportunities with her father, but became the sympathetic friend she could confide in as she watched her mother slowly deteriorate from the cancer ravaging her body. Clifton understood her fears, having lost his father to the dread disease. He had given her a shoulder to lean on at the time—like the one Gavin lent to Clifton in the portrait, but was that as far as their emotional attachment went?

Gavin wasn't as opportunity-oriented as Clifton, but he offered a caring thoughtfulness and creative skill she'd grown to admire. And dare she admit … to love. She could get ready to join her friends outside, but would changing her clothes change the feelings inside?

"Renata, try this sandwich," Bianca said. Renata accepted the napkin with a triangle of whole wheat bread. "The filling is fresh cucumber and tomato with dill, yummy."

The chef had set out a chilled tray of sandwiches. Carbonated drinks and water were available in a tub of ice.

Renata, Bianca, and the other bridesmaids had changed into swimsuits to enjoy the afternoon poolside. Preparations for the evening's barbeque filled the warm air with the savory smell of meat slow-cooking on the rotisserie behind Colonnades. Larissa and Ana took turns trying to outdo each other's diving skills. Camilla and Marina sat at the pool's edge, dangling their feet in the cool water.

Renata, coated in fragrant coconut sunscreen, perched on a lounge chair, drinking in the sun's rays. She bit into the soft bread with the seasoned veggies. "This sandwich may be good, but I don't think my stomach will be able to handle much."

"Are you okay? You look friendless even though you're sitting with your best friends."

"I'm okay." She paused and wiped her hand on the napkin. "Maybe."

"All right." Bianca plunked down on the patio chair beside her, "Give it up. What's bothering you?"

Renata looked at Bianca, shading her eyes with her hands. "I've been trying to figure that out myself."

"What are you talking about?" Bianca squeezed her brows into a frown.

"Clifton and I were a twosome after we met in Brazil. We shared meals whenever we could, took weekend hikes, and confided our inner struggles about him losing his father and me losing my mother to cancer."

"And that's why you make a perfect couple. So, what's wrong?"

"You know we had to text or email over the last couple of months, while I was in Brazil."

"Same for me and Jason when I was in Brazil. What's the point?"

"The point is, separation is supposed to make the heart grow fonder. For me, the separation did that. I began to feel closer than ever to Clifton."

Bianca sat next to Renata on the lounge chair. "Okay. Sounds good so far."

"Since I got here Monday, Clifton seems different—distant." Renata rolled the used napkin between her palms. "I'll mention something we discussed, and he acts like he's hearing it for the first time."

"Maybe he's preoccupied with work."

Renata shook her head and pressed her lips together. "No, it's more than that."

"What do you mean?"

"Like today. I mentioned he picked out the color for our room, and he said I picked out the color."

"Maybe he just wants you to get credit for choosing the color since your aunt and granny said they liked the color."

"Yes, but in our emails, Clifton made a big deal about choosing lavender phlox for the pillows in our bedroom. Today, Clifton obviously didn't know what I was talking about."

"Maybe wedding jitters are toying with his memory."

"I don't know." Renata picked up the beach towel slung over the arm of the chair and dabbed at the perspiration on her forehead. "I think I smell a mouse."

"Rat."

"What?"

"A rat. The saying when something sounds suspicious is, I smell a rat."

Renata and Bianca had gone to college in the States and spoke fluent English, but Bianca had better command of the slang.

"Yeah, that."

"What do you suspect?"

"Clifton seems to lean on Gavin for everything. He wasn't like that when I first met him."

"Why don't you ask Clifton about your concerns. My guess is he's overloaded by trying to run the nursery business while preparing to get married."

But could she share her heart when it was thumping out confusing messages? How could she discuss the smoldering feelings that she couldn't admit to herself, much less Clifton? Was the experience that gave her a roller coaster rush a dream or had Gavin really kissed her?

"What do you think?" Renata had asked Gavin when he helped zip the summer dress she'd tried on during Tuesday's shopping trip.

"I think you're lovely in whatever you have on."

She stood in front of the tri-fold mirror and inspected the dress from different angles, but her eyes strayed to Gavin's watching her. Bianca and the others had gone on to another store.

She turned to face him, his face only a breath away. She should have stepped back, but her feet wouldn't move. Stirrings raced over her body. All warnings and inhibitions tumbled away. She lifted her chin. His lips met hers, sending shock waves from head to toe. He stepped back, his hands still grasped her arms, then slid to his sides.

"Sorry," he whispered.

"But I don't think I am."

"Please don't say that. I was wrong."

He walked away and steered clear of her the rest of the shopping trip.

Renata sat up and grabbed her phone from the poolside table. "I think I will ask, but I'm sending the questions to the one who seems to have all the answers."

She brought up the text screen and began tapping a message to Gavin.

"She's in the park across the street."

Clifton had asked for Emme after parking behind the Flower Cottage and being greeted by an older lady, who introduced herself as Mellie.

"I used to own this shop, and I help out from time to time."

"Of course. I've talked to you on the phone before. I'm Clifton Davenport."

"Of Davenport Nurseries?"

"The same."

"Why, yes. I've placed many an order at your business. Would you like me to get Emme for you?"

"No, no. I don't want to bother her."

Clifton held up the Lionel rail car and check and walked past the work table to the front customer counter. "I just wanted to bring her a payment for the ladies' luncheon and this railroad car for Richie to thank him for the loan of his model train."

"That's sweet. He loves anything to do with trains." Mellie continued shaping bows, her back to Clifton.

As if a picture framed by the front display window, Clifton could see Emme in the park across from the shop. A policeman stood behind her. He was tall, his broad shoulders and arms wrapped around Emme, helping her toss a ball.

The policeman turned, and he caught sight of his full face. Wasn't that …? It was. Tony. The FSU campus cop Emme introduced as a friend when they were in college. Had he been more than a friend? Was he Richie's father? She had a son. She must have had someone else in her life. Now seeing them together … how could he have been so blind?

A sparkle at the end of the counter distracted him. Afternoon sunlight reached in the window, spotlighting glittery gem stones in a plastic bag. Was that the family ring? He stepped closer. His breath caught. No question. His grandmother's ring sat on the counter with an appraisal tag of $5000 attached. Emme said she'd lost the ring. Was she trying to sell it?

Rrring.

Startled, Clifton's elbow sent the train car he'd brought for Richie clattering to the floor.

Mellie answered the shop phone. "Flower Cottage, may I help you?"

He stooped to pick up the model train car. Mellie's voice droned in the background. Outside Emme chatted with Tony, who had knelt down to Richie's height. Had she been pregnant and needed their engagement to get a father for Richie? If Tony was Richie's father, were they married and divorced or never married? Dizzying questions swirled in his head. He had to brace himself against the counter when he stood.

Had his mother been right about Emme using him? Or worse, had his good instincts—the ones his father thought Clifton had—been so totally wrong about her? He placed the gift for Richie on top of the check, gave a nod to Mellie still on the phone and made his way out the back door.

His hand trembled as he pressed the remote button activating the familiar "beep-beep" to unlock his car. Intense suffocating heat inside the car overtook him. He feverishly pressed the car fan to high and loosened his collar.

Gavin's phone rang. His own number came up on caller ID.

"Gavin?"

"Hey. I just got a call on your phone. Dollar Mart. They want you to call them back. It might be about your proposal." Gavin gave him the number to call. "Good luck brother."

"Thanks."

"He placed the call, which reached the regional director's office. His secretary answered.

"Mr. Davenport?"

"Yes, I had a message to call."

"I've been instructed to tell you that the director looked at your contract proposal with interest, but regretfully declines the proposal at this time."

"I see."

She added a consoling, "He didn't rule out discussing your ideas in the future."

"I appreciate the call."

His hand went limp; he let the phone drop on the seat next to him. There went his chance to raise the funds to purchase the Davenport property, his best chance to not be beholden to Mendes. Could this day get any worse? A message alert chimed. Probably Gavin. He turned the fan, blasting his face, down a notch.

Clifton swiped the screen to check the message. Highlighted in yellow, a message from Renata to Gavin was hard to miss.

I care for Clifton, but you need to know I've fallen in love with the man I've been corresponding with these last two months. Since we kissed, my heart has been telling me it's you. Am I right?

Since they kissed? The air conditioning fought to cool the hot air in the car. Sweat beaded on his brow, but a chill gripped his insides. Everything was topsy-turvy. Renata ... in love with Gavin?

The only constant was his poor judgment. He grasped the steering wheel and leaned to rest his forehead on his hands. "Lord, I've made a mess of things," he whispered. He wasn't worthy of Renata or her father's trust. For that matter, he wasn't worthy of his own father's trust. He couldn't manage the family's corporation, much less a relationship. "I need direction now as never before."

Suddenly, he realized he was still sitting behind Emme's flower shop. He glanced at the back entry. He could at least be thankful Emme wasn't standing there staring at him. He couldn't sit there waiting for direction. For now, he'd follow the last shred of instinct he could muster which was to clear out of there. He cranked his car, flipped the gear into drive, and left the Flower Cottage, along with some unidentified hope he had harbored, behind.

Emme entered the shop and was greeted by the perpetual smell of springtime.

Ding.

Emme side-stepped the mat, but not Richie. He loved to step on the Say it with Flowers doormat to activate the ringer, meant to be a customer alert.

Mellie turned from her work to greet them. "You two have a good session out there?"

"We did." Emme spotted the train car left on the counter. "Where did the rail car come from?"

"Clifton Davenport brought that by."

Emme wrinkled her forehead. "He did?"

She stepped to the counter and picking up the model train car, spotted the check.

"He said he wanted to bring payment for the luncheon," Mellie said. "And that railcar is for you, Richie. To thank you for letting him borrow your train set last night."

"Neat."

Richie reached up for the car brushing against the plastic bag that held the ring. The $5,000 tag stood out like a beacon. If he saw the ring ... and the tag what must he have thought?

"Did Clifton see the ring on the counter?"

Mellie glanced at the bag clutched in her hand. "I ... I don't know for sure. My back was to him." Her face went ashen. "I suppose he could have. Probably not a good thing?"

"Choo, choo, choo." Richie pushed the rail car carrying a toy mouse toward the back door.

"How long ago was he here?"

"Not long. I was just finishing this arrangement." Mellie pointed to the flowers ready for delivery.

Emme started toward the back entry.

Richie pointed out the window. "There's a big truck out there."

"A truck? I wasn't expecting a delivery." She stepped to the window and peered out to see a tow truck and a large burly man wearing a T-shirt that didn't quite cover his pot belly. He was hooking a tow line to the rear of her florist van.

Emme snatched the back door open, "Stop!" But the man kept walking to the driver's door on the truck.

"Sorry lady, just doin' my job." He climbed into the idling truck and, with the grinding of gears he pulled out of the parking lot. The Flower Cottage van followed like prey being dragged away by its attacker.

Emme tried to wave away the gravel dust, swirling about her face.

"Mama." Richie stood framed in the doorway. "Why did that man take our van?"

"I'm going to find out." The chalky taste of parking lot fallout made Emme choke on her words. She marched back inside and looked at the clock. One-thirty. She was to meet her mother and Frank with the payment at four o'clock. Emme grabbed the phone book and searched for the Low Price Auto Sales' number.

"Mellie, could you take Richie upstairs for a snack?"

"Of course."

Emme punched numbers into the phone and called after them. "There cheese sticks in the fridge."

"Low Price. Come see how low we can go. Larry speaking."

"I just found out how low you can go." Emme picked up a stray stem from the floor and tossed it toward the trash can. The clipping hit the top edge of the can, ricocheted, and rolled under the flower case. She rolled her eyes upward and slumped to the stool. "This is Emme Matthews. Why did you take my van?"

"Non-payment. It's in the..."

"I know. I know. It's in the contract. But the payment is due today. I was bringing the money to you this afternoon." Her voice strained under the effects of the inhaled dust.

"Just going by the terms of the contract. Payment's due at noon."

"Since when?"

"Since you signed the contract."

"But..."

"The agreement clearly states that balloon payments are due by noon on the due date."

"Fine." She swallowed a bitter taste in her mouth. "So how do I get my van back?"

"It's mine now. But I tell you what I'll do. I'll hold the van for a week. You bring me the five thousand dollars plus the interest and cost of towing, and the van is yours."

"You'll get it." Her statement came out like a threat.

She mashed the button to end the call and ran trembling fingers through her hair. How was she going to make her deliveries?

As if on cue, Izzie walked in the back door and started speed-talking. "Did you talk to your parents? How did the meeting go with Big Brother

Tony? Can he help with the hearing tomorrow?" She did a double-take, eyes on Emme, then to the vacant spot where the van normally sat, and back at Emme. "Wait. What are you doing here? Where's the van?"

"The van just got hauled off by low-life Larry."

"How can he ... the day's not over yet."

Emme could picture her blood pressure soaring to unhealthy heights. "You know him and his contracts. He says balloon notes must be paid by noon on the due date." Emme kicked at a stray petal underfoot. "You have every right to say I told you so."

"No point. Now what?"

"Now?" She stood and pushed her hair away from her face, but the strands kept tumbling forward.

"Oh, let me see if I can bring us up to date." She spread the fingers on her right hand and used the index finger of her left hand to enumerate.

"First, on top of the five thousand dollars, there's a towing fee plus interest to pay. Second, I got fired from the wedding job that would have paid for the van and my mounting bills. Three, I have no way to deliver flower orders. Four ..." Emme grabbed the bag holding the Davenport ring and held up the incriminating evidence for Izzie to see. "Mellie found the engagement ring I lost. Clifton was here and likely saw the ring with a valuation tag. He must think I'm a thief."

She set the ring down, tears stinging her eyes. "And five, with no proof I can support Richie, tomorrow I could lose my son."

Chapter 17

Gavin stepped down from the ladder in the chrysanthemum house and wiped the perspiration from his brow with the bottom of his grimy T-shirt.

"Only one more row of pipe to replace, and we'll have this house fully functioning," Carlos said, carrying a section of new pipe.

"Good. Hand me the pipe."

Gavin repositioned his ladder and set to work, relieved to have repetitive work as a diversion. For weeks, he'd tried to ignore his growing feelings for the woman his brother had asked him to correspond with. He labeled his attachment to her as common interests and friendship. But when they kissed, he knew his emotions ran deeper. Far deeper. Deep enough to stir to life feelings he'd never experienced before and didn't want to acknowledge—couldn't acknowledge. What if Clifton guessed? What if Renata's father noticed? For the good of the Davenport heritage, the nursery business, and loyalty to his brother, he couldn't succumb to his desires.

He would go on no more target practice sessions, shopping trips, plantation tours, or spend an evening consoling her. All those events had made him learn to appreciate her sweet spirit, her love of learning and nature, and her spontaneous laughter. The occasions also revealed he and Renata were born of the same fiber, yet worlds apart since she was marrying his brother. Renata stirred his heart, making breath come hard when she was close. He had to lose himself in work and steer clear of her.

Gavin took a long drink from his water bottle, then poured the remainder over his head.

"How much inventory do you think we lost?" Gavin asked.

Carlos surveyed the battered plants they had trimmed and re-staked. He shook his head. "Hard to say. A lot of the developing buds were destroyed."

Gavin nodded. The cell phone in his pocket sounded. The caller ID showed he was calling. He still had Clifton's phone.

"Hi, brother. Need any more interior design information?"

"What I need is to talk to you."

"Go ahead."

"No. I mean in person."

Gavin knew his brother. His voice carried a note of alarm. "Of course. I'm finishing repairs with Carlos in the chrysanthemum house."

"I'll be there in fifteen minutes."

Gavin punched the button to end the call.

"Something wrong?" Carlos asked.

Gavin wrinkled his brow. "I don't know. Clifton wants to talk to me. He'll be here shortly."

"Good time for me to go round up more potting mix. One more load should do us."

With Carlos gone, Gavin washed his hands. He wished he could wash away the yearnings in his heart as easily.

Clifton walked in, his expression hard to read. He reached in his pocket and handed Gavin his phone and pressed the screen to reveal a text message. "It's from Renata. She thought she was texting you."

Gavin accepted his phone and read. The phone turned hot in his hand—his knees, weak. He leaned against the end of a plant table. "Cliff, I never intended—"

"The point is … she's fallen in love with you. What I want to know is how you feel."

"She's pledged to you."

"Put that aside. I want to know if you feel the same about her."

"It's just … over time … the more I've communicated with her, the more in tune I seemed to be with her."

Clifton the priest. The hearer of his confession.

"Do you love her?"

"I care about her … a lot."

"Do you care about her enough to marry her?"

Perspiration beaded on Gavin's forehead. "What do you want me to say?" He straightened his stance, wishing all the circumstances could be wiped away.

Clifton laid his hand on Gavin's shoulder. "All I want is the truth. Don't you see? She doesn't love me. And I don't love her. The marriage had turned into one of opportunity we were both willing to accept. But if you two …"

Gavin's neck muscles tightened. "Yes." His response barely perceptible. "What's that?"

"Yes." His voice came stronger. "Yes, I think I love her, but I didn't want it to happen."

"Do you want to marry her?"

"And if I did? What are you suggesting?"

"I'm suggesting the two who have corresponded and have fallen in love should be marrying one another. You selected the colors and accessories for the marital bedroom for heaven's sakes."

"And what about Renata ... and her father?"

"One thing at a time." Clifton looked at his watch.

"I asked Renata to meet me at the office, but I wanted to talk to you first. Give me an hour then join us." Clifton patted Gavin's sweat-soaked T-shirt. "If you take a shower, you will be a lot more appealing." He winked, strode to the door, and exited.

Gavin stared after his brother, his gaze transfixed on the greenhouse door.

After leaving the Flower Cottage, Clifton had gone to the one place where he could get reliable answers—Davenport Community Church. He'd knelt at the altar and prayed in earnest, laying out his questions and concerns. Was Renata's text the answer to Pastor's prayer? He had prayed the answer be clear. Whether the text was initiated by the heavenlies or not, Clifton did not want to hurt either Renata or Gavin.

Would this situation ruin the business relationship forged with Mr. Mendes? Likely.

But now was the time—the right time—to make things right for Renata and Gavin, regardless of the outcome with Mendes. Clifton would have to live with the property loss and carry on from there.

Returning to the late afternoon quiet of the office, Clifton looked at his dad's portrait. His gentle, all-knowing smile brought back his admonition to look for the right timing for using his God-given instincts. He was beginning to understand.

Clifton heard the office door open and Renata's sing-song "helloooo."

"Renata, come in." Clifton went down the hall to meet her half way.

"Thanks for leaving your friends and the barbeque."

"Of course. Everyone was wondering where you were."

"We've had so little time alone—we need to talk." He gestured for her to have a seat in front of his desk. He took the chair next to hers. She gave him an inquiring look.

Clifton cleared his throat and leaned toward her, clasping his hands.

"We've been separated and communicating by texts and emails the last couple of months, but I have to confess—and I know you suspect—I asked Gavin to help with our correspondence."

She folded her arms in front of her and pressed them to her stomach. "How do you know I suspected?"

"Gavin's phone and mine got switched by mistake. I saw the email you sent Gavin."

She straightened. "Clifton, I—"

He held up his hand. "Please let me finish. I want to apologize."

Renata raised her head and sniffed. "You should."

"I was so busy getting the nursery business back on track, I asked Gavin to handle correspondence with you as though the messages were from me. He tried to brief me, but ..."

At his admission, Renata's eyes grew large as a deer's. "You pawned me off on your brother?" She jumped up and paced, then stopped and confronted him. "Ever since I arrived, when we're together, I don't even know you. You're distant." She jammed her fists to her hips. "I was right. That's why you act like you don't know about things we've shared at length these past months ... and Gavin does. Being apart should have helped bring us closer together." She poked her index finger at Clifton. "I thought that was happening to us. Well, surprise! Your little charade made me fall in love with your brother."

She wasn't finished. "First, I'm shocked to hear you're married, then I learned that your ex-wife is the florist. Now, I've apparently picked out the colors for our wedding, not to mention our bedroom, with someone else because you were too busy for me. I was still willing to make our marriage work. But now ..." She broke off her tirade, defiant eyes glistening. "What next?"

Her words cut deep into his soul exposing his guilt.

She turned away, throwing her hands up in an I-give-up gesture.

Clifton debated. Should he try to comfort her or leave her alone?

A long minute passed.

Renata sniffed and turned back to him. Her eyes softened. "I suppose I should be thankful the truth came out now—before the wedding."

Clifton measured his words carefully. "You said, just now, that you had fallen in love with Gavin."

Renata stared at him. Was she checking for some spark left in their relationship?

"I believe I have."

A weird sense of peace crept over him at her admission. Clifton gave a single nod of acceptance. "Gavin will be here shortly. He wants to talk to you."

She took in a quick breath. "Gavin ... why?"

"I showed him your text. He admits there's a bond between you that he can't deny."

Renata plunked back into the chair next to Clifton. "Oh, Clifton, what a mess. Where does this predicament leave us? What about the wedding?"

"I think you should have your wedding." Clifton said as he thumbed a text to Gavin to come on up when he arrived at the office. "You just need the right groom."

She sat upright. "Are you suggesting—"

"I'm suggesting you marry the one you're in love with."

Renata slumped back in the chair.

For the first time since she arrived on Monday, Clifton relaxed in her presence with an odd kind of peace. As if on cue, he heard the office door open and footsteps in the entry hall. Clifton stood as Gavin entered.

"I believe it's time you two talked."

Clifton gave Renata's hand a squeeze and she responded in turn.

"I'll break the news to Mom and your father. Just let me know your wishes and when you're ready."

Gavin's eyes locked onto Renata's. "Give us a few."

Clifton shook his brother's hand and patted him on the shoulder, saying more than words could express at the moment.

Mr. Mendes's face flushed crimson as he jumped up from his chair in the Colonnades living room. "You're betraying my daughter?"

Gavin, Renata, and Clifton had formed an agreed upon alliance to try and explain the turn of events to their parents. The love seat, once Clifton's traditional hot spot, was occupied by Gavin and Renata.

Clifton stood in front of the fireplace. Music with a Brazilian flavor streamed from the patio, and the aroma of barbeque provided an inconsistent backdrop to the grave emotions that hung heavy in the room.

"Sir, I'm trying to do what's right for your daughter."

Renata stood and planted herself between her father and Clifton. "Oh, Papa, there's no betrayal." She grabbed Clifton's arm and crooked her other arm around her father's. "I don't know what I would have done if Clifton hadn't been there for me during Mother's illness. We'll always be friends, but I'm glad Clifton asked Gavin to correspond with me or I might be marrying the wrong brother."

Clifton's mother sat on the edge of her chair, wringing her hands. "But … You can't mean …"

Gavin spoke up. "Sir. I've asked your daughter to marry me. We'd like to have your blessing."

Mendes squinted his eyes at Clifton then Gavin. Renata grasped her father's arm.

"Papa, say yes. Don't you see? We can still have the wedding as scheduled and keep the property agreement."

Musical strains of "Wedding Bell Blues" filtered into the room. Rosemary sank back in her chair and clasped her hands to her forehead. "Lord help us."

Chapter 18

The mission was hers, and hers alone, to make. She might not be the best contract negotiator, as evidenced by having her van repossessed and not being able to make a custody suit disappear, but she could keep her integrity intact.

Emme steered her van—liberated by her mom and Frank—past the Davenport Community Church. A ray of sunlight tweaked the tip of the cross on top of the little white frame building adding a spark to the late afternoon sky.

She slowed. The night four years earlier, when she went with Clifton to break their engagement news, Clifton explained the church had been cut from cypress trees on his family's plantation. "It's the place where I received the Lord, and it's where I want us to be married."

He had squeezed her hand that sported his grandmother's ring. "I wish Grandmother was still alive to hear our news. As first grandson, she gave strict instructions that this ring must go to my one and only."

Big problem. His one and only had changed. Emme looked at the ring on the seat next to her. Shrouded in plastic with the valuation tag still attached, the ring lay entombed, morgue-like. "I'd best remove the tag. I need no more wrong impressions." Ahead, the sight of the *Davenport Plantation and Nurseries* sign made her stomach lurch, but not quite the same way as the sign for *Larry's Low Price Auto Sales* did earlier. The sight of the plantation sign made her want to throw up. The sign at Larry's pushed her more toward heartburn.

Larry had greeted Nan and Frank as if they were family arriving at a homecoming. "Well folks, what can I help you with?" When he spotted Emme, he shuffle-stepped back to his desk.

Frank had taken off work a little early to meet her mother at the bank. While there, he got the news the van had been repossessed.

"We've come for the Flower Cottage van. Here's the pay-off in full plus fifty which should cover the towing. I want the van and title, now." Frank used his no-nonsense cop voice, which sent Larry scurrying. Emme stood a little taller. Her mom had her back, and Frank, her front.

It did her heart good to hear Frank and her mother assure her that she was not alone in her problem with the van. Accepting their help was humbling—a trait she'd have to continue to work on.

Emme pulled into the oak tree-lined road to Colonnades. A giant spider web masterpiece, attached to some shrubs, sparkled in the sunlight. The ornate weaving was the handiwork of the Creator's creature but wouldn't stand up to pressure. *Lord, is that an object lesson to go with Izzie's web-weaver accusations? Just so you know—I'm banking on your help, not mine, right now.*

Along with the ring's return, she wanted Clifton to know she had not lied about its loss and to understand why the ring had been appraised. She could manage the drive to Colonnades, but she was going to need supernatural help to speak the right words when she got there.

The road yielded to the open expanse cleared for the plantation home and nursery business. The rosebushes that formed a skirt around the rail car had been working overtime producing blooms since she was there in the spring.

She pulled up front, flipped the gear shift into park, removed the valuation tag from the ring, and exited the van. If she hesitated or over-thought what she was doing, she might drive around the circle and head back home. Determined, she climbed the steps made of old brick. Clifton had once explained they were salvaged from the chimney of the old 1800s kitchen that had been separate from the house.

Discards made useful. There might be hope for her.

She approached the door and rang the bell, setting off cathedral chimes. From somewhere toward the rear of the house, strains of an old Elvis song, "Are You Lonesome Tonight," played. The sun slipped behind an oak and peeked through the trees. The spicy odor of cooking meat permeated the air. The aroma, normally mouth-watering, made hers go dry.

She'd forgotten. According to the wedding events list, tonight was barbeque night by the pool, catered by Chef. What on earth was she doing? Could she slip away before someone saw her van with the Flower Cottage plastered on the sides? She turned to leave when the latch rattled, the front door swung open, and Mrs. Davenport stared her in the face.

Eyes wide, Rosemary Davenport took a quick step backward.

"Mary Elaine. What—"

Emme must have portrayed a mirror image of surprise.

"Mrs. Davenport, I'm so sorry to bother you. I ... I just needed to return something to Clifton."

His mother tilted her head and frowned. "Return? You picked a bad time."

"You're right. I'm sorry to interrupt ..." *Don't retreat. Take a stand.* Complete your mission. "... but I misplaced and just found the ring Clifton gave me." She pulled the ring from her pocket.

Mrs. Davenport narrowed her eyes and cocked her head, making Emme want to find a good-sized rock to crawl under.

Izzie's voice popped up somewhere inside her head. Show her what you're made of. "I was going to explain to Clifton, but you can tell him." Emme pointed to the ring. "I kept the ring in a safe at the flower shop. I discovered a folded piece of notepaper wedged in the safe, and assumed the paper belonged to Mellie Tidwell, the former owner."

"I know Mellie." Mrs. Davenport relaxed a bit at the sound of her name.

"Somehow the ring got caught in the folds of the paper I gave Mellie, so she thought the ring might belong to the original homeowner."

"Regina Hamilton?"

"Yes. You know the background of the house?"

"Some. I've done business with Mellie over the years, and she told me the history of her shop."

Emme let the words flow. Her account unfolded as if she were sharing her story with an interested friend.

"Please tell Clifton what happened. Renata should have the ring."

Mrs. Davenport took the precious heirloom. "Yes ... Renata ... um ... thank you for returning the ring. I ... I'm sorry for the way things ... I'll see that Clifton gets the message."

Emme turned to leave. As she returned to the van, her steps felt lighter. The heaviness that had pressed against her soul in Mrs. Davenport's presence had lifted. But what Clifton thought of her still weighed on her heart.

The office was quiet and cavernous at seven a.m. Clifton flicked on the desk light. The Coast Line Train Reactivation file he'd worked on until two a.m. still lay open. Though short, he had a good night's sleep and was ready to review his work and make certain everything was clear before his seven-thirty appointment with Frank Bruckman, representing Coast Line.

The encouraging presence of his father's portrait on the wall and Emme's WWJD bracelet hanging from his desk lamp energized his work. He revised the declined Dollar Mart proposal, revamping stats and charts to make both the Dollar Mart and railroad projects synchronize. He was tired, but realized he'd been able to work without feeling the ball-peen-hammer weight of Mendes about to drop on his head. When his relationship to Mendes was strictly business, they had worked well together, but when Renata joined the mix, personal and business lines blurred, stifling his abilities.

He'd already prayed over and faxed a copy of his amended proposal to Dollar Mart. He incorporated Emme's ideas to have Dollar Mart the only place to purchase tickets for the Christmas train and offered a percentage of each ticket sold to go to the company's annual toy drive for needy children. Plantation tree prices would not undercut those sold at Dollar Mart. Of course, the early morning meeting with Bruckman was key.

The call for an appointment from Emme's stepfather came last night in the midst of the barbeque at Colonnades. The DJ's lively music apparently proved a good match for the spirits of the group from Brazil. Only his mother, who had disappeared back into the house, seemed to be having a bit of trouble with the quick turn of events.

Clifton had announced the change in grooms with Renata interpreting. "Friends, you've come to celebrate a marriage. Renata and I are grateful for your presence and want you to know plans for the wedding are proceeding, but with a slight change."

He motioned for Gavin to step up. "After a great deal of soul searching, Renata and I, and of course, Gavin, agree that she and Gavin are the best match." Renata reached for Gavin's hand. She snort-giggled. Gavin looked at her with adoring eyes while the bridesmaids squealed in delight.

"Please join me," Clifton continued, "in wishing these two the very best." His last words didn't get interpreted, but everyone seemed to get the message and gathered around the newly featured couple. Uncle Jorge, Aunt Sophia, and Granny seemed less shocked than he had been when he read Renata's text.

He apparently hadn't been the only one with gut feelings their marriage wasn't quite right. With Clifton, Renata, and Gavin linking arms, Mendes rose to make an impromptu speech in Portuguese. The small gathering cheered, and Renata interpreted for Gavin and Clifton.

"If my daughter is happy, I am happy. Since my girl will still carry the Davenport name, the property gift to the plantation remains." Mendes spoke and lifted his cup in the air. Everyone else followed suit and raised their drinks in a toast, then cheered some more.

Gavin grinned. Bianca slid in beside Clifton. "You could have knocked me over with a feather. I texted Jason. He wants to know if he's still a groomsman."

"I ... I don't know. That's up to them." He pointed to Gavin and Renata.

Clifton sat down, and Bianca joined him. "Should I be grieved or relieved this transition is going so well?" he asked.

"From the look on your face when you made the announcement, I'd say relieved. I've been concerned about you. Do you know tonight is the first time since we arrived from Brazil that I've seen a genuine smile on your face?"

"I didn't realize my ... preoccupation showed. I really want what's best for Renata ... and my brother." Larissa and Camilla grabbed Gavin and Renata and insisted they all join the DJ's call to dance the Macarena.

"Well, from the looks of things, you did a good job. Come on." Bianca pulled Clifton to his feet. "I'll show you some dance steps."

Clifton dutifully followed her lead. At dinner he sat alongside Gavin and Renata to show they were all still friends. Receiving Bruckman's call gave him reason to escape. Mendes was actually tapping his toes to the music when Clifton slipped out and headed to the office.

The downstairs intercom sounded.

"Yes?"

"Frank Bruckman."

Seven-thirty. Right on time.

"Come on up." Clifton walked down the hall to unlock the door.

Frank cut a commanding figure, a few inches over six feet, with broad shoulders and a no-nonsense demeanor. Definitely a cop sort of guy. He'd only met him once when Emme and he graduated from college.

"Clifton. It's been a long time." He seemed a different man—his handshake, firm.

"Yes, sir. So, you're in charge of security for the Coast Line Railroad?"

"I am. My boss was impressed with your presentation and sent me with a list of points to go over on your proposal for reactivating train service to the plantation."

The meeting was fruitful, points of question were answered, and an agreement was signed.

Bruckman rose from his chair. "Thank you for agreeing to an early meeting. Emme has a custody hearing at the courthouse in Hamilton Harbor at ten-thirty, and I promised to be there."

"Custody?"

"Richie's aunt suddenly turned up to challenge Emme's guardianship."

"The child is not Emme's?"

"She has legal custody of the boy and plans to officially adopt him."

"I thought the child was hers."

"No. I guess you were overseas at the time of the accident."

Everything Frank said spawned another question. "Accident?"

"Richie's father was Emme's cousin, Jason—on her father's side. He was a pilot. His wife, Kimberly, was pregnant with Richie when she won a family trip to Disney World. He rented a plane that crashed in bad weather, killing Jason and both sets of grandparents. Kimberly was critically injured and wanted Emme to take the baby. She died shortly after he was born."

"I had no idea."

"That doesn't surprise me. Few people around here know Emme is not Richie's natural mother, and she wants to keep it that way."

"But why?"

"I think being adopted herself... she has notions of her own. Protective." Frank hesitated. "My past is no secret. I've changed, but she doesn't allow me to keep him by myself." He glanced at his watch and took a step to leave. "Thankfully, she's softened some of late."

Clifton remembered Emme describing the giant black question mark that was etched on her soul when she learned her birth parents gave her up. Her desire to shield Richie made sense.

"Is there any chance she could lose him?"

"As blood kin, the aunt claims to be the better person to raise him. Since Emme is adopted she can't claim blood relation. In her favor, Emme is the only mother Richie has known, and a policeman friend has agreed to be a Big Brother for Richie. But she's still got to prove she can support him. Not easy since she lost your wedding job and then her van."

"She lost her van?"

"She'd be upset, me telling you, but her mother and I got the van back for her. Frankly, she's in a bad spot. You never know what a judge will do, and she doesn't have an attorney. I hate to think what will happen to her if she loses that boy."

The desk chair screeched under Clifton's weight. The picture of Richie injured in the park, bleeding and reaching for Emme, crossed his mind. Losing him in a custody suit would be devastating to both of them.

"She's trying to handle the hearing without representation?"

Frank nodded and extended his hand. "So, you understand why we want to be there for support. My boss said to tell you he used to take his kids on the Christmas train and is glad you wanted to start service to the plantation again."

Clifton closed the door on his meeting with Frank, but not on Emme's plight.

Grandmother's ring. Did she have the ring valued because she needed the money? He checked the time, eight-thirty, and hurried to his desk. Was there any way he could help her? He searched his contacts for Attorney Horowitz's number. He glanced at his father's portrait. If his gut was right, he should make this call.

"Lincoln Horowitz' office."

"Is he in please? Clifton Davenport calling."

"He's at the courthouse."

"That's where I need him. How long will he be there?"

"He's filing some motions. Should be back before noon. Can I have him call you?"

"Please. Tell him I need his help at a ten-thirty hearing at the courthouse and to call me ASAP."

Ms. Peacock's short, mincing steps clicked down the entry hall. She had a slight build, thin face, and always dressed in a skirt and blouse. She'd changed little since he'd first seen her in the office almost twenty years ago. Straying from her usual raised hand greeting before entering her office, she instead walked to Clifton's desk.

"Have you seen today's food page?"

"No. Was I supposed to?"

"I think you'll find the article interesting."

As frugal with words as she was with the business accounts, she placed the newspaper on his desk, then returned to her office. Clifton's phone sounded. His mother.

"Clifton, have you seen the morning's paper?"

"Ms. Peacock asked me the same question. What am I supposed to see?"

"Look at the food section." Clifton frowned as he scanned the front-page index for the food section. His mother sounded ... pleased.

"Do you see? We got a full-page spread."

The headline—*All Aboard for an All-American Dinner*—stood out with red, white, and blue lettering. Featured on the top of the page was a close up of Richie's Lionel train with the sign—*Davenport Express-A part of America's Rich Heritage*. Below the picture read: *The revival of an old area favorite, the Davenport Express, was a unique and fun way to present an American menu for the wedding party staying at Gulf Haven.*

"I do see, and I believe the full-page piece is thanks to Mary Elaine," Clifton said.

"Any chance we could get her back for the wedding? She does have everything ordered."

"You fired her. You should be the one to rehire her—if she'll accept."

"I suppose you're right. I was a bit ... hasty. Speaking of Mary Elaine ... she returned the ring."

"What? When?"

"Last night. You were at the barbeque. She said the shop owner found the ring, that's the previous florist, Mellie. I dealt with Mellie for flowers—"

"Mom, too much information. Mary Elaine returned the ring last night, and you're just now telling me?"

"You were busy out back and—"

"Listen, I have to go to Hamilton Harbor. Put the ring on the table by the front door. I may need it."

Clifton buzzed Ms. Peacock. "You can reach me on my cell phone." He grabbed the newspaper and headed out the door.

Clifton stopped the ATV abruptly in front of Colonnades and took out his key remote. He hurried up the columned porch steps as his mother snatched the front door open.

"Clifton, what's going on?"

"I'll explain later. The ring?"

His mother handed him the ring. He turned to leave, then turned back around and kissed his mother on the cheek. Mouth open, she touched her cheek. No words came out.

Clifton pulled out of the drive and drove past the old Davenport Express rail car. The roses surrounding the car were in full bloom. He stopped, backed up, hurried across the trimmed grass, clipped off one of the flowers, and slipped the bloom into his pocket.

"Little flower, I think you bloomed at just the right time."

Chapter 19

Emme sat in the judge's chambers on the third floor of the Hamilton Harbor Courthouse. The narrow room held a long conference table polished to a high sheen. Judge Sapp, a blunt-faced man with serious eyes and thick silver hair combed straight back, sat at the end of the table. A clerk of court and stenographer were seated on either side of the judge.

If Emme hadn't been on the opposing side, the eloquent attorney might have convinced her that Aurora Kemp was the most logical choice to be awarded custody of Richie.

Aurora appeared all business in a cream-colored suit. Her perfect auburn hair just touched her collar; her earrings were ivory ovals. She sat with her attorney on the left side of the table. Emme, her mother, Frank, and Tony sat on the right.

How could she compete against Aurora's offer of money, home, and heritage as a blood relative? Emme's claim for custody rested on a struggling business in a rundown neighborhood where she often relied on babysitters, as Aurora's attorney pointed out. What she had on her side was the moral support of her mother, stepfather, and Richie's Big Brother, Tony, along with a nice newspaper write up Izzie had scrambled to show her before she left for court. Never mind that she had just been fired from the job.

"I'm ready to hear from the defendant," the judge said to Emme. "Do you have counsel to represent you?"

Mouth dry, Emme pushed herself up, using the arms of the chair. Her knees were feeble, and she stuttered. "You ... your honor. I ... I will be representing myself."

The door to the chamber opened, and the judge's secretary appeared in the doorway. "Sorry to interrupt, Judge, but Attorney Horowitz is here regarding this case."

Judge Sapp pulled down his glasses and peered over the rims. A tall man of medium build, dressed in a light gray suit, erect posture wide-ridged brow stepped into the room.

"Your honor, I'm offering my services pro bono if the defendant will accept."

Emme caught a glimpse of someone standing in the outer office behind Horowitz. She did a double take. Clifton. He smiled at her. Emme stood frozen, dumbfounded.

"Tell him yes," Tony prompted.

Emme blinked and turned to the judge. "Yes." Her damp palms dropped to the table, smudging the shiny surface.

"Could I have five minutes to confer with my client?" Horowitz asked.

The judge removed his glasses. "The hearing will be in recess for five minutes."

Horowitz motioned for Emme to join him at a small table in the rear of the room.

"Are you really here to argue my custody case?" Emme asked.

"I wouldn't be here if I weren't."

He unlatched his briefcase, took out the food section, and pushed the paper, along with a handwritten note, in front of her.

"Read the attachment."

Scrawled in Clifton's handwriting, the note read like a telegram. *Renata is marrying Gavin. Wedding still on. Mom wants to rehire you as wedding florist. (Over).* Emme's shaky fingers lifted and turned the paper over. Taped to the back was Clifton's grandmother's ring. *The ring is yours to sell if you need the money or to keep. Either way, you remain my one and only. Will you marry me again? I'd be honored to be a father to Richie. Clifton.*

Emme's gaze went unfocused as tears came and sniffles followed.

"We haven't got long." Horowitz, all business, pressed a clean handkerchief into her hand. "Here," he said, his demeanor, serious—his eyes, kind.

"Your response is?" he asked.

Emme blew her drippy nose on the handkerchief and squeaked out, "Yes."

"You accept the wedding job, and Clifton's proposal?"

The questions rushed at her with freight train speed. No time to dally. "I do, but the hearing—"

"Just leave that to me. Clifton has filled me in on many of the details. What was the argument presented by the plaintiff's attorney?"

"He made a case that Aurora has money, can provide a nice two-parent home in a good neighborhood, send him to the best schools, and she is blood kin. Her sister was Richie's mother. I am Richie's aunt on his father's side, but since I was adopted, I can't claim him as a blood relation."

"How old is the boy?"

"Three."

"Has Ms. Kemp been involved in Richie's life?"

"She sends him gifts, but she never laid eyes on him until a couple of months ago."

"You've had him four years, and she's just now trying to get custody?"

"Yes, I have legal guardianship." Emme pulled a paper from her pocket. "Richie's mother was specific that she wanted me to raise Richie and made the request official before she died. I can't claim blood relation, but I love him as my own."

Horowitz scanned the paper Emme gave him, then looked at her with eyes bright. "Let me handle this."

Emme held out his handkerchief.

He waved off her gesture. "You keep it."

From that moment, Horowitz took control as if he'd studied and prepared his argument for months.

"Your honor, I think we can agree the most time-honored and recognized relationship in our society is the love of a mother for her child. I have here the wishes of a dying mother for her unborn child, holding onto life by a thread in order to give that baby boy life. Her plea is dictated to a nurse, witnessed by her doctor, and signed by a notary. I quote: 'It is my desire that Mary Elaine Matthews, my husband's cousin, raise my baby as her own.'"

Aurora's lawyer jumped up. "I object. The document has not been properly introduced as evidence."

"This is a hearing, not a trial. Sit down. I'll see that you get a copy." The judge wrote something on a pad in front of him, then looked up. "Proceed."

Horowitz motioned toward Aurora—her eyes were focused on her clenched hands.

"I'm sure the child's aunt has good and noble intentions, but we must look to the biological mother's wishes, and the fact that Mary Elaine Matthews has honored the mother's request since the boy was born. He's three years old now. I understand some concerns were presented about Ms. Matthews' ability to provide for the child as a single parent while running a struggling business in a rundown neighborhood. But look at the flip side of those arguments. Ms. Matthews' struggling business is taking off." He lifted the newspaper in front of Emme and held up the food page. "As evidenced by the full-page feature article appearing today."

Aurora's lawyer popped up again. "Your honor, I object—"

"You'll get a copy, take your seat."

Aurora's lawyer looked at his client and made a slight shrug.

Judge Sapp held up his head to view the page through his glasses. "Looks just like the train I had as a kid. Continue."

"Her florist services have been retained for the highly publicized Mendes-Davenport wedding, so she'll be well-positioned to provide for the boy. In addition ..." He motioned at the three on her side of the table. "... she has supportive parents, and this policeman gives of his time as the child's Big Brother. As for the neighborhood they live in, I happen to be a member of the Downtown Reconstruction Board. I personally know plans are underway for revitalization of that area. Furthermore, without specifics until family is notified, I can assure you there will be a positive fatherly influence in Richie's life as well."

Eyebrows shot up around the table. Emme felt heat flush over her face.

"My client has kept her word to her dying cousin and is working hard to support the child. Would you deprive the boy of the only mother he has ever known?"

"You may inquire now," the judge said to the opposing lawyer.

"May I have a moment with my client?"

Aurora huddled with her attorney briefly before he stood to address the group. "My client, being made aware of certain facts, has decided to withdraw her request for custody."

The judge made a decisive nod. "So be it. The court instructs the clerk to draw up an order to be signed by the court. The custody of said child will remain with the defendant. This proceeding is adjourned."

Outside the judge's chambers, Clifton waited, sitting in a hard-plastic chair. The smell of strong coffee, thickening on a warmer, colored the air of the waiting area. He alternated praying for the proceedings to go well for Emme and staring at fishing magazines stacked on a corner table. The clickety sound of fingers tapping on a computer keyboard served as white noise, a background on which to hang questions. Would Emme think Renata's switch to Gavin weird? Would she think his proposal insensitive? Presumptuous? Inane? Crazy?

If she accepted his proposal, where would they live? She had her shop and home—he lived at Colonnades and had the plantation to run. Thank goodness, he no longer had to sleep in the green bedroom with the jungle print bathroom. He would move back to his room in the west wing, which meant his mother's room was nearby. But he was getting way ahead of himself.

She could turn him down. She'd have every right, hurting her as he did. To think, she had sacrificed to raise a child not even hers, while his selfish concern was believing she had betrayed him. Under conviction, he stood and began to pace. If she rejected him, he'd understand. When he started counting his steps, he sat back down.

"Would you like some coffee? I can make some fresh." Clifton noticed the secretary's name plate on the desk, Shirley Goss. She had short black hair and understanding eyes.

"Thank you. No."

"A family member meeting with the judge?"

"No. A friend. She's trying to retain custody of the child she's raising. We've known each other since we were kids."

"Nice you've remained friends so long."

"I haven't been a very loyal friend."

"But you're here now."

"Do you think that will count?"

"I'd say so. How about some water?"

"That would be nice." He must look needy.

Shirley disappeared into a back room and returned with a bottle of water. He unscrewed the cap and swallowed. The cool water refreshed his dry throat. "You must deal with relational issues all day long."

She smiled. "I do indeed."

"Have you ever heard of a guy who loved a girl, but put his own interests first and lost her?"

She folded her arms and rested her elbows on her desk. "Selfishness. The root of most conflicts the judge has to rule on."

Selfish. She'd nailed his problem. He'd thought of himself and never bothered to find out or even ask about what Emme was feeling. If only she'd give him the chance now.

"Do you have any idea how long—"

Before he could get the question out, the door to the judge's chambers opened and Tony walked out. His facial expression was hard to read.

"Man, was that lawyer your doing?"

"Depends on the job he did."

"Are you kidding? He knocked it out of the park."

"So ... that means good?"

Beyond Tony, Clifton could see the others milling around in the conference room.

Nan and Frank emerged as Clifton asked the question. "Good isn't the word," Frank said.

Clifton frowned. He could see Emme now talking to a woman in a light-colored suit. "What is the word?"

Frank smiled. "I'd say fantastic."

Relief washed over him. "Everything is okay for Emme and Richie?"

Emme's mother grasped Clifton's arm, her face glowed. "The lawyer did such a good job, the aunt dropped the custody suit."

Tony spoke up. "I have to get back to work, but I guess I'll be seeing you on Big Brother visits." He gave Clifton a friendly jab to his shoulder.

"Speaking of work," Frank said, "I'd better get going. Clifton, my boss wants to meet with you soon on the rail service. I'll call you." Nan and Frank made their farewells.

The woman in the suit and a man came out, apparently the aunt and her lawyer. They departed deep in conversation, leaving Horowitz and Emme standing in the doorway.

Horowitz extended his hand. "Young lady, nice doing business with you." Emme bypassed the handshake and went for a big hug. He grinned.

"Clifton, I believe this case sets a record for shortest notice and quickest results."

"I can't thank you enough."

"My pleasure. You have quite a girl here." Horowitz placed Clifton's hand on Emme's. "I'm thinking you two have much to discuss. I've got to run."

Emme opened the newspaper tucked under her arm and pulled out the note he had written. She dangled the paper, the ring still attached, in front of him. "Sir, I think I need an explanation. You walk out of my life, get engaged and apparently unengaged, then send me a proposal on paper?"

Clifton dropped his head. "You never answered my calls. And I thought you'd ... I saw you had a baby ... I've been a miserable cad."

Emme took a step toward him. She raised the paper. Was she going to slap him? His face twitched.

"Especially since you returned with a Brazilian beauty attached to your arm."

"Turns out mine was the wrong arm. Renata and Gavin discovered they were meant for each other."

"And what did you discover?"

Emme stepped closer, her smugness softened. Shirley's white noise stopped. The walls and floor receded. All he could see was Emme. Her presence enveloped him as her lips grazed his, then lingered and she melted into his embrace.

Shirley cleared her throat. "Uh ... would you like to do your conferring in the judge's chambers?"

Emme flushed crimson and pulled away.

"Sorry," Clifton said. "No, I'm not sorry, but is going in there okay?"

"Don't worry. There's a back door to that room. The judge has returned to his office."

They stepped into the conference room, and Clifton's phone buzzed on vibrate. He reached in his pocket to retrieve the phone, touching the soft petals of the rose he'd picked in haste. He recognized the number. "Dollar Mart."

Emme grinned and held up crossed fingers.

"Clifton Davenport."

"Mr. Davenport, I'm Mr. Gentry's secretary at Dollar Mart. He asked that I call and see if you can meet today at two-thirty. He likes your revisions and wants to discuss the proposal."

"Of course. I'll be there."

Emme raised her brows in question as he ended the call.

"I submitted your suggestions. The regional director likes the revised proposal and wants to meet with me."

Emme wrapped him in a hug. "Congratulations." The press of her embrace tumbled him back to old times and released a rosy fragrance from the flower in his pocket.

"I need you to see something." Clifton pulled out the rose, a bit scrunched but still intact. "You remember the time I fell into the rose bush and broke off a limb?"

"I do. On our last visit to the plantation before Daddy died." She took the rose and touched the white petals tinged with crimson. "Is this ...?"

Clifton nodded. "Dad and I grafted a stem from the broken red rose branch to a white host.

"Amazing." Her whispered word traveled from upturned lips to her glistening azure eyes drawing Clifton back to the first time he'd proposed. He lifted the paper she'd laid on the table and peeled off the tape holding the ring.

"Grandma said to give this ring to my one and only. Mary Elaine ... Emme, you are my one and only." He held up the rose and ring. "I can't think of any better way to prove that I love you. Have since I first laid eyes on you. Will you marry me?"

She flashed a smile. "Again?"

He cradled her face, soft to his touch. "Yes, again."

Her kiss on his lips gave her answer. The sweet fragrance from the red-tinged rose, encompassed their past, released its perfume and confirmed that first love did indeed have a second chance.

Chapter 20

"It smells like Christmas," Gavin whispered to Clifton as they followed Pastor Hanover and took their places in front of the altar. Red cedar boughs, entwined with white lights and satin ribbon, charged the air with their pine scents and adorned the ends of the pews along the central aisle. Red and white roses, the result of the grafts made by Clifton with his father, decorated the altar.

Lanterns by the stained-glass windows of Davenport Community Church cast flickering light, wrapping the sanctuary in a warm glow. The violin melody of "The Prayer" completed the setting for the Emme Matthews-Clifton Davenport December wedding.

Clifton's eyes fell on Renata who gave him a thumbs up. Since marrying Gavin, she radiated an inner glow, still contagious. Their sunset wedding—a beautiful event—had taken place four months earlier.

Clifton scanned the rest of the tiny gathering awaiting Emme's entrance. Sitting next to Renata was his mother, fiddling with her fingers. She never could be still. Behind her, Carlos wore a silly grin. Like an elbow jab to the ribs, he was reminding Clifton that he knew Emme was the right one for him all along. Eduardo, Carlos's son and a camera buff, snapped pictures from the rear of the church next to Mellie who played Emme's music selections on a CD player.

On the right side, Tony sat behind Nan who was on the front pew. She held up a handkerchief for Clifton to see. She'd warned him she cried at all weddings.

Was he going to do the same? When Mellie shifted the background music to "Ave Maria," an adrenaline rush hit his head and tears threatened as he caught his first glimpse of Emme. Flanked by Richie to her right and Frank on the left, she was stunning with her golden hair flowing onto the shoulders of a white lace dress. Barely aware of Izzie making her way down the aisle, his laser-lock on Emme's eyes never strayed until she reached his side.

"You are beautiful."

Her blue eyes glittered. "Thank you. Not too bad yourself."

Clifton was only halfway aware of Frank and Richie kissing Emme and going to sit beside Nan.

"Friends and family," Pastor Hanover began, "we have gathered during this glorious season to witness the union of Clifton Richard Davenport and Mary Elaine 'Emme' Matthews." After explaining the sanctity of marriage, saying "I do's," and exchanging rings, Pastor said, "The couple has prepared special remarks for each other."

Clifton turned to Emme, the glint of soft candlelight in her eyes.

"Even though I may call you Emme, as others do these days, deep in my soul you will always remain Mary Elaine—the girl who rode in on the Davenport train with her family to find a Christmas tree and left with a piece of my heart. Today, you honor me by agreeing to make my heart whole again. I pledge to never take that love, or you, lightly or for granted." The blue and white threads of the WWJD bracelet Emme had made for him peeked out from the cuff of his dress shirt.

Tears escaped Emme's eyes. Clifton brushed them away with the tips of his fingers. As Emme spoke, her chin quivered. Endearing. "Clifton, the boy in the red and green cap. I fell in love with you at age six and I love you now. When I first saw you, a voice inside me whispered, 'He's the one.' You still are the one and always will be."

Clifton squeezed her hand. Her return squeeze sent shock waves straight to his soul.

"By the authority of God and laws of the State of Florida, and with few dry eyes among these witnesses," Pastor dabbed at his own eyes and beamed, "I pronounce you husband and wife. May God bless this marriage. You may kiss your bride."

Emme's smile blossomed into a grin. Clifton slipped his arms around her, every nerve at high alert as her arms encircled his neck. He claimed her sweet lips, sending electric currents to his toes. Wrapped in the peace of the sanctuary, Clifton soaked in her warmth and that of their applauding family and friends as Mellie played "Ode to Joy."

"Hey brother, save some for later," Gavin whispered behind Clifton.

"Must I?" Clifton winked.

Emme blinked and loosened her grip on Clifton, then motioned to Richie to join them. Clifton swooped up the boy, loving the touch of Richie's arms snugged around his neck.

Pastor Hanover made the official pronouncement. "I present to you Mr. and Mrs. Clifton Davenport, and I'm to remind you of the special reception following at Colonnades."

At that, Richie pulled a handful of rice from each of his pockets and released the grains on top of Clifton and Emme's heads. The room erupted in laughter. Clifton, still holding Richie, grabbed Emme's hand and they scurried down the church aisle into the crisp, clear night air.

Showers of more rice stung Emme's shoulders, and Richie squealed in delight as they scrambled into the church yard.

When Clifton set Richie down, he ran to Nan, asking, "More rice?"

Nan shook her head. "Sorry, they got the full load. Looks like you have some on you too."

Richie began searching his shirt sleeves for stray rice and tossed them toward Emme and Clifton.

"I think Richie has discovered a new favorite game," Emme said.

"Seems we just went through this ritual, only they used bird seed on us." Gavin said as he and Renata joined them. Gavin stooped to give Emme a kiss on the cheek. "Welcome to the family."

After Eduardo positioned various family groupings and took photos, Renata gave Emme a hug. "We're going to be sisters now."

Emme got a whiff of her perfume and relived placing guest bags and flowers in her room at Gulf Haven. Her wildest wishes could never have entered this scene into her dreams.

"Right." Emme stepped back to get a good look at Renata. "You're wearing the chocolate sauce dress. That scarf is gorgeous with the lavender."

Renata gave Gavin an adoring glance. "Gavin picked the scarf out for me."

"My brother, the fashion consultant. He even picked out this tie for me," Clifton added, lifting his deep burgundy tie.

"Emme," Gavin said, "you'll have to take over for me. Your husband has no color sense."

"Don't be talking about my bro." Izzie joined the group with Mellie at her side. "He picked the color scheme for this wedding."

"I did?" Clifton's forehead wrinkled.

Izzie opened her arms, displaying her red dress, then swished her head from side to side, setting her shimmering white earrings in motion. "Red and white." She pointed to the flowers Emme held. "Clifton ordered the bridal bouquet made of the white, red-tipped roses from the plantation. Of course, florist emeritus, Mellie, added her special touches." Izzie stepped back to showcase Mellie. The twosome presented a whimsical study in contrasts—Izzie's tall height to Mellie's short, Izzie's stand-up black hair versus Mellie's permed white.

"I was happy to be pressed back into service. The bouquet is specially designed to reflect the stones in the heirloom ring you gave Emme."

Clifton stooped to give Mellie a hug of thanks. Emme wiggled her ring finger next to the bouquet while Eduardo moved in for a close-up shot of the roses with greenery and glistening picks of garnet and silver.

"Nice color scheme. There's hope for you yet, big brother," Gavin said.

"I have a big brother," Richie said. He wriggled out of Clifton's arms to go see Tony.

Emme leaned to hug Mellie, who spoke in a hushed voice, "You know the map you found in the safe?"

"Yes."

"Marigold called and said she made an interesting discovery related to it but couldn't talk over the phone. She's coming next week and said she would see me then."

"Sounds mysterious."

Mellie gave a furtive nod, her eyes darted from side to side, adding to the secrecy.

Intrigue at Feldman Square? Or was she watching too many Murder, She Wrote TV reruns? Emme took her cue to keep her news quiet but squirreled the tidbit away.

Conversation had shifted to the topic of living arrangements. "The flowers from Gavin and Renata's wedding were still fresh when Mom insisted Emme and I start making plans to move into the west wing, since she'd moved back in the main house."

"Is the color scheme red and white?" Gavin teased.

"Any color changes I wisely have left to Emme, and there hasn't been a quiet moment around Colonnades since."

"Talking about me?" Rosemary joined the group with Pastor Hanover at her side.

"In most glowing terms." Clifton gave his mother a side hug.

"Emme, you will be a welcome addition to help Renata and me keep these boys in line."

Surprising Emme with an embrace, Rosemary, smelling of sweet lilac, brushed Emme's cheek with a tear. When she pulled back, Rosemary dabbed at the moisture and straightened her posture. "You kids hurry now. The reception is ready. Pastor, ride with me, won't you?"

"Will do." Pastor turned and, tipping his head, said, "It's a Christmas blessing to see you boys happily married."

"Amen to that." Carlos had been talking to Nan and Frank. All three joined the newlyweds. "Frank has some exciting news."

Frank had been a wonderful support, and Emme had begun to see the endearing qualities her mother saw in him. He truly had a kind and tender heart, and Richie loved playing with his Gram and Gramps. "What news?" Emme asked.

"My boss at Coast Line said to tell you the supplies and permits to reopen the train spur have been secured. By this time next year, the Davenport Christmas Express will be running."

Carlos let out a whoop. Gavin and Clifton high-fived.

Clifton's Dollar Mart contract had already put the plantation in the black with enough to purchase the Davenport property back from Mendes, but he wouldn't accept the money. "A gift is a gift," he'd insisted.

"Richie, you'll be the only kid in school who will have a train that pulls into his front yard," Tony said.

"Whoo-whoo!" Richie brought smiles with his high-pitched attempt to imitate a train whistle.

"I think another kiss is warranted from my new bride." Clifton swept Emme close, the scent of his cologne and his tender touch encircling her.

And sometime in the space of sighs and sweet applause from the little group of spectators, Clifton's kiss sealed the joy in Emme's heart, and love bloomed all over again.

Colonnades' Orange Sweet Rolls

Ingredients
Dough:
1 pkg. active dry yeast (2 ¼ tsp.)
½ cup warm water
Fresh orange zest from 1 medium-sized orange
½ cup orange juice
¼ cup sugar
1 tsp. salt
1 egg
2 Tbsp. butter softened
3-31/2 cups all-purpose flour

Filling:
2 Tbsp. sugar
2 tsp. ground cinnamon
1 Tbsp. butter softened

Glaze:
1 cup powdered sugar
1 Tbsp. orange juice
Fresh orange zest from 1 medium orange
1 tsp. vanilla extract

Directions:
<u>Dough</u>—Dissolve yeast in ½ c warm water for about 1 minute. Stir yeast and water. Add orange zest, orange juice, sugar, salt, egg, butter and 1 ½ c flour. Beat everything together on low with mixer, scraping down sides as needed. With a wooden spoon, stir in enough of the remaining flour to make dough easy to handle. (Dough should not be sticky and should spring back when poked.) Transfer dough to a lightly floured surface and knead 5-6 minutes. Form the dough into a ball and transfer to lightly greased bowl. Cover the dough and let sit in a warm place until doubled in size, about 1 ½ hours. Line 9 x 13 baking dish with parchment paper, leaving room at the sides. Turn the dough out onto a lightly floured surface. Use rolling pin and roll evenly into 10 x 15 rectangle.

Filling—In a small bowl, mix together sugar and cinnamon. Spread the rectangle with softened butter and sprinkle with cinnamon-sugar mixture. Tightly roll up the dough and cut into 16 even rolls with sharp knife. Arrange in baking pan, cut sides up. Cover the rolls and let them rise in a warm place for about 30 minutes-1 hour. Cover with aluminum foil. Bake at 375 degrees, 25-30 minutes, until light golden. Cool on rack about 15 minutes.

Glaze—In small bowl, mix together glaze ingredients and drizzle over rolls. (Note: dough may be made the night before, cover with plastic wrap, let rise in fridge overnight. The next morning, remove from fridge and let rise about 1 hour.) Yield 16 rolls.

About the Author

Sally Jo Pitts writes what she likes to read—faith-based stories of romance with an unusual twist. She grew up in central Florida and now lives in the Panhandle of Florida with her investigator husband and feisty schnauzer. She graduated from Florida State University, taught home economics and served as a high school guidance counselor. Currently, she is a private investigator in her husband's agency and writes between cases. More about Sally Jo and things she investigates can be found at www.sallyjopitts.com.

Dear Reader,

Thank you for joining me in the fictional town of Hamilton Harbor. Emme and Clifton's story is the first in the Hamilton Harbor Legacy series where the town is awakening to revived businesses, new friendships, and budding romances.

In my Florida Panhandle hometown, there is a park that mirrors Feldman Square where old homes once stood. Now, only two remain. It was fun to use the magic of the pen to resurrect the homes on the square, and you'll find my make-believe houses hold more secrets in the upcoming series.

When I wrote this story, I only knew I wanted to have a guy and girl be legally married, but somehow not know it. My first storyline had the hero marry the heroine on a fraternity initiation dare. She learns it was a joke and they break up after a honeymoon night that results in a pregnancy. The heroine kept the child a secret until it was discovered the marriage papers were authentic. But I hated to have my hero, Clifton, be such a cad. I scrubbed that idea and opted to have them both surprised to find out they were married and complicated matters with the ward, Richie, who Clifton believes is Emme's natural child.

Emme's character is written to be fiercely independent and determined to do things on her own. I created Izzie to help her realize that God expects us to do our part but also wants a relationship.

Clifton has God-given talent for management, but after making a poor decision, loses faith in his intrinsic ability. Emme helps Clifton restore his confidence and Clifton encourages Emme to accept his help.

I hope you enjoyed watching Emme and Clifton get a second chance on love. And keep an eye out for another romance brewing in Hamilton Harbor.

In Stumbling Upon Romance, dog groomer Claudia Stewart buys the dog grooming shop from Mellie's sister and more is learned about the mysterious map Emme discovered at the Flower Cottage.

I'd love to hear from readers. Visit my website at www.sallyjopitts. com where I investigate lots of things, from leaving a legacy, researching commands to write in the Bible, and time management, to my favorite books and recipes.

Reading Group Discussion Questions:

Emme Matthews defines herself by her success in her independence as a single mother and floral designer. When Clifton Davenport looks at himself, all he sees are his past mistakes. Do you identify with either character? Explain.

Do you find it easier to define yourself by your successes or failures? Do you ever define yourself by who you are in Christ?

Using her nickname, Emme, Mary Elaine has attempted to closely guard her private life until an investigator locates her. Do you think she was right or wrong to conceal her identity to keep the Davenport wedding job? What would you have done?

When Clifton learns Emme's identity, he agrees to keep her secret so that she can remain the wedding florist. Was that the right move? Should he have been up front with his fiancée and family?

After Clifton finds Emme and sees Richie, he assumes the boy is Emme's biological child. Have you ever believed something to be true only to find out later that you were mistaken? Has your first impression of someone ever been wrong? What changed once you got to know the heart of the person?

In chapters six and eight, Izzie accuses Emme of depending on herself and weaving a web. In chapter eighteen Emme responds in prayer when she sees a giant, ornate spider web and is reminded of Izzie's web-weaver accusation. What truth is Izzie is trying to get across? Have you ever been guilty of web-weaving—leaning on your own flimsy strength?

Emme and Clifton were friends as youngsters. Is there a friend in your life who draws you out in ways others don't? Describe that friendship.

Emme has devoted her life to raising Richie and keeping her vow to care for him as her own. Clifton is determined to make amends for putting the family plantation and legacy in jeopardy by his unwise choice in managers. Is there a special cause or need you pursue (or have pursued) that is close to your heart?

In chapter eight, Emme learns, from a whispered conversation, that she is adopted. She wants to shield Richie from the hurt she experienced. What do you think of her decision to let Richie and others believe the boy is her natural child?

Clifton believes it's too late to break off his engagement to Renata when his pastor prays for God's will in the situation. Have you ever been in what seemed an impossible situation when God opens a door?

The Davenport Plantation Christmas train tradition ended when the railroad rerouted. Have you had to let go of a family tradition? What was it? Has a new tradition taken its place?

When Emme designs the All-American dinner with the model train, she believes she has planned something special, but Mrs. Davenport thinks she's trying to sabotage their party. Scripture tells us that all things work together for good to them that love God, to them who are called according to his purpose (Romans 8:28 KJV). Was Emme being fired by Mrs. Davenport a good thing? What might have happened if she hadn't been fired?

When Emme makes the step to reconcile with her mother and Frank, what truth does she learn?

Clifton asks his brother to handle communication with Renata which leads to confusion and misunderstandings. Have you ever taken an easy way out only to complicate matters?

In the end, Emme sacrifices for Clifton by returning the family ring for Renata. Even though Clifton believes he's lost Emme, he is willing to give up the family ring if Emme really needs the money. He also sacrifices for his brother and Renata's happiness even though it may risk the future of the family's plantation. Have you ever sacrificed something for someone else? Has anyone sacrificed for you? Explain.

As a single parent, Emme seeks help from the Big Brothers organization. Have you ever been mentored? Or a mentor? What was the experience like? Discuss mentoring opportunities in your community. Would you be willing to serve in that capacity?

The Davenport's family legacy included property and a special ring. Leaving a legacy is often thought of as a tangible inheritance, but it can also refer to leaving behind what you contributed to humanity during your life. Emme wanted to leave Richie the legacy of a happy childhood. Values can be more precious than valuables. Share the legacy you would like to leave.

What do Emme and Clifton finally learn about who they are?

www.ingramcontent.com/pod-product-compliance
Lightning Source LLC
Chambersburg PA
CBHW070459260626
47161CB00004B/1379